DEAD LINES

A LYDIA BARNWELL MYSTORY

JAMES H LEWIS

DEAD LINES

by James H Lewis

ISBN-13: 979-8-9902037-6-1

For Delores Casali, who introduced me to the life of Therese Rocco, Pittsburgh's first assistant police chief.

CONTENTS

"JOHN LAROCCA SPENT his winters in Florida, toasting his body into a golden glow and leaving Mike Genovese in charge of the mob."

Delores Tavener, prolific author of gothic bodice rippers, looked through her stacks of unsold books to the writer's stage where crime writer Parker Stevens held court. While Delores had attracted a group of middle-aged women whose numbers hadn't topped two dozen, Stevens had filled all one hundred seats set up before the stage in the church parking lot that adjoined the library. Others stood behind them of all ages and both sexes.

"Whereas LaRocca was a cautious man who shunned the limelight and ruled by reputation, Genovese was impulsive and reckless," Stevens continued.

His story of the mob's rise and fall had drawn nearly everyone from the rectangle of authors beneath the large white tent the library had erected over the asphalt. It was as if a giant vacuum cleaner had suctioned up all the potential buyers, leaving only crumbs for the twenty-seven other writers. Nothing sold in Pittsburgh like true crime, she thought to herself, especially if the crime was committed here.

"One of LaRocca's soldiers was a young man named Alphonse Marano, a two-bit hood who dealt in gambling and prostitution," Stevens told the crowd. "Marano befriended another man, a newcomer to Pittsburgh, and introduced him into the family. When the Feds descended on two of the mob's gaming parlors across the border in West Virginia, Genovese learned Marano's friend was an undercover IRS agent. Someone had to pay, and with LaRocca sunning himself in Miami, retribution would be swift and bloody."

He lowered his voice and bent into the microphone, his listeners matching his posture by leaning forward to catch every word. "Twelve days before Christmas 1967, Genovese ordered one of Marano's friends to take him on what would prove to be his last road trip. A passing motorist found him slumped over the wheel of his car on a blacktop road near Mt. Pleasant. No twelve drummers drumming, only a washed-up hood with a bullet where his brain should have been."

Delores heard a collective exhale from the crowd. "Time doesn't permit me to tell you what that reckless act did to Frank Amato's empire, but you can read it all in my book, *Death in the Steel City*. I'll be at my table to sign copies."

That man knows how to sell better than he writes, Delores thought. He was in his late-fifties with a silver mane and a Van Dyke beard, not a hair out of place. Before the audience, he seemed to stand over six feet tall, but she'd seen him at his table and put him four inches shy of that.

An introvert, Delores found it difficult even to interact with fans who approached her. She watched as Parker

Stevens—whose real name, she learned, was Steven Parker —gathered up the pages of his manuscript and stepped away from the podium, raising himself on the balls of his feet.

"What are you working on now?" a voice called.

Stevens—or Parker, depending on how you looked at it —paused mid-stride and seemed to consider whether to answer. A dramatic touch, she decided, assuming the questioner was a shill. The crime writer returned to the microphone.

"I've been reluctant to discuss this before," he said. Sure you have, she thought. "But I'm investigating a murder that took place in 1993. The Pittsburgh Police Bureau never solved it, but I have."

He turned to leave, while a chorus of voices followed him with questions. "I can't say more about it yet. I may have revealed too much already. But this time next year, you'll find answers to all your questions in my forthcoming book." Proclaiming his thanks to everyone for listening, he took the four steps off the temporary stage and made for his table, the crowd trailing him to form a line.

They blocked access to Delores's space, but as she looked around at her fellow authors of mystery, science fiction, romance, thriller, gothic, young adult, and historical novels and the equally ignored nonfiction writers, she said aloud, "We're in the wrong business."

Allegheny County Police Detective Lydia Barnwell sat at the foot of her dining room table, facing her fiancé, South Hills Police Chief Calvin Mayfield. Though he was only eight feet away, she felt a chasm separated them.

Calvin's mother Ruth and Ben, his father, ate in silence between them. They had not revealed what time they would arrive from Toledo, only that they would do so. Lydia had prepared a shrimp salad with capers, fresh celery, and herbs on a bed of romaine lettuce with lemon vinaigrette dressing. She'd peeled and deveined wild Gulf shrimp — nothing farm raised for her future in-laws — but Ben stared at it as though it were a foreign dish.

"This is delicious," Ruth said even though she only picked at it. She looked across the table at her husband as if encouraging him to break his silence and agree.

This was not the first time she'd met the pair. They had visited when Calvin was still deputy chief and she a detective on the force of a borough in Pittsburgh's South Hills. Then, she'd only spoken to them in passing, since she and Calvin were not yet together. Lydia was living with one of the borough's patrol officers, a man who later died in the line of duty. In the wake of his death, Calvin and Lydia had fallen into bed together. She had considered it a mistake the next morning, but they repeated it a week later, and soon they were a couple.

Now, with plans for a wedding in the vague future, she faced what felt like a cross-examination, but no defense attorney posed questions.

As though in response, Ben asked his son, "How's the new job?"

Calvin, oblivious to his father ignoring her, reviewed how he'd become chief of Boyleston Borough following the retirement of the man who had served as a mentor to both of them, Karol Novak. Boyleston was then negotiating with two neighboring communities to combine their police departments into a regional law enforcement agency. Now, two days away, Calvin would be sworn in to a position he'd occupied in an acting capacity for six weeks.

Echoing a complaint Novak had often voiced, he told his father, "I love the job, but not the politics."

"You'd better get used to it," Ben said. "Politics is a part of life."

Lydia thought he might ask about her work, how she'd joined the Allegheny force, which investigated crimes of violence for all 117 police departments scattered throughout Pennsylvania's second-largest county except Pittsburgh, but he did not.

"We're so proud of you," Ruth said.

And why wouldn't they be? If her father were at the table … No, he wouldn't acknowledge the path she'd taken. He might even find fault, tell her how she might have done better if she'd remained in San Antonio.

Placing her knife and fork atop the half-eaten salad, she pushed it back a few inches and studied the three faces engaged in conversation. Dark faces. Almost pure black, an image driven home by the contrast with the string of pearls around Ruth's neck. She shuddered as a terrible thought careened through her body, her tight blonde curls shivering.

Calvin's father had emigrated from Jamaica when he was a child. While his ancestors may have inherited the English surname, one look at him revealed no trace of a white bloodline. Ruth's family had lived on Toledo's east side for generations, working in the petroleum and manu-facturing industries that defined the downwind side of the city. She had worked as an administrator in the public school system while raising Calvin. Lydia could not detect a wrinkle on her face. She always misjudged the age of Black people.

Facing them was this white woman whose children, if

she and Calvin were blessed with them, would break the blood line. Was that what made Ben turn away from her and Ruth pick at her food?

Excusing herself, she collected her plate, retreated to the kitchen, and let tears flow.

***

STEVEN PARKER PRESSED the remote control clipped to his visor and eased his Honda Odyssey into the garage, tapping the brake as his front bumper neared the wall. The ten-year-old vehicle had less than a foot of clearance when parked. He had nailed old sleeping bags to the drywall to protect both it and the car, but he sometimes misjudged the distance, usually on gray days when visibility was low.

It had been a mistake to buy a minivan, but between the time he'd purchased it and admitted Lois had been right all along, he'd been swept aside by the *Pittsburgh Herald* and didn't have the money to downsize.

He put the vehicle in park, got out from behind the wheel, and walked to the front to check the distance. Satisfied, he shut off the engine and raised the tailgate, which extended beyond the garage door. He was fortunate it wasn't raining, because he would then have had to back in to unload his unsold books. No cloud broke the surface of the blue sky on this autumn afternoon, and while the sun hung low at this hour, the air was still a pleasant sixty-eight degrees.

Parker removed two empty plastic cartons from the van and set them aside. He'd sold over forty copies, netting him almost six hundred dollars. If the number of those who'd scanned the QR code on his banner was an indication, more would come from sales of the ebook version. The day had been well worth his time.

He hauled out another container full of books then a fourth that contained his promotional sheets, pens, and the notepad containing the sign-up sheet for his newsletter. As he placed this box atop the full one, he felt a movement behind him, a rustling of air, a slight change of temperature. Parker half-turned and was about to speak when his eyes fastened on the raised arm and the object held in the gloved hands.

"Don't—" His was not a cry of alarm but a whispered plea, cut off mid-sentence as the blade of the shovel cleaved his skull.

The assailant stood over him, his chest heaving. Without a word, he dropped the tool, closed the tailgate, and pressed the button on the keypad to lower the garage door.

"You okay?" Calvin asked. Lydia nodded but didn't answer. "You left so suddenly."

She turned and faced him. "They drove five hours to visit you. I didn't want to interrupt."

"They also came to meet you."

"Did they?"

"Yes," he said. "What's wrong?"

She took the plates from his hand and scraped the leftovers into the garbage. "Let's talk about it later. I don't want to upset anyone."

"But something's bothering you. I can tell."

"It will keep," she said. "Later."

He uttered a small moan, conveying his helplessness.

Lydia stared out the kitchen window at her garden, withering in the fading autumn light.

"That was wonderful, dear." She turned to find Ruth donning a pair of rubber gloves.

"I can do that."

"No, you cooked for us. I'll clean up."

"Calvin often does that. You trained him well."

Ruth chuckled. "Ben and I worked full-time. We gave him jobs to do."

They worked side by side for a moment without speaking, breaking the silence simultaneously.

"Did you—"

"Calvin tells me—"

"Sorry," Lydia said, glad to have her seize the initiative. "You go first."

"No, I—"

"Please," she said. "Go ahead."

"I hear you lost your mother at quite a young age. I suspect you had a lot of responsibilities too."

"Yes, I barely remember her."

"You had no brothers or sisters?"

"I was an only child. My father was an Air Force officer. We lived on bases all over the world. He didn't know what to do with me. I kind of raised myself."

"I'm sorry to hear that."

"I sometimes regret not having a normal childhood, although some of my friends raised in two-parent homes had lives that were even more unsettled. It made me resilient. I'll say that much."

"I'm sure your father did the best he could. We can't wait to meet him." When Lydia's face betrayed confusion, Ruth added, "At the wedding."

"I'm not sure we—"

"Oh, did I misunderstand? I thought you were getting married."

"We are, but we're not planning a big ceremony."

Ruth peeled off the gloves and grasped Lydia's arms. "But you must. My mother is still alive. Calvin has aunts, uncles, and lots of cousins. We're a big family. Everyone will want to attend."

Lydia's Motorola interrupted the torrent. She picked it up and listened. "All right," she said. "On my way." She returned to the dining room, where Calvin's face was planted next to his father's.

"Suspicious death in Scott Township." She dialed her password into the gun safe to retrieve her weapon. "I may be late."

"You have to leave?" Ruth said.

"She's a homicide detective," Calvin explained. "When duty calls, she responds. We both do."

"Take your folks out for steak," she said. "They'll be hungry."

Never had she been more grateful for work to interrupt her personal life.

———

SEVEN POLICE CARS and an ambulance ringed a mustard-colored ranch-style home, their blue and red flashing lights attracting the attention of neighbors and passersby. Scott Township officers directed traffic on McMonagle Avenue while county officers held back curiosity seekers. Two news vans had pulled across the street, reporters speaking earnestly into cameras as they communicated their ignorance.

The house was at the base of a hill that wound up

Fairhaven Drive. Local cops had established an outer perimeter to keep the crowds back and marked off the immediate area in crime scene tape. The medical examiner's van was backed into the driveway of a garage on the lower level, alongside a white Honda Fit. Lydia parked behind a patrol car, flashed her ID at the officer, and advanced toward the garage, bending over to step inside, since the door had been pulled halfway down.

A blue sheet covered a body on the stone-tiled surface. Blood splatter arced behind it, staining a pile of books from an overturned plastic carton. The photographer had finished his work. Brandy Timmons, the crime scene investigator, crouched over the body. She glanced up as Barnwell hovered over her. She pulled back the sheet, revealing what remained of a man's skull. Timmons volunteered no information, and Barnwell did not quiz her. What had happened was apparent.

Other members of the team had bagged both ends of a round point shovel, laying it alongside a small pool of blood. An iPhone was alongside the body. Timmons's crew had bagged it as well. Two dusted for prints, while a third swept a broom across the floor, picking up leaves, debris, and potential evidence. The victim's left hand extended beyond the sheet, an indentation on his ring finger. Had someone stolen it?

As she prepared to question Patrol Officer Barry Barnes, who'd been first to arrive, Lydia's partner, Detective Lyle Jeffrey arrived, dressed in jeans, a denim jacket, and a cap from his son's baseball team. He took in the scene and joined her in questioning the patrol officer.

"He's Parker Stevens, the crime writer," Barnes told them. "His wife discovered the body when she came home.

She's upstairs now. Neighbors are with her. She's in quite a state."

Lydia told him to take another officer and question nearby residents to learn if anyone had spotted suspicious-looking individuals or vehicles lurking in the vicinity.

She led Jeffrey up the interior steps to the living area, entering a long-narrow hallway lined with family photographs. They followed the sound of weeping to their left. Three figures sat clustered around a circular coffee table. Two women held hands on a sofa, while a man who appeared to be in his fifties leaned toward them from an armchair. All looked up as she entered.

Barnwell introduced the two of them. "Which one of you is Mrs. Stevens?"

The older of the two women replied in a shaky voice, "I'm Lois Parker. Steven inverted his first and last names. It sounded more literary." Her light-brown hair was flecked with gray. A silver necklace interrupted her tan knit top. Neither looked expensive.

"And you are…"

"Joanne Schuster and my husband Ron," the other woman said. "We're neighbors."

A young man entered the front door, shoving his phone into the hip pocket of his chinos. Before either detective asked, he said, "I'm Bill Parker, Steve's son. Mom called me when—" He fumbled for the right word as his thumb massaged the index finger of his right hand.

"We'll interview all of you, but we'll begin with Mrs. Parker."

"I'll stay with her," the son said. "You can see she's in shock."

"I know this is difficult," Lydia said, "but I'll speak with her alone. We want to find who did this to your father, and I need to get her information while it's fresh in her mind."

He seemed about to protest, but Jeffrey ordered that he follow him toward the kitchen. The neighbors remained in their places. Lydia turned toward the husband, fixing her azure eyes on him. Her long nose and tight blonde curls completed the impression of a bewigged British judge staring down a barrister who had overstepped his bounds.

"We'd better leave them alone," Ron Schuster said to his wife. "Lois knows how to reach us if you need to speak to us."

"We will. Give me your address." She added it to the names she'd already recorded in her notebook.

Lydia waited until the front door closed then donned a reassuring smile as she turned toward the now-widowed woman. "I'm sorry to make you go through this, but we need to catch whoever attacked your husband. Every minute that goes by makes it more difficult."

Lois Parker covered her face with a tissue and nodded without speaking.

"How did you discover his body?"

"I opened the garage door and found him lying there." Her voice trembled as she spoke. "At first, I thought he'd had a heart attack, so I stopped the car and ran toward him, but I only took a few steps before I realized ..."

"What time was this?"

"I don't know exactly. Four-thirty? Four-forty-five? I called my son right away, and he phoned the police, so they'll have it."

She shuddered and wrapped her arms around herself, rocking back and forth. "Do you need water?"

"No, thank you. Joanne looked after me. She found a—" She pointed to an amber bottle resting alongside a half-filled glass on the end table. Lydia raised it and saw it contained lorazepam, a mild sedative. It had been prescribed for Joanne Schuster. "She returned to her house to find this?"

"No, I think she had it in her purse. I'm not certain. I'm not sure of anything." She tried accompanying this with a chuckle, but it deteriorated into a spasm of coughing.

Lydia asked if she needed a break, but the woman told her to continue. "The sooner you've asked your questions, the sooner I can lie down."

In response to her gentle questioning, Lois explained her husband had spent the day at a book fair in Mount Lebanon while she'd attended a movie in Robinson Township. As often happened with people under stress, she gave Lydia the name of the film. "It's the first time I've been to a theater since COVID. I wasn't that interested, but Jane was eager to see it and didn't want to go alone." Jane, she explained, was a woman she knew from church.

Not wanting to seem adversarial, Barnwell resisted the temptation to halt the torrent. "As you arrived home, did you see anyone else in the vicinity? Anyone near your property? A car parked on the street?" To each question, the woman shook her head.

"Your husband was a crime writer?"

Lois took her through his career, his years at one of Pittsburgh's dailies, the buyout that left him with far less than they could live on, and his turn to true crime articles and books to scrape together a living. "It's still two years before he can get social security and touch our retirement savings." As was true of many who were suddenly bereaved, she spoke of her husband in the present tense.

"Did he have any enemies? Someone he'd worked with at the paper? A character in one of his stories?"

Lois replied with a series of nos, adding that the crimes

of which he wrote were so old that none of the principals were still alive.

"Have there been any neighborhood disputes? Did he owe anyone money?" Keeping her voice level, Lydia ran through most of the reasons someone might want another person dead.

That left only one possibility. "I'm sorry to have to ask this, but I need to find a motive for what's happened. Were the two of you happy?"

To her surprise, she didn't react, appearing to give the question serious consideration. "What's happy?" she said. "We've been married thirty-four years and have been together since college. We've had good times and bad. At our age, I guess you'd say we've grown used to each other."

"Were there other women in his life?"

She looked away and inclined her head. Lydia waited, knowing she'd hit a nerve. "One," she said in a voice so soft that Lydia had to lean forward to hear her, "but it ended years ago. Another reporter. I'd heard rumors. A friend saw him together with a woman at a restaurant downtown. I went through his pockets and found a hotel receipt wadded up in his jacket. I confronted him. He denied it at first, but I made him confess." She met Lydia's eye for the first time since beginning the story. "He promised to end it. I heard she left the paper."

Wasn't that always the way? Two had tangoed, but when the music stopped, only the man remained on the dance floor. Lydia had to pry the other dancer's name from her. Lois claimed to know nothing else about her. "It was a long time ago," she said.

"There was only the one?" Barnwell asked.

Again, the woman gave the matter some thought before answering. "As far as I know."

"Can you think of anyone who would have done this to your husband? Someone with a grudge that festered?"

"No, I can't." She melted into the cushions and studied the ceiling. "I've realized... Well, no. I realized it back when he cheated on us that I don't know all that much about him. Do you believe that?"

Lydia did. She'd heard others say the same thing.

Detective Jeffrey almost had to push Bill Parker through the dining room and into the kitchen as he turned to check on his mother. "She'll be all right," Jeffrey said. "Barnwell has a gentle touch. If she needs you, she'll call out."

His shoulders slumping in defeat, the son relented. He led the detective into a spacious kitchen that looked out on a sloping lawn and oak trees parading their colors in the autumn breeze. "Hold on a sec. I need to make a quick call." He stepped into the hall, cupping his hand over his cell phone. Jeffrey stood near the door to eavesdrop. What could be so important?

"Someone entered the garage as he was unloading his books and struck him over the head with something heavy," he said. "It looks like a shovel." He answered a few questions and promised to keep in touch as Jeffrey retreated.

"Thanks," Bill said. "Do you want a cup of coffee? I can sure use one."

"That would be fine." He didn't need a jolt in the late afternoon, but if it put the man at ease, it was worth it.

The detective studied him as he dropped a pod into a coffee machine. He was of medium height, five-nine by Jeffrey's estimate, which, after a quarter century as a cop, was usually dead on. His wavy dark hair, steel-gray eyes, and pointed chin reminded him of an actor whose name he couldn't recall. Perhaps no one in particular, he thought as Parker slid a mug toward him and repeated the routine for himself. He wore an open-necked, short-sleeve blue shirt that displayed muscled arms.

"Cream?" he asked.

Jeffrey declined and took a chair at the breakfast table at the kitchen window, indicating with a nod of his head that Parker should join him. He propped his body worn camera on the surface and explained he was taping their conversation. "It saves you a trip to headquarters." Parker waved his hand, accepting the explanation.

"Who did you speak with just now?" Jeffrey asked.

"Christie, my sister. Mom asked me to alert her, but I waited until I got home to assess the situation for myself. It was all Mom could do to call me."

"That's how you learned?" It may have seemed like a silly question, but if one of the Schusters had conveyed the news, that put them on the scene early.

"Right. She was...not hysterical but confused. She said Dad was lying in a pool of blood in the garage and she didn't know who to turn to."

"And you..."

"Called 911. She was in no shape to do so. Then I left work and came here."

"Where's work?"

Parker told him he was development director for a small theater company in Pittsburgh's Oakland neighborhood. "It's opening night of a new production, *Good Day*, by a Texas writer. It concerns an exterminator who comes to clear out a wasp's nest. We've scheduled a donor reception after tonight's performance. I was setting up tables and putting up posters of the cast members—"

He stopped mid-sentence. "Christ, I need to cancel that. Can you give me another minute?"

Jeffrey waved him on and listened as he spoke to someone, barking out a chain of instructions. "Go to the office and get into my computer. Send out a broadcast email to the mailing list. Regrets. Family emergency. Will reschedule."

Jeffrey overheard a woman's voice responding but couldn't make out the words. He rose from the table and looked out the window as he listened. "No," he said, "do it now. I'm sorry, but I'm—"

The woman made a quick reply. Jeffrey watched his back tense. "Damn it, Jenny. Someone murdered my father. Do it!" He stared at the phone. "Fucking students with their heads up their asses. Where were we?"

Jeffrey thought he might have led with the news and requested the woman's help, but stress did strange things to people. Or was it his way to be brusque and demanding?

The detective led Parker through questions similar to those Barnwell was posing to his mother. He could not think of anyone who wanted to kill his father. He knew of no disagreements the man had with others.

"What about criminal figures he mentioned in his books?"

"They were about old cases," he said. "He rewrote stories he'd published over the years in his columns. If someone felt threatened by them, they would have been after him long before."

"What was he working on now?"

"I don't know. He never discussed his work with us. The first we knew of it was when he'd finished a book." No matter how Jeffrey approached the subject, the son could think of no motive for the slaying, but he volunteered an additional detail. "He's always tight-lipped about his projects, but on this one he was downright secretive. I think it was something special."

"What sort of person was he?" Jeffrey asked.

Parker seemed to give the matter inordinate thought. "He was a proud man. Over his years at the paper, he'd attracted a devoted following. He enjoyed meeting his fans. Many gave him leads for stories. When they laid him off, it punctured his ego. He couldn't understand how they could do that to him, of all people."

"He was bitter?"

The young man rose again and made himself another cup of coffee, not bothering to ask Jeffrey if he'd like a refill. "He'd convinced himself many folks subscribed to the paper only to read his column," he said over the gurgling of the machine. "When they let him go, he predicted their circulation would suffer. When it did, he took grim satisfaction." He brought his coffee to the table and stared into the cup. "It didn't occur to him the same thing was happening to most local papers. He thought he'd done it."

"When was this?"

"It must have been..." He did some calculations on his fingers. "Four years ago this Christmas. Can you believe they'd do that to someone on the holiday? Say, do you want another cup?"

Jeffrey declined the belated offer. "Did you get along?"

Again, Parker considered before answering. "We didn't fight, if that's what you mean."

"So you disagreed."

He looked over the detective's shoulder at the fading light. "Dad was a man of set opinions, which he was unafraid to express." He snorted, and Jeffrey decided his hesitation had less to do with uncertainty than with finding the most elegant way of expressing himself. "He didn't much care for my career plans."

"Fundraising?" Jeffrey asked.

"No, acting. I was a drama major at Point Park. It was all I'd ever wanted to do. He thought I was a dreamer, not that he put me down. He thought success on the stage was less about talent than luck. Perhaps he was right." Bill turned from the window. "He never questioned my talent but was concerned about my future."

He looked at Jeffrey for his reaction. When he got none, he said, "I landed this fundraising job. The pay's poor, and I'm not sure how effective I am. The arts are tough. People think the price of a ticket covers our costs. It doesn't come close. Without donors..."

"Was he happier about that line of work?"

"He didn't say. That wasn't his way. But he seemed pleased I was bringing in a steady paycheck." He peered into his empty mug. "It's funny how things worked out. He was always the breadwinner. Now my sister and I are employed."

"What does she do?"

"Christie's a professor of American studies at Smith College. Pretty good for thirty-two, don't you think?"

"Did that impress your father?"

The man stared at Jeffrey as though he hadn't been listening. "The only person my father impressed was himself." Parker shook his head as though warding off a thought. "That's too harsh. Don't get me wrong. He loved us, sent us to college, and let us follow our own paths, even if they weren't what he wanted for us. He could be a hard man, but he was fair. None of us is perfect."

He clasped his hands and bent as though in prayer. "I will miss him."

———

"I'll be late," Lydia said. "Give your parents my regrets."

"That bad?" Calvin said.

"Worse, and not a clue who's done it."

"We'll see you when you get here. Tommy's taking Howie out for a walk. I'm cooking out on the deck."

Howie was the West Highland terrier bequeathed her by the father of her late lover. Lydia paid Tommy, a fatherless neighborhood boy whom Calvin had informally adopted, to walk him twice a day. He'd offered to do it for free, but Lydia had insisted. Anna, his mother, was a good friend who showered them with homemade food whenever she got the chance. A diabetic, her meals were always healthy. Lydia liked her for that but loved her for her friendship and bright spirit.

"Everyone's taken care of except for yours truly," she said.

"You want to tell me what was bothering you this afternoon?" Calvin asked.

"No es importante."

"All right," he replied. "Suffer in silence."

She gave him a laugh she didn't feel, told him she loved him, and ran off as they reached the door of the Schuster house.

"I'm fixing dinner," Joanne said. Her eyes were red, and she carried a crumpled tissue in her hand. "I'm making extra for Lois and Bill."

"This will take a minute. We can speak while you cook."

The neighbor backed into her home, raising her eyebrows in an exaggerated display of annoyance. Her husband sat at the kitchen counter nursing a glass of red wine. "Can I get you anything?" he said.

"No, thanks," Jeffrey said. He removed his camera and gave the pair the same explanation for recording their interview he'd provided to Bill Parker. "How long have you known the deceased?"

"The deceased?" Ron Schuster said. "Christ! His name was Steven."

"How long have you been acquainted?"

Joanne responded, "We bought this house—what, Ron? —twelve years ago. Lois welcomed us with a big casserole. We've been friends ever since."

"The closest," her husband said and gulped from his glass.

"Put that down. You don't need to finish the bottle." She turned to the detectives. "He's upset. We both are. Lois is my dearest friend."

"You were also friendly with them?" Jeffrey asked the husband.

"Very close," her husband said.

"They golfed together. Tell him, Ron."

"We hung out. Made up a foursome with a couple of others. Took in a few Pirates games." He pulled the bottle toward him.

"Did he have any enemies?" Lydia asked, eager to break through the back and forth between the pair.

"How would I know? He kept to himself," Ron said. Was he always this belligerent, or was the alcohol talking?

"Everyone liked Steven," she said. "He was a local celebrity." She reached for another tissue, sobbed into it, then cast three chicken breasts into a sauté pan, flinching as the grease hit her arm.

"Everyone," Ron said.

Joanne shot him a look of contempt. "It had to be a random thing. Nothing like this happens in our neighborhood. Not to someone like Steven. It scares the hell out of me."

They jockeyed with the pair for another ten minutes, but Joanne was consumed with frying the chicken while Ron, ignoring her instructions, polished off the bottle and opened a replacement.

"What have we learned?" Jeffrey said as they returned to their cruisers.

"Not a damned thing. He's drunk, she's preoccupied, and Officer Barnes says none of the other neighbors saw a thing. The garage opens on McMonagle, and no homes front on the street for a block in either direction. We have no eyes or cameras on the murder scene."

"And everyone loved the victim."

"Everyone except his wife," she said, reviewing her conversation with the widow. "And she and her son are accounted for."

CHAPTER TWO

LYDIA AWOKE before Calvin or his parents. She made herself a cup of espresso and perched on the barstool while she jotted notes on a yellow pad. Bill Parker had given her the name of his father's agent, and she'd left a message on his voicemail. She'd speak to whoever organized the book fair to get a list of other authors at the event. This being a Sunday, she'd have to wait until one o'clock when the library opened, and it might be difficult to reach potential witnesses. She hoped she and her partner didn't have to interview every writer, but they had to start somewhere.

"Any leads?" Calvin placed a beefy hand on her neck and gave her a ten-second massage.

"Apart from an affair fifteen years ago, he seems to have had a blameless life. Everyone loved him, or so we're led to believe."

"Speak no ill of the dead," he said.

"And leave nothing for us to go on." She brewed a pot of coffee then cracked eggs into a Pyrex pan, sliced mushrooms and sautéed them for a half minute, added milk, cheese, and broccoli, shoving the stirred mixture into the oven. "If you and your dad want sausage, it's up to you."

Ben rumbled in and collapsed into a chair at the breakfast table. "Bad night?" Calvin asked him.

"I only sleep well in my own bed," he replied.

Lydia poured him a cup of coffee. Ben carried it into the living room, turning the television set loud enough to awaken neighbors. As she set the table, Lydia heard a KDKA reporter detail what was known about the crime writer's murder. "County police say Parker's wife discovered the body when she returned from an afternoon with a friend. They've questioned friends and neighbors but so far have no leads. Parker had long been a crime reporter for—"

"Hey," Ben called, "it's you."

Lydia followed the sound of his voice and caught a fleeting image of her walking away from the camera toward the Schuster's residence. "You want me to back it up?"

"No, thanks," she said with a chuckle. "It's not my best side."

"You're working on this murder?"

"She's in charge of it, Dad."

Ben turned toward her, his eyes round and his mouth open. "You investigate things like this?"

"She's a homicide detective," Calvin said. "It's her job, and she's good at it."

"Well!" he said. Lydia was certain this was not the first time Ben had heard this, but with an active case being splashed across the television screen, it registered. "Will you find the killer?"

"That's why they're paying me," she said. "Come on. Let's get you fed."

He followed her into the kitchen, sat at the foot of the

table, and watched as she freed a slice of casserole from the pan. "And she cooks," he said to his son.

"She has to," Ruth said, sliding into the seat near the window. "Your son never learned how."

"Au contraire," Lydia said. "He's gotten pretty good at it."

"I lived on my own for a few years before she found me," Calvin said.

They sat in silence, Ben devouring what seemed a pound of sausage links Calvin had overcooked. His wife ate with dignity, averting her eyes from the ravenous display taking place alongside her. "Where are we going to services?" she asked.

Calvin and Lydia locked eyes. Neither of them were churchgoers.

"I have to report in," she said.

"You have to work on Sunday?"

"She's a detective," Ben said. "She's working on a murder."

"I know, dear, but on Sunday?"

"She has to get right on it. Every hour that goes by makes it more difficult to solve."

"Well..." his mother said.

Lydia rose from the table to dress for work. She had no intention of adding salt to the wound by explaining that her partner always took his family to Mass on Sunday, leaving her, on this day, the officer in charge.

LYDIA WAS NOT the only one working on the Lord's day. She arrived at headquarters to find a message from Brandy

Timmons, the crime scene investigator, enclosing her report and a cryptic note reading, "Call me when you've read this."

The document was three pages long, not including the photographs taken at the scene. The victim had been found lying on his back with a deep wound to his head, both arms spread as though warding off an attack. A round, pointed instrument of the sort used both as a spade and a shovel was near his feet. An analysis showed the blood found on the blade matched that of the victim. His were the only fingerprints on the handle and were smudged, suggesting the killer wore gloves, though none were found in the garage.

Parker had been unpacking books from the trunk of his vehicle when he was attacked. Because the garage was only inches longer than the SUV, the report suggested the door had been raised at the moment of the attack. Blood splatter was found on the plastic containers, the wall behind the victim, and his clothing. A partial footprint in the victim's blood showed the killer had stepped forward after administering the blow.

Reconstructing the attack based on the victim's height and the angle of the wound, the team estimated the assailant, either male or female, stood between 5'7" and 5'10". There was no blood on the doorsill leading to the inner stairway or on the steps themselves, indicating the attacker had not entered the house. They matched fingerprints in the garage to the victim, his wife and son, and the Schusters, who were frequent visitors. It would take days, if not weeks, before the FBI could process recovered DNA samples to find a match, if it existed.

Besides books, one of the two containers held a faux-leather bag containing $212 in cash. The victim's wallet, holding another thirty-six dollars, had been in the right front pocket of his trousers, along with his wedding ring and key fob. Robbery did not appear to have been a motive. Parker's cell phone had been found alongside the body and turned over to the ACPD's digital forensics team for examination.

Among the sweepings from the garage floor, the team recovered a golf scorecard, an instruction manual for a power drill, and a crumpled receipt from a Mexican restaurant. She glanced at the scanned images and set them aside. Timmons had sealed the originals in a plastic bag and deposited them in an evidence locker.

Lois said the garage had been closed when she arrived. While the keypad required a four-digit code to raise the door, one had only to push the enter button to close it. Brandy's team found no fingerprints on the victim's Odyssey other than his own.

In short, the killer had come and gone, leaving little physical evidence except for a partial shoe print, which they were working to identify.

Lydia leaned back and imagined what must have occurred. Parker had arrived home and begun unpacking his books and display items with the garage door open. Someone had slipped in behind him, grabbed a shovel, and landed a single blow. Taking nothing, the assailant had stepped outside and pushed the enter button on the keypad. Had the killer known he didn't need the code to lower the door, or had he been lucky? The garage was set back from McMonagle Avenue at such an angle that passing drivers might not have witnessed the attack. No security cameras were trained on the spot.

Having digested the report, Lydia called Timmons, as

the investigator had requested. After discussing her find-ings, she said, "There's one thing I didn't include because I don't speculate in my reports, but I'm sure I'll be asked about it when I'm called to testify."

Barnwell knew she was about to alert her to a point a defense attorney might use to undermine their case.

"Parker had his back turned when the assailant entered. Something caused him to turn around, perhaps a sound as the shovel was raised. The blade caught him above the temple." This, Lydia knew, was the most vulnerable point on the head. Only a thin layer of bone covered critical blood vessels and nerves. "We don't know whether the attacker led with the blade or the flat of the shovel, in which case the victim turned into it."

"Meaning that whoever did this might have meant to injure rather than kill him."

"You got it."

The attacker's intent could determine the charge on the continuum of homicide. "Thanks, Brandy."

"Any time," she said. "No, I take that back."

They enjoyed their dark humor and ended the call.

BARNWELL WAS DIALING Parker's agent again when her phone rang. A squeaky voice asked if she was the detective in charge of the crime writer's murder. When she confirmed it, the woman said, "I think I know why he was killed."

Lydia listened for a few seconds and said, "Where can we meet?"

She identified herself as Delores Tavener and gave her address. Ten minutes later, Barnwell arrived at her home, a rectangular brick structure on Earlsmere Avenue in

Dormont. She took the four steps from the sidewalk to the front yard, noting that they were canted toward the left. The house appeared otherwise in decent shape.

Before she could knock, the door sprang open, revealing a small round woman, looking not unlike one of Santa's helpers. "I'm Delores, but everyone calls me Dee." She stuck out her hand, forcing Lydia to stoop to grasp it. She was not over four-foot-ten, and her high-pitched voice, hooped earrings too large for her face, and cotton dress with floral prints completed the cartoonish image.

"Please come in," she said. "We don't get many visitors, do we, girls?"

As she stepped into the vestibule, Lydia's eyes watered. The girls, she knew without spotting one, were neither children nor roommates, instead those of the feline variety. She took the offered seat, an overstuffed armchair whose beige corduroy upholstery had been denuded by the persistent sharpening of claws. The detective reached for a tissue paper and filled it.

"Oh dear, are you allergic?" Dee asked.

"Very." She'd once held a hairless cat without the accustomed sneezing and watering of her eyes, but any other breed sent her rushing to her medicine cabinet for Benadryl. She never had the same reaction to dogs, leading her to suggest to her allergist it was all in her head. He'd agreed, though not in the way she meant it.

"You can get shots for that, you know," Dee said. "They desensitize you."

"I'll look into that." A gray tabby leapt from nowhere and took possession of the back of the chair. She turned to see the animal, which glowered at her. "I take it this is her spot."

The woman giggled. "Everything is." An orange tabby ventured into the room, eyed the stranger, and retreated.

Eager to get the interview over, Lydia placed her camera between them and explained why she was recording it. "You said you saw the victim at yesterday's book fair. Were you acquainted with him?"

"Sort of," she said. "I sign up for as many of these events as I can. I'm self-published, and it's the best way to meet readers and make sales. He attends most of them, so we've seen each other but haven't exchanged two words. I write gothic romance novels. Most take place on secluded islands or in old homes. My latest, The Shroud of Walpole, is set in Massachusetts before the Revolution. My heroine..."

Lydia listened to as much as she could take, waited for Delores to catch her breath, and said, "And Mr. Parker wrote a different sort of book."

"Yes, his were nonfiction, so our paths didn't cross. That's not his real name, by the way."

"I'm aware he used a pen name. So how did you come upon him yesterday?"

"The way it works, we each rent a table," she said. "It's fifty dollars, but if you want electricity, it's one hundred. You set out your books and promotional materials. Some writers erect big cloth banners behind them. I use posters, because my titles are always changing. I write four a year."

"Did you speak to him," Barnwell asked as the gray tabby ventured onto her shoulder, "or did he approach you?"

"Nothing like that. The organizers pick six or seven authors to give presentations during the day. There's a stage set up at one end of the church parking lot. They let the library use it except for Sunday morning. The library's closed then anyway."

Lydia wished the woman had an editor. "And Mr. Parker was one presenter."

"He has—he had, I guess, a big voice. They had a microphone and loudspeakers set up, but we couldn't make out most of the presentations from where we sat. We could hear him though. He was discussing his latest book, something to do with the Mafia in Pittsburgh. It was a story about how one mobster had another killed. People flocked to hear him tell it. No one came to my table while he was speaking, even though mine is a totally different genre." She sighed and threw up both hands. "I wish I could do that, but I'm too shy to speak to people."

She was doing a decent job at the moment.

"So you think there's a connection between his underworld story and his murder?" Lydia blew her nose again.

"No, it was after he'd finished. Someone asked what he was working on. We often get that. 'What's your next book about?' But this seemed a bit … contrived. Like he was waiting for the question."

"He'd put someone up to it?"

"Exactly. That's when he said he thought he'd solved a murder from several years ago. He was cagey about it. The police hadn't caught the killer, but he'd figured it out. Someone asked for details, but he said they'd have to read about it when his book came out."

"This was a local murder?"

"I think so. I don't recall the details, only that someone had been killed, the police hadn't solved it, but he had."

The woman could recall nothing else, not where the murder had occurred or when. "But if the killer heard him say that and followed him to his house... You see why I called you."

Lydia suspected Delores had an overactive imagination.

She was a novelist after all. But she assured her she'd done well to notify them, thanked her for her time, and took herself and her allergies with her.

***

"THANKS FOR HOLDING DOWN THE FORT." Jeffrey slipped into the desk alongside hers in the bullpen. He raised his coffee mug to his lips before asking his question. "What's up?"

She shared the CSI report, the fingerprint evidence, cash and cell phone found along the body, and the three items swept up from the garage floor. "According to the scorecard, Stevens, Schuster, and two others played at the Mount Lebanon course on Wednesday. Stevens won. Schuster had the high score."

"Probably hungover," Jeffrey said.

"And two people went out for Mexican food the night before."

"Taco Tuesday," Jeffrey said as he eyed the receipt. "We go there."

"I'm also watching something on YouTube," Barnwell said. He slid his chair closer to her and saw a figure behind a podium stabbing his finger into the air as he spoke.

"Another writer heard Parker discuss his next book yesterday. I talked to the head librarian and learned they'd streamed the presentations. You need to see this."

She scrubbed the video back once, twice, then a third time. Parker thanked the audience for listening and stacked one set of papers atop the other. A breeze caught a page and tried to make off with it, but he snagged it with one hand and returned it to the stack. He turned as though to leave when a shouted question made him pause. Neither officer could make out what the person had asked, but the context was clear.

Parker seemed to consider before returning to the microphone. "I've been reluctant to discuss this before now," he said, looking out on the audience as though searching for something. Permission to go ahead or a specific person?

"I've been investigating a murder that took place here in 1993." He paused again as though considering whether to continue. "The Pittsburgh Police Bureau never solved it, but I have."

He turned to leave, but a chorus of voices halted him. "I can't say more about it yet. I may have revealed too much already." He told the crowd they could read his solution when his book came out the following year.

"My witness thought this was staged," Lydia said, "that he'd planted the question."

"It has a theatrical flourish," Jeffrey said.

"She also thought it might provide a motive for his murder. Someone in the audience might have heard him, decided he was referring to them, and followed Parker home. What do you think?"

"It's a possibility."

"I put little stock in it when she told me, but this is the third time I've watched this clip, and I'm no longer sure."

"So what's our next step, Detective?"

"We go through the victim's papers to find any notes he might have on this murder. We get a search warrant for his phone and computer. I look through the files for unsolved homicides occurring in Pittsburgh during 1993." Jeffrey nodded in agreement. "I've placed another call to his agent, but he hasn't returned it. The librarian is forwarding still shots they took at the event. Perhaps we can identify someone."

"I'll have the public information officer issue an appeal," he said. "There are likely to be a few dozen others who snapped photos."

"Not that it will do us much good," Lydia countered. "A slew of nameless individuals wandering around at a book far."

"Once we identify which case Parker was investigating, we can grab Pittsburgh's file and match their suspects to these images."

"It's a long shot," Lydia said. Jeffrey agreed, but it was all they had. No one to whom they spoke had hinted at a motive. The only blemish on the writer's reputation was an affair he'd had more than a decade ago.

"His daughter, Christie, is flying in from Hartford in the morning. We'll question her as soon as she gets here. Meanwhile, Bill Parker is asking when we'll release the body for burial. I told him it's up to the coroner. He's not happy."

"He'll have to get over it," Jeffrey said. "Meanwhile, we have somewhere to start."

———

They divided the work. Jeffrey would check the alibis of both Lois Parker and her son while Lydia searched through the author's notes. She notified Mrs. Parker that she was on her way and was about to close her link to the ACPD database when a message came through. Tyrell Brown, the pathologist, had filed an autopsy report.

"That was quick," she said aloud. She opened the file and began reading.

Steven John Parker was a white male, fifty-eight years

old, sixty-eight inches in height, weighing 163 pounds. He had blue eyes, white hair, and had been circumcised. Rigor mortis was not present, as the body had been transferred to the medical examiner's office on Penn Avenue and refrigerated within two hours of his death. Brown listed every item Parker had been wearing when killed, down to the color of his socks. There was nothing remarkable about any of it.

Parker had been "well developed and well nourished," the report said, with "a laceration of the face and scalp and a fracture of the left laterosagital arch and the laterosagital accessor arch caused by the sharp edge of a blunt object." He'd been struck in the temple, in other words, as Brandy had told her.

She read through the pathological diagnosis, which showed he had been struck only once with sufficient force to cause his death. In falling onto the tiled floor of the garage, he had fractured his right forearm. Clay dirt was found in the temporal lobe, identical to debris on the shovel's blade.

The coroner listed the cause of death as laceration of the brain and blunt-force trauma. Death had been instantaneous. He estimated the attack had occurred between 3:30 and 4:30 p.m. Bill Parker had called 911 at 4:47. Given the estimated time when Lois had discovered the body, she had missed the intruder by minutes, perhaps avoiding the same fate.

The report listed the gross description of the cadaver, the condition of every organ from skin to bladder. Here she found two items out of the ordinary. Steven Parker had suffered from a mild form of atherosclerosis caused by plaque accumulation in the arteries. While there was no sign of cancer, he had been suffering from steatotic liver disease. While this didn't prove he was a heavy drinker, alcohol was a frequent contributor to what was commonly known as fatty liver.

Brown indicated that his report was incomplete. He had sent out tissue samples to detect the presence of drugs in his system. This could take days. But she had new questions to ask of the widow. Was he being treated for his heart condition and was he an alcoholic?

She hadn't yet formed a clear picture of the victim, but a few snapshots were falling into place.

JANE BRANSCOMB BEGAN NODDING before Jeffrey finished his question. "*Killers of the Flower Moon*," she said. "I loved the book and wanted to see what Martin Scorsese did with it. Lois wasn't interested, but she called me Friday and agreed. I think she was doing me a favor. She seemed to enjoy it, but Molly—the role Lily Gladstone played—her story was so sad. And for Lois to drive home and see her husband like that—"

Jeffrey interrupted the onslaught, "And she drove?"

"Yes, I'd offered, but she insisted."

"What time did you leave the theater?"

"It started at noon, and there were no previews. That's unusual. I guess it's because the movie is so long. Even so, we stayed through the credits. It must have been close to 3:45."

Jeffrey knew it took about twenty-five minutes to get from the mall in Robinson to Scott Township. "Did she drop you off?"

"No, I asked her to come in for coffee. She didn't want any, but we sat and discussed the movie for a few minutes. I offered her my copy of the book, but she wasn't interested.

Then she got worried her husband would need her help unpacking his books, so she left."

"What time was this?"

"I don't know, around 4:30. She wasn't here fifteen minutes."

The Parker home was five minutes away, so Jeffrey estimated she'd opened the garage door at about 4:35. Twelve minutes later, Bill Parker had called in the emergency. Lois's story fit. He asked Jane if she had saved the stubs. She replied they were electronic tickets and handed him her phone, which confirmed she'd bought two tickets to the noon showing.

He drove to the Janus Theater Company, a small space in a former Methodist church off Fifth Street in Oakland. Intermission of the matinee performance of Good Day had ended, and there was no one at the ticket window. Stepping inside, he found a pair of college students sitting on a stairway to what had once been the choir loft, now the theater's balcony. He asked for whoever was in charge, and one nodded toward a door on the opposite side of the lobby.

Jeffrey entered and encountered a woman only slightly older than the students seated at a cheap metal desk, wearing a worried expression. He identified himself, and she did the same, stating her name as Rachel Waldman. "I'm glad you've come."

When he asked if she was the director, she corrected him. "Interim director. Todd left in late summer after getting crosswise of the board. So I'm it."

"Were you here yesterday afternoon?"

"Until about 3:45. I left to take a nap and get dressed. I always do that before an evening performance. We premiered a new play last night."

"Was Bill Parker here?"

Her face fell. "That's why you're asking. I should have guessed. I thought it was something else. We had a break-in last week. Someone stole all our costumes and props. I can't imagine what good it did them, but it sure screwed us over. We rent the costumes, so we'll have to pay for them if they don't turn up. When you introduced yourself, I hoped …" She sighed then collected herself. "Bill. It's a goddamn outrage what happened to his dad. Have you caught who did it?"

Jeffrey ignored her question, repeating his own. "Was he here when you left?"

"Yeah, we were supposed to have a reception following last night's performance. He was setting up tables and the bar downstairs."

"But he had to cancel it?"

"He sent out a notice in the afternoon. It didn't tell you much, only that there was a family emergency. We'd ordered hors d'oeuvres and champagne. Prosecco, really. We can save the booze, but the food…"

"I thought someone named Jenny sent it out."

"Jennifer Tillman. She's a student at Point Park. Maybe she did, but it went out under his account. We don't provide her with one. She's an assistant."

"Is she here now?"

"I haven't seen her since yesterday. They were both here when I left. We're a small company. We don't have spare hands."

Jeffrey thanked her and rose to leave. "I hope you catch whoever did this."

"Rest assured, we will."

"We need those costumes. We're on a tight budget here and can't afford the expense. I don't know how I can keep the doors open much longer."

Barnwell turned off Greentree Road, shielding her eyes from the sun hugging the horizon. The days were growing shorter. Soon, Southwestern Pennsylvania would be wrapped in a gray blanket for months on end. Two Scott Township patrol officers directed traffic around the crime scene. One blocked the entrance to Fairhaven Drive, allowing only residents to enter. Another stood at the driveway leading to the garage, urging traffic on. There was nothing to see here, but drivers slowed as they passed, hoping to glimpse something they could share with their ghoul friends.

She parked on Fairhaven and crossed the street to the front door. Joanne Schuster answered her ring and stepped aside. "Lois is trying to rest," she said. Beyond her, Lydia saw bags of vegetables and fruit vying for space on the dining table. "The neighbors have been generous. Too much so. We don't know what to do with all this food."

"Who was that at the door?" Lois Parker appeared at the top of the stairs, wearing a robe and slippers. Her hair hung straight to her shoulders, and her skin looked gray. It was a contrast to the makeup and dress she'd worn the day before. "Oh, it's you. Have you caught whoever did this?"

"I'm afraid not," the detective replied, "but a fellow writer gave us what may be a promising lead. Do you know what story your husband was working on?"

Lois descended the thirteen steps and eased herself into a dining chair. She lowered her head and rubbed her fore-head. "No, Steven never discussed his work. He went into his office, closed the door, and sat there doing whatever he did. Three hours every morning. He even had a coffee maker there."

Barnwell posed two more questions, but Lois maintained she knew nothing about his writing. "I haven't even read his books. The subjects don't interest me."

"Mrs. Parker, was your husband under a doctor's care?"

She sat erect, her face contorted in a frown. "He sees his doctor once a year. We both do. Why?"

"Was he seeing a cardiologist?"

"A heart doctor? Not that I'm aware of. Why?"

Joanne Schuster, who'd been hovering in the background, took a seat alongside her. "The pathologist found evidence of blocked arteries. Were you aware of this?"

"No," Lois said.

"He never mentioned it to us," Joanne said. "Was he about to have a heart attack?"

"I'm not a physician. Ask his PCP." She took down the doctor's name and number.

"Was he a heavy drinker?"

"What kind of question is that?" Joanne asked.

"I asked Mrs. Parker."

She tossed her head over her shoulder toward a wheeled cart stocked with liquor bottles. "He only drank bourbon but liked to keep something on hand for friends."

"Did he drink to excess?"

Again, the friend interrupted, "What does that have to do with his murder?"

Lydia took that as an answer to her question. "Something else found during the autopsy," she said.

"He was always under control," Lois said, "never abusive, the way some men get. But yes, he liked to drink. He always did, but after the paper let him go…"

Lydia waited, but his widow had nothing more to say. "I'm not trying to be intrusive, but we have so little to go on.

We're trying to form a picture of your husband. Anything that helps us understand him may be relevant."

"He was a decent man," Joanne said. "He loved his country, his church, and his family."

Was she preparing a eulogy? "I'd like to see his office," Lydia said. "I need to know what story he was writing."

Lois waved toward the stairs, and her friend said, "I'll show you the way." She led her up and pushed open the door to a small room along the back of the house. Had it been a family home, it would have served as an infant's bedroom. A window overlooked the trees at the edge of the hill, but the desk faced away from it. "You shouldn't upset her."

Lydia stared at the woman until she lowered her eyes. "This is a murder investigation. My job is to solve it. To do that, I have to ask questions. Sometimes they're far more intrusive than these."

"All right," she said. "I'll leave you to it, but try to be considerate. Lois has just lost her husband. We're in mourning."

Lydia didn't respond, and the neighbor retreated, muttering to herself. An integrated computer rested on the desk. She touched the keyboard, and an image of a mountain range appeared on the screen. An icon across the bottom contained the single word "Parker." She clicked on the mouse and found it demanding a password. Ross Sutton, who headed digital forensics, had instructed all officers to leave electronic gear as they found it. If it was off, leave it off. If it was on, leave it that way. She didn't touch the keyboard.

A black laser printer rested to the right of the monitor. The power was off, and the out tray was empty. A desk lamp with an articulated arm was attached to the desk. A mesh container held a handful of pencils, an assortment of red and black pens, and a pair of scissors. A yellow writing pad was to the left of the keyboard. None of the pages contained writing, but she found an impression on the top sheet. She dropped it into an evidence bag and sealed it.

Beneath the window, a small bookcase held a dictionary, thesaurus, instruction books on writing, and copies of Parker's previous books. A coffee maker, similar to the one in the kitchen, sat atop it. She opened the folding closet doors on the far wall. Built-in shelving held reams of paper, a replacement cartridge of ink toner, and file folders. Lydia pulled them out and thumbed through them. Most contained newspaper clippings of stories Parker had written over the years. She spent most of an hour combing through them but found nothing regarding an unsolved murder from 1993.

Whatever she was looking for wasn't here. And something else was missing. Who sat at a desk for half the day and didn't have some photos? Children's first Christmas. Trip to the Grand Canyon. Parker's workplace was sterile.

She left the office, passing a bedroom door. Cracking it open, she saw a queen-size bed, a side table with a reading lamp and a stack of Parker's books, and a highboy dresser. She opened the latter and found men's clothing—socks, underwear, short-sleeve shirts, and pajamas. Lydia closed the door behind her and looked into the master bedroom at the head of the stairs. Another queen-size bed, matching nightstands with only lamps on their surfaces, a table at the window with a Queen Anne-style chair alongside it. Throw pillows everywhere. Perfumes and a jewelry box on the dresser, which was filled with women's clothing.

They slept in separate rooms. There was nothing unusual about that. Many couples did. But given what Lois had told her the day before about her husband's past affair, she wondered if the arrangement told a larger story. Descending the stairway to the main floor, she found her seated at the dining table with a bowl of soup before her. Joanne was in the kitchen making what appeared to be a sandwich. Lydia heard her weeping and saw her draw a sleeve across her nose as she worked. None for me, thanks.

"Do you know the password to his computer?" she asked.

Lois looked up from her lunch and shook her head. "No idea."

"Your husband played golf with Ron Schuster and two others on Wednesday."

"They often do."

"Do you have the names of the others?"

Again, Lois shook her head. "I do," Joanne said, stepping in from the kitchen. "I'll get them for you. Is it important?"

"Everything is." Turning to Lois, she said, "You went to a restaurant Tuesday night?"

"No. We almost never go out these days. Not since he retired."

"Totopos?" Lydia prompted.

"That's us," Joanne said. "We go there every Tuesday."

"We found the receipt in the garage."

"It must have fallen out of Ron's slacks when they left to play golf. A banker friend of ours says to never leave the customer's copy on the table. He always scoops it up and stuffs it in his pocket. I keep finding them when I wash clothes."

She thanked the women, told them not to touch anything in the office, and explained that they'd issue a warrant to take possession of it. "Take it now," Lois said.

"No," she said. "There's a procedure I must follow to protect the chain of evidence." She thanked her again and expressed her regrets. Lois appeared not to have heard her.

LYDIA RETURNED HOME to find Calvin at the dining room table alongside Tommy Molnar. "What treaty ended the Revolutionary War?" he asked.

"Ghent?" Tommy asked.

"Close, but you're about three decades too late."

"Paris." Lydia said as she breezed toward the kitchen, shedding her jacket and rolling up her sleeves.

"Hey," Calvin called after her. "No fair. Besides, there's nothing for you to do."

Ruth and Anna Molnar, Tommy's mother, were bent over a sheet pan filled with chicken thighs, small potatoes, and lemon. "You're busy," Ruth said. "This is my specialty."

"I see you've met my best friend," Lydia said.

"Mine now," Ruth replied.

She changed out of her work clothes and returned to find the table set and everyone ready to take their seats. Ruth served plates in the kitchen, and Anna brought them to the table. Ben asked the blessing without an introduction. "And Lord, we are so proud of our son and all that he has accomplished. Protect him in all he does."

"And Lydia too," Ruth piped up.

"And Lydia," he said.

The food was delicious, and Lydia said so, but the meal caught in her throat. Why had Ben excluded her? Did he resent the fact his son was marrying a white woman?

Later, as they were side by side in bed, she said, "I don't think your father likes me."

"He does," Calvin said. "It's just his way."

"He doesn't speak to me."

He stilled for a moment. "Have you tried speaking to him?"

If there were a spare bed in the house, she would have moved to it, but they were all filled. Instead, she stayed awake, wondering if her relationship with the man she loved was doomed.

CHAPTER THREE

LYDIA PARKED her cruiser in front of headquarters, facing a day in which devotion and duty vied for her time. As she approached the steps to head upstairs to the detective division, a familiar figure stopped her in her tracks. "Nadine?" she said. "Is that you?"

A young Black woman fixed her with a broad smile. "One and the same."

Nadine Foster, a patrol officer with the North Fayette Police Department, had helped her on her first case with the county. Now she was wearing an ACPD uniform. "You've joined us? Why didn't you say something?"

The young woman tossed her black curls and laughed. "It's only my first day since completing training. I knew I'd eventually run into you. I was saving the surprise."

"Well, welcome. I'm glad you've made it." Lydia now had a patrol officer she could trust. The woman had helped her face down a recalcitrant county officer during the case they'd worked together. They stood at the base of the stairs and talked for a moment before Lydia bounded up the stairs, telling the young officer they'd catch up later. When she entered the bullpen, Lyle was already at his desk, his usual mug of coffee beside him, eyes glued to the monitor. It wasn't often he beat her in. As hours passed without a lead, both shared a sense of urgency.

"Sutton has something for us," he said. Lydia hadn't even taken her seat as she followed her partner across the hall to the lair of the digital forensics detective. Sutton was an immense man, standing well over six-two and stocky, built more for breaking down doors than breaking into electronic devices, but the latter was his forte. When he plowed a wake through the bullpen, loose paper flew from desks and the floor trembled in awe. He spun around in his drafting chair as they entered. "Four-thirteen," he said.

Jeffrey wrinkled his face in bewilderment and was about to speak, but Barnwell got there first. "How can you be so sure?"

"When he fell, his watch posted an alert. Because he didn't respond, it alerted 911. Scott Township sent out a cruiser but found nothing awry." Steven Parker had arrived home to be struck down at 4:13 p.m. His wife discovered the body about twenty minutes later and called her son. He had placed the emergency call at 4:47. It wasn't often they could fix a time of death to the second, not that it got them closer to a suspect.

"Have you cracked his computer?" Jeffrey asked. "He was investigating an unsolved murder that may point us toward whoever killed him."

"I'll get on it," Sutton said. "Right now, we're trying to crack his phone." He explained that the victim's cell phone still had battery power when they received it. In such cases, the procedure was to plug it in and keep it alive then throw number combinations at it until it unlocked. "He used six figures, rather than four, so it'll take us a bit longer, but we'll get into it. We always do."

"We always do," Jeffrey chuckled as they settled into their desks. When all else failed, Sutton and his team broke the phone apart and removed the chips inside. Rarely did they encounter something impenetrable.

"Calvin's investiture is at eleven," she said. "I need to be there."

"Yes, you do."

"Parker's agent has finally returned my call, and Christie Parker, the daughter, is on a flight from Hartford now. I'd intended to meet her at the airport, but—"

"You handle the agent, and I'll take the daughter," Jeffrey said. "You can't miss Calvin's ceremony."

It wasn't the division of labor she favored. Lydia often got more out of female subjects than did male detectives, but she couldn't argue with his logic. "Meanwhile," he said, "the PI officer has issued an appeal for anyone having information or pictures of the book event to contact us. We'll see what it pulls in."

JERRY YARBOROUGH PEERED at Barnwell over a pair of reading glasses, his elbows resting on his oak desk, his fingertips steepled together. "What can I tell you?"

Behind him, two windows, looking out on the fall colors of a nearby hill, flanked shelves lined with dozens of books, framed photos of film posters, and audiobook covers. A stack of file folders and notebooks was to his right. "You represented all these projects?" she said.

"My three associates and I. Two of them live in New York. I prefer it here. That wasn't possible when I set out on my own. You had to work in the city. Now, you can be anywhere. But you didn't come here to discuss my business."

"In a way, I did," she said. He raised his eyebrows, inviting her to continue. "I've been trying to reach you since Saturday evening."

He waved it away with a flick of his hand. "I only answer my cell phone on weekends, and only publishers, editors, and producers have the number."

"I would have thought you would have called us when you heard of Parker's death."

"My wife and I were at Deep Creek. I didn't hear the news until we returned last night. Besides, there's not much I can tell you. Parker wasn't one of our more important clients." He straightened up in his chair. "That didn't come out right. What I mean is that we dealt by email and phone. I think he's been here once."

"You represented him through, what, four books?"

"Yes, but ..." He raised his hand to adjust his glasses, which did not need adjusting. "We represent a range of authors. Fiction, nonfiction, self-help. We also work with playwrights. We have two sorts of clients—older, established writers with solid reputations who produce regularly and have devoted followers. That's our bread and butter. We market their books to editors at the big houses and present their work to film and television producers for adaptation to those media.

"The second group are younger writers who we feel have promise. We invest more in them than we get back, but the key word is invest. Out of several dozen whose work we're handling at a given time, we may find a market for about a third. Of those, a few will bring us an immediate return. And one—sometimes two—become successful enough to repay the time and talent we devote to them over the years."

"The cash cows," she said.

"I'd never put it that way, but if it works for you, fine."

"To which of these two did Steven Parker belong?"

His snort was barely perceptible. "To neither." Lydia didn't hide her confusion. "He came to us with a contract in hand. No, let me back up. He approached me at a writing conference four years back. It's one of these events where every author who signs up gets ten minutes with an agent. We seldom come away with much, but it's a service to the community, and every so often ..." He did not finish the thought.

"Anyway, he pitched me a crime story. I told him it had some promise, which was generous, but it wasn't the sort of thing we handle, which was the truth. He sent me a letter thanking me. Few do that. It stuck with me. A year later, he called and told me he'd approached a publisher of regional history paperbacks on his own. They'd offered him a contract, but he wanted to parlay that into a multi-book deal. He also wasn't certain what rights he was signing away. He asked me to represent him for our standard fifteen percent."

"And you agreed," she said.

"I knew the publisher and told him they don't operate that way. A lot of their business is work-for-hire. You work for them, they pay you a fee, and their name goes on the cover. I was tempted to dismiss him, but recalling how thoughtful he'd been in writing me back, I promised to see what I could do. I told him to sign this one-book deal and draft a proposal for three more. He did, and we got him the contract."

"Sounds like a win-win," Lydia said.

Once more, he scoffed, "I don't think the four books have made ten thousand dollars, which means less than fifteen hundred to us. I wasn't exactly doing him a favor, but it was close."

She was about to ask another question, but the agent leaned toward her as though in confidence. "He wasn't much of a writer, to tell the truth. His books were rehashed columns he'd done for the paper over the years. Reversion-ing, we call it. But he was an outstanding marketer. Every book fair, every bookstore, and every writing conference, he was out there promoting his work. I wish all my authors were as comfortable with that part of the business."

"This new book he was writing sounds different from what he'd done in the past."

"You know more about it than I do."

"He didn't discuss it with you?"

"He emailed me and said he was working on something big. An unsolved crime, unlike anything he'd written before. I wasn't certain what to make of it. He was a bit of a promoter. I asked him for an outline. If it was that good, I thought I could get him an advance. He wanted to finish it first."

"He gave you no idea what the nature of the crime was?"

"None. He was tight-lipped, which was unusual for him. He said he'd told no one, not even his family." The agent spread his hands, searching for the right words. "It was almost as though he was afraid someone would steal his idea and get the story out before he did."

Lydia pressed him, but Yarborough insisted he knew nothing about the project. "I've only seen him a handful of times, mostly at conferences. Truth is, I hardly knew the man."

CHRISTIE PARKER APPEARED to be in her early thirties, trim with light-brown hair and a pert nose. And, most surprising to Detective Jeffrey, who had expectations of what a college professor was supposed to look like, unkempt. She wore an old pair of jeans and a T-shirt bearing the logo of Seattle's women's soccer team. She stood at the entry with her hands on her hips.

"I just got home. Come back at a better time."

Jeffrey didn't apologize. "I'm investigating your father's murder. I don't have a better time."

"I know nothing that will help you."

"Then this won't take long." He stepped past her and into the foyer, still holding his ID folder in his hand, and was enveloped in the perfume of flowers. Floral baskets, vases, sprays, and even wreaths occupied every flat surface he could see—roses, lilies, carnations, and tiny white flowers he couldn't identify. Potted plants, their cards attached, crowded the windowsill. "Where can we talk?"

Lois stepped into the long hallway from the kitchen. "I'm going up to my room," she said. "You can visit with her here." She came toward them, as disheveled as her daughter, and ascended the stairs, gripping the railing as though it were a life ring buoy and she was hauling herself to safety. Which perhaps she was.

"Ms. Parker," Jeffrey began as he pointed to a chair by the front window.

"Dr. Parker."

"Okay, Doctor." He removed his camera, placed it before her on a coffee table, and explained why he was recording the conversation. "I'm sorry for your loss."

"Don't be. We were not close. I'm here for my mother. And my brother," she added as an afterthought.

Jeffrey had a half-dozen questions he wanted to ask before getting into the touchy subject of family dynamics, but she had opened the door, so he barged in. "The two of you didn't get along?"

"He ignored me, and I ignored him. I'd prefer not to go into it."

"I'm afraid I must insist. We're trying to learn everything we can about him. Someone murdered your father, and whoever did so may target others. I need to find who did this and why." He leaned toward her. "I require your cooperation."

She chuckled and smirked at him. "You *require* it?"

"I do. You can answer my questions here or at headquarters. Your choice." He slid his reading glasses down on his nose and stared at her until she looked away.

"He cheated on my mother and almost destroyed this family. She would have been better off if she'd left him, but he had friends in high places and could have made things difficult for her. He belittled both my brother and me. Bill aspired to be an actor. Has he told you that? He poked fun at him and told him he didn't have the talent. When he wanted to take a semester studying theater in London, he threw every impediment his way until he gave up."

"Yet he paid for his education," Jeffrey said.

She smirked as she planted both knuckles on her hips. "He did not. Grandpa Dorsey established a trust fund for us. Our father didn't lift a finger to help. Where did you get that idea? From Bill? He's too forgiving. I am not."

"Did he disapprove of your career choice?"

"Not as much. He didn't think much of American studies. Why didn't I go into something practical like journalism? But when I got on as an assistant professor, he acknowledged it brought a regular paycheck."

"And when you became a full professor?"

"We weren't speaking by then."

"Because…"

Her smirk turned into a sneer. "He didn't approve of my marriage." He waited, sensing more was about to come. "I have a wife. You have a problem with that?"

"Where were you Saturday afternoon?"

She snorted. "I was waiting for you to ask that. I led a colloquium from two to four. Forty-one students attended. You can question them all. Better yet, sign onto YouTube and watch it."

She was trying to intimidate him with her snotty disposition, but Jeffrey refused to be drawn in. "Dr. Parker, do you have any idea who might have wanted to kill your father?"

"Any of us," she said then amended it. "Not really. Mom loved him, despite what he'd done to her. Bill's a softy. You know how boys are about their fathers. Always trying to measure up. And I…" She held her arms out, knowing her alibi was unshakeable.

"Other than the family?"

She scoffed again, her arms crossed in front of her. "I don't know enough about his life to tell you anything. Maybe Susan Nance's husband. She's the reporter with whom he cheated on Mom. But that was like nine years ago. If he was going to do something to Dad, he would have done it then. No, I can't help you."

He tried to probe, asking about Parker's decades as a crime reporter, his new career as a struggling writer, any friends he'd had, but she professed ignorance. "We haven't spoken in years. What he was doing, who he knew, why someone might have killed him, it's all a mystery to me."

Jeffrey rose to conclude the interview, but she said, "When you find him—or her—thank them for me, will you?"

———

LYDIA DIDN'T HAVE to travel to attend Calvin's investiture. To avoid the implication that any of the South Hills municipalities had precedence over the others, the ceremony was held in the first-floor conference room of ACPD headquarters in Greenfield, a few miles from all three communities.

Calvin appeared in a gray uniform, to which a Vietnamese couple who ran a local tailoring shop had affixed a cloth badge embroidered with the initials SRPD, Southern Regional Police Department. His father wore a dark wool suit with a tie bearing stripes of red, white, and blue. His mother was dressed in a flowered, ankle-length dress. They'd worn the same clothing as they dressed for church the previous morning. Ben's Sunday best, she suspected, though she knew Ruth, given her past position in Toledo's public school system, had more than one.

For her part, Lydia wore her workaday clothes, dark slacks, a white blouse, and a plain blue jacket. For the fifteen-minute ceremony, she'd signed out and secured her Motorola radio-telephone in her locker. She joined Calvin's parents in the black armchairs ringing the large table that dominated the room. Someone had seated them at the end of the table closest to the podium, which was flanked by the ACPD logo and the US and Pennsylvania flags. Ruth, sitting alongside her, covered her hand with her own, while Ben only nodded.

She turned away and found her boss, Inspector Andrew Morris, conversing with the county councilor for the district. She had shown up to support the merged police agency and the man who would lead it, and, Lydia was sure, to get her face on the evening news. Behind her, District Judge Violet Bartleson, her black robe trailing, said, "It's past eleven. We need to get this underway. I have cases to try this afternoon."

Morris rose to his feet and welcomed the gathering, most of whom were councilors and mayors of the borough and two townships. As he spoke, the door to the conference room opened, and Karol Novak, Calvin's predecessor as borough chief, entered. He smiled, nodded to her, then took a seat at the far end of the table.

Morris gave a brief history of how the new agency had been formed, without mentioning the event that had precipitated it, the shooting of an unarmed Black teenager by a rookie officer from one township that had sparked a near riot. "And as its first leader," Morris said, "the three communities selected Calvin Mayfield. Come join me, Chief."

Calvin rose and stood to one side as Morris praised him. "A young man with exceptional leadership skills and proven integrity, who has led the Boyleston Police Force since Karol Novak retired."

Novak waved a paw as four dozen pairs of eyes swung toward him.

The inspector recounted Calvin's educational background and his fight to join Boyleston as a patrol officer. "His path was not easy," Morris said. "Despite his outstanding credentials, he was denied positions with many law enforcement agencies. I'm pleased to say much has changed over the past few years."

She saw Ben stiffen. Too much had not changed, and no brush of fulsome flattery could paint over the fact.

Morris introduced Judge Bartleson, who administered the same oath she'd read to Calvin months before when he'd succeeded Chief Novak at Boyleston. "I, Calvin Benjamin Mayfield, do swear," he repeated after she fed him the opening words, "that I will support, obey and defend ... the Constitution and the laws ... of the United States, ... the Commonwealth of Pennsylvania..."

Ben sat erect, as though at attention, as the oath dragged on.

"... and that I will uphold, obey and enforce the law ... without consideration to a person's race, ... color, sex, religious creed..."

As he lowered his right arm at the close of the oath, the judge extended her hand and the onlookers gave polite applause, but Calvin's Boyleston officers rose in a raucous cheer. The others came to their feet, some leaving the room, a few gathering in groups, and most approaching Calvin to offer congratulations. Lydia slipped behind them, heading toward Novak.

"He's come a long way," the chief said as she approached him.

"And you brought him here." Novak's grin cut a swath through his face, as she acknowledged the role he had played in mentoring this man. He had believed in Calvin and supported him against the doubters in his own department. He had been sworn into a position Novak had been promised, but the eventual oversight hadn't bothered him. "I've tried to retire three times," he'd said then. "I have no regrets. It's time."

"If you have a moment, I have a question for you," Lydia said. Novak didn't answer, but his eyebrows shot up in curiosity. "I'm leading the investigation into Steven Parker's murder."

"I read that. Good for you."

Across the room, Inspector Morris engaged in conversation with Ben Mayfield. He seemed to point toward her. She ignored it and returned her attention to Novak. "It may be tied to a Pittsburgh cold from 1993."

Novak's smile disappeared, replaced by a scowl that could have darkened the room. "Little Jeanne Holman," he said through clenched teeth.

She stood with her mouth agape. Here was a man whose concussion during a soccer match made it difficult for him to remember events from a few days ago, yet he'd pulled this name out of the air without prompting. "Tell me about it."

Novak looked from one side to the other, reached for her elbow, and turned her away from the table. "Not here," he said. "Let me pull my thoughts together, and I'll come to your place."

"Fine," she said and thanked him, but he stalked out. She had never seen him react to anything this way.

Before she could think about it, she heard Calvin's voice at the far end of the room, summoning her. She navigated through the hangers-on and joined him. One officer held Calvin's personal phone and motioned him, the judge, and his parents to stand together.

"Get in the picture," he ordered.

She took a spot to the right—Judge Bartleson, Calvin, his mother and father, and then herself. For an instant, she felt she didn't belong. "Hold on," Ben said, holding up his hand to the officer as though ordering a traffic stop. "You stand next to Calvin."

"No," she said, "you two should be closest to him."

"Stand next to Ruth," he ordered. "You're family now."

She did as she was told, marveling at his change in attitude.

———

Scoglio's, a restaurant near headquarters that both Calvin and Lydia frequented, was closed on Mondays, so the four headed to a diner in Robinson Township for a celebratory luncheon. "If you like pork chops," Lydia told Ben, "theirs are delicious." She was only repeating what Calvin had told her, having never touched the dish herself.

"Thanks," he said. "I'll try it." She ordered the pasta fra diabolo, brimming with seafood. "You don't eat meat, do you?"

"I try not to, but I'm not dogmatic about it." She smiled to herself, recalling the bacon-wrapped scallops she'd devoured the evening Calvin proposed. "My father used to eat anything that walked on hooves. It earned him a heart attack."

"He's in the military?"

"Retired now, but he served in the Air Force and rose to the rank of colonel."

"We look forward to meeting him," Ruth said.

Lydia said nothing. The two had not spoken in some time. They weren't estranged. They just had little to say to one another. She had yet to tell him she was engaged.

"He must be quite proud of you," Ben said. "The inspector says you're one of his best detectives."

So that was why Morris had looked her way while she was pumping Novak for information. Did this explain Ben's sudden act of recognition, placing her next to Calvin in the photo? If so, she'd take it.

Their food arrived, and as hungry as she was, she only picked at it, eager to return to headquarters and follow the lead Novak had given her. "Duty calls," she announced halfway through the meal. She'd already slipped her credit card to the server. "My treat."

"Has something come up?" Calvin asked.

"Novak remembers the 1993 case. He's provided a name."

Calvin chuckled. "The bloodhound is on the trail. We'll see you tonight."

Fifteen minutes later, she settled into her swivel chair and opened an internet browser. Before she could search for Jeanne Holman, however, Jeffrey interrupted her. "There's no love lost between Christie Parker—Dr. Parker to me— and her father."

"Like that is she?" Lydia said, noting the emphasis he'd placed on the title.

Over the chatter of other detectives and the clatter of a dozen sets of fingers on keyboards, he described her resentment over Parker's treatment of her mother and his psychological abuse of her and her brother. "When I interviewed the son, he gave Parker a pass, said that even though he hadn't encouraged his acting, he paid his tuition. Dr. Parker says that's not the case. Their grandfather's trust find picked up the tab."

"Why did he lie to you?"

"She doesn't say he lied, rather that he puts a positive spin on a negative experience out of misplaced loyalty. She gave us one other thing. The reporter he screwed is Susan Nance. I'm trying to locate her."

"It might also be worth speaking to someone at the paper. Was he as contemptuous of his fellow workers as he was of his children?"

"I'll handle that," he replied, "while you speak to the girlfriend. Meanwhile, our appeal for photos of the book fair brought us more than we'd bargained for." He opened a file of shots attendees had sent in. "A few think they may have seen someone acting strangely. We'll need more boots to interview all of them."

"The librarian sent me a list of the authors who took part." Lydia leaned back in her chair and stroked her lip. "I ran into a recruit this morning who worked with us on the North Fayette murder. You remember Nadine Foster?"

"The Black girl?"

"Woman," Lydia corrected. "I want her working with us."

"The uniform division makes those assignments."

"I want *her*," Lydia repeated. She picked up the interoffice phone and dialed an extension.

AT BARNWELL'S INSISTENCE, the uniform division assigned Nadine Foster and one other patrol officer to the case. Chief of Detectives Glen Carpenter added another detective, Scott Ullrich, who had worked with them before. Jeffrey assembled the team in the conference room and reviewed what they knew about the murder.

Parker had spent the day at a book fair sponsored by the Mt. Lebanon Public Library. During a presentation, he'd claimed to have solved a cold case from the 1990s. Someone who heard him might have felt threatened and followed the crime writer to his home. He handed out assignments. The two patrol officers were to interview as many writers as they could.

"Focus on the four who sat to either side of him and the

three other crime writers in attendance," he said as Lydia distributed a map showing their assigned places at the tables.

"Five witnesses saw people at the fair who raised their suspicions. Ullrich and I will question them," Jeffrey continued. "We're looking for anyone who showed an unusual interest in what Parker said during his fifteen-minute talk. Anyone lurking around his table before or after his presentation. Someone who followed him when he packed up his books and left."

He concluded by explaining what would come next. "If anyone identifies such an individual, invite to headquarters to view the videos and stills we've assembled. We're looking for a needle, but it's not a huge haystack." He dismissed them and huddled with Ullrich to split the list between them.

Lydia returned to her desk to find a message from Brandy Timmons. "The indentation on the notepad you submitted read, MJ-'He is capable of it. Left after arrest.' There's nothing more. No prints. All other tests negative."

Once, an investigator would have rubbed the edge of pencil lead over the paper, darkening the surface so that whatever had been written on the preceding page would stand out in relief. Now, Brandy had used a combination of side light and imaging software to accomplish the same thing. She'd also subjected the paper to chemical tests to find any trace evidence.

Despite all this, the terse note Parker had made to himself told her nothing. Who was MJ? Who'd been arrested, and of what was he capable? She puzzled over it for a few seconds and gave up, opened a browser, and typed in the name Jeanne Holman. Her search returned several listings, including archived news reports from three decades before. She clicked on the first and found a photo image of a newspaper story from June 9th, 1993.

Beneath the headline, "Body of Shadyside teen found in Highland Park," she saw the byline, Steven Parker. When, she wondered, had Steven Parker become Parker Stevens?

Shelving the thought, she enlarged the image and read the story.

> The body of a thirteen-year-old middle school student was found in a wooded area of Highland Park yesterday morning by two youngsters. Parents of the teenager identified her as Jeanne Holman, who had been missing since Monday night.
>
> Detective Anthony Grico said the girl had been assaulted and then strangled with her own blouse. He said they've made no arrests but are questioning another minor who was seen in her company on the previous afternoon.

"Assaulted," she suspected, was a euphemism for rape. Newspapers had been more delicate in their terminology years before, and police were more willing to identify an underage victim. What she knew about such cases, including the fact that her attacker had at least partially undressed her, sent a chill through her body. What someone had done to this girl ... could do to any woman ... made her angrier than anything else she encountered. What gave any man the right to attack a woman, let alone rape and strangle her?

As she paged through subsequent reports, she learned Jeanne's parents had returned from separate jobs on the first Monday in June to find her not at home. This was not unusual, they said. It was the first weekday of the summer break, and she had several girlfriends she hung out with. When she didn't return for supper, they still weren't alarmed. It was a glorious evening with clear skies and temperatures in the low seventies. They figured she'd lost track of time, perhaps even stayed with a friend for dinner.

At eight o'clock, they began calling the homes of her classmates, but no one knew where she was. One girl recalled seeing her at Mellon Park, five blocks from her home, at mid-afternoon. Growing alarmed, the couple reported her disappearance to Pittsburgh Police. Reading between the lines, Lydia suspected they hadn't taken it too seriously at first. A thirteen-year-old girl on a summer evening ... kids were running loose all the time. Jeanne might have ridden the bus downtown to wander through department stores. Perhaps she was hanging out with a boy and was concealing it from her parents. She was a teenager, after all.

By morning, however, police mounted a search, branching out from Shadyside south to Squirrel Hill and east to Oakland. They did not turn north, reasoning that a white girl would never wander alone into East Liberty and that if someone from that neighborhood had abducted her, an informant would have spotted him.

Shortly after nine, however, a pair of youngsters playing in the trees at the edge of Highland Park found a body. They told their nanny, who alerted Pittsburgh police. The first officer on the scene ...

Lydia stopped reading and reached for her phone. Karol Novak answered so quickly he seemed to have predicted her call. "You discovered her body," she said.

"No, a couple of pre-school youngsters did. But when their caregiver reached us, I was only a few blocks away."

"What can you tell me about it?"

"I've spent the afternoon recalling Jeanne's murder and the aftermath. I've made a slew of notes. Can we get together at your place tomorrow morning?"

It was the second time that day he'd suggested coming to her house. When they got together, it was always at his. "Done," she said.

———

LYDIA SLICED two chicken breasts while telling Calvin what she'd learned. She heated a pot of water for pasta while she smashed garlic and quartered mushrooms. Ben and Ruth were upstairs packing for a return to Toledo in the morning.

"Your dad came out of his shell after the ceremony," she said.

"He's never in a shell. If anything, we'd like him to curb his enthusiasm."

"You know what I mean. The way he repositioned me for the photo. He finally seems to accept me."

"He accepted you the moment he met you. Even before that. As soon as I told him I'd asked you to marry me, he decided you were okay."

Lydia tossed a salad and shook her head. "Then why did he seem so distant when he first got here?"

"You should ask him." Before she could protest, Calvin moved his face closer to hers, demanding that she meet his gaze. "Ask him."

"All right, if you're sure."

She broke strands of linguine into the boiling water, set the bowl of salad on the table, and heated olive oil. Once the pan was hot enough, she sautéed the chicken strips. As they sizzled, Ben clambered down the stairway. "Something smells good."

"Just you wait." She added garlic then tossed in the mushrooms, finishing the sauce with a generous measure of white wine, salt, and pepper. Ruth joined her husband as Lydia stirred al dente pasta into the mixture, ladled it onto plates, dressing each serving with Parmesan and parsley.

Ben shoveled a mouthful into his maw and chased it with a swallow of wine. She grinned, recognizing where Calvin had inherited his eating habits. They made small talk while they ate, neither officer discussing cases in progress. When they finished, Calvin removed the plates, and his mother joined him in the kitchen, leaving her with Ben. She suspected this had been planned.

"Something's been bothering me, and I need to ask you about it. I don't want to offend—"

"Ask away," he said.

"When you arrived here Saturday, you didn't speak to me. I was afraid you didn't like me. I thought maybe ..." She raised her hands in surrender, not wanting to voice what she'd suspected.

"I was born in Jamaica, as you can tell that from my flat Midwestern accent."

She returned his smile. "I knew right away. Jamaican men speak from deep down." She pointed to her midsection. "They have these bass notes."

"You're a linguist?"

"I've lived all over the world. I'm fluent in Spanish and can get along in a few others, but let's return to Jamaica."

"When I was five, my father got a job in a shipyard in Jacksonville. You heard anything about that town? Know what it's like to be Black there?"

"I've heard it called South Georgia," she replied. "It's

why the Florida-Georgia game is played there, rather than at one of the two universities."

"Nuff said. From my earliest days, I was taught not to speak to a white woman until she speaks to you, and then only with deference. Eighteen years of having that drummed into me ... It's a tough habit to break." He leaned forward and laid his hand on hers. "I think you're special. Calvin is lucky to have found you. He doesn't deserve you. Oh, heck. He does, but you get my meaning."

"Mr. Mayfield ..."

"Dad. You better start calling me that."

"Dad," she said, wiping a telltale tear from her eye, "thank you."

Calvin's words came back to her: "Have you tried speaking to him?"

She rose and joined him and his mother in the kitchen. "Get out of here," she told him. He shrugged and joined his father in front of the TV while she turned to Ruth. "I've been thinking about your wedding plans."

"Your wedding plans," Ruth replied.

"It's important to you, isn't it?"

His mother folded the towel and leaned against the counter. "Our first child was a girl. We named her Nyah. She passed away soon after Calvin was born, not for any of the usual reasons Black children die. She caught pneumonia and was gone before we knew it. He was a year old then. We had no more after him. I was too old. So he's our only child, and we — I've always been protective of him. I don't like this police business, but it's his choice."

She waved an arm as though batting away a fly. "Anyway, when he told us he was engaged, I thought how wonderful it would be to have all our relatives attend our service. We've been to so many of theirs. It's selfish of me, I know."

"Then you shall have it."

"No," she said. "You're the bride. You get to do what you want."

"What I want," Lydia said, "is to be part of this family. I won't go into the reasons it's so important to me, though someday I may tell you. But if a church wedding means that much to you, I want it too."

Ruth shook her head, and Lydia knew she was about to burst into tears. "The problem is, where to hold it? I'm not a churchgoer and, I hate to tell you, neither is your son."

"I'm sure you can find a place."

"Where did you attend yesterday?"

"You wouldn't want to go there. It's in what they call the Hill District. Ebenezer Baptist." She interrupted herself and looked at Lydia. "A Black congregation."

"So?"

"I'd think you'd want something more — where your friends feel comfortable."

"Anyone who is uncomfortable attending my wedding in the church of my choice is not my friend. Consider the matter settled. Will you help me put it together?"

Her laugh came from somewhere deep inside. "You know I will."

CHAPTER FOUR

BEN MAYFIELD DRAGGED a suitcase down the stairs. "Let me help with that," Calvin said.

"It's okay, Son. I'm not dead yet." He took the stairs again and returned with a second bag, the case for a CPAP machine slung over his shoulder.

"Have a seat, Dad," Lydia called out. "I'm making omelets." She brought him a glass of orange juice, which he sipped as he took his morning pills.

"There's a shorter route home than heading up I-79," Calvin said. "Take I-376 out past the airport—"

"Son, I traveled between Toledo and DC before you were born. I know the way."

Calvin gave up. Lydia served him a mushroom omelet, two strips of bacon, and a slice of whole wheat toast then sat across from him while she downed the one cup of coffee she allowed herself each day. Karol Novak would arrive in an hour, and she wore a distracted expression as she made a mental list of things she needed to know.

Ruth joined them as her husband wiped his mouth with

a napkin and leaned back in his chair. That hadn't taken him four minutes, she thought.

As Lydia rose to prepare a plate for her, she said, "Just toast for me, thanks. I don't eat much when I'm going on a long car trip. It makes me sick."

Lydia nodded to acknowledge the instructions and rose from the table. Ruth followed her and poured a cup of coffee as she settled in behind the counter.

"You lost your mother when you were quite young," she said.

"Yes, I hardly knew her. My father raised me." Which wasn't quite true. Captain Barnwell, who was later to attain the rank of colonel, hadn't accepted the role of parent. Wives of other officers had looked after her until she'd turned nine, at which point she'd raised herself. The experience still rankled, but it had taught her self-reliance.

"I don't want you to worry about a thing," Ruth said. "If I had a daughter, I'd be planning this wedding. I'm doing the same for you."

"That is so sweet of you."

"I won't overstep my bounds. I'll check with you on every detail. Consider me your willing hands. What's wrong, dear?"

"Nothing," Lydia said, wiping away a tear. "Thank you. You have no idea what this means to me."

***

BRIAN RANSOM LIVED in a three-story home built at the turn of the last century on Squirrel Hill's Shady Avenue. Lyle Jeffrey rang the doorbell and, hearing no sound from within, knocked. The man who answered had a square face and close-cropped gray hair. He invited the detective in with a gravelly voice, the result of too many cigarettes, too much bourbon, or both.

He led Jeffrey into the front room, where an odor testified to the former, motioned him to a leather sofa with a nod, and said, "Coffee?"

"Please." While Ransom fumbled in the kitchen, the detective examined the framed photos interspersed among hardcover books in a massive oak cabinet built into the outer wall. He recognized past presidents, senators, mayors, entertainers, and a parade of Pittsburgh sports figures, each wearing a forced grin and gripping the hand of the man who returned holding a mug with the masthead of the *Herald* wrapped around it.

"So," he said, dropping into a leather-covered armchair facing the couch, "Steve Parker."

"Or Parker Stevens," Jeffrey replied.

Ransom snorted, raising his shoulders as he did so. "An affectation."

"I understand you were his editor."

"Managing editor," he corrected. "Seventeen years. I started as a copyboy back when we had that position. I worked my way up the ladder and stayed until I retired." He looked around. "My wife died eighteen months ago. This place is too big for me. I'll have to do something about it, but I won't leave the neighborhood."

It was an old story. Native Pittsburghers tended to stay close to where they were born. The late president of the Steelers, Dan Rooney, had been born, lived, and died in the same North Shore community, walking between his home, church, and school. He'd married a woman who lived only a few blocks away. When Fred Rogers opened each program singing, "It's a beautiful day in the neighborhood," it held special meaning for his fellow Pittsburgh residents, his neighbors.

"So you knew him well," Jeffrey prompted.

"I did." He waited, volunteering nothing.

"What sort of person was he?"

"A good journalist. He started off working the courts. We used to have the resources to station reporters at the courthouse. The best would find a story without being assigned. Parker was a natural. He got to know police officers, schmoozed them, as they say here in Squirrel Hill, and they fed him leads. He soon focused on crime. Editors recognized his talent and gave him free rein. He sold newspapers. People couldn't wait to read his stories."

Ransom recounted some of Parker's best articles, his many scoops, and a few occasions when his digging had sent detectives in a new and promising direction. He'd eventually earned his own column, which gave him the freedom not just to report the facts but to offer opinions.

"That's when he took the pen name."

"Why?"

Ransom issued a sardonic chuckle. "He fancied himself a target of bad guys. The mafia was gone by then, but he convinced himself others were out to get him. At one point, he grew a beard. Another time, he dyed his hair and curled it. He wore outlandish disguises."

"How did his colleagues take this?"

"The young ones bought into his myth-making. His contemporaries laughed behind his back."

"Was he aware of this?"

"If so, he didn't show it. He's not the first journalist to write his own news releases and accept them as fact."

"Still," Jeffrey said, "someone murdered him who either

feared or hated him. Do you have any idea who that might be?"

"Early in his career, maybe. He questioned everyone involved in a case and was sometimes ahead of the cops. But later? No. He was dredging up old stories and breathing new life into them."

"He'd become lazy?"

"I wouldn't say that. He'd lost his touch. It happens."

"Is that why he was laid off?"

Ransom leaned back, his face twisted in something between a scowl and a smirk. "Laid off?"

"His family tells us he was let go as part of a staff reduction."

"That's what he told them, is it? I guess he could hardly tell them the truth."

"Which is…"

"In another time and place, you'd have to issue a subpoena to get me to talk. Our lawyers would challenge it based on freedom of the press. We'd fight it out in court, and I'd win. But I no longer work there, and since this is a homicide case…" He tapped his fingers on the arms of his chair. His left knee danced as he sat. Jeffrey suspected the man needed a cigarette. "We fired him. They gave him a nice severance check, so generous he could have represented it as a buyout. But we let him go and showed him the door."

"Because?" Jeffrey said.

"Remember I told you he impressed some of the younger ones with the legend he'd built around himself? He'd impressed one too many of them."

Jeffrey caught the double entendre. "Women?"

"Yeah. He carried on with one reporter for over a year. Susan Nance. She's still around somewhere. Her husband crashed into the newsroom one day, yelling and threatening him. It took security to get him to leave. They fired her but kept him. It was the wrong move, but I was the editor, not the publisher. He made the call, and I had to deal with it."

"What did the husband say when he confronted Parker?"

"He didn't threaten to kill him, if that's what you mean. He wanted to rough him up. 'You're always fighting for justice? Come out from behind that desk. I'll show you justice.' He stood four inches over the guy. Parker was a pipsqueak. Did I mention that? Things got pretty tense."

The incident had occurred ten years before, the retired editor told him. He wasn't sure whether Nance had ever followed through on his threat. Was he angry enough to have killed him? "At the time, yes, but I doubt he'd still be that angry. How long can you hold a grudge? They divorced after she left."

"She was fired back then. Why did it take so long to get rid of Parker?"

"She was neither the first nor the last. He had one more affair that we know of, but time aged him, and the younger ones didn't find him as attractive. Besides, women woke up to the fact they didn't have to put up with that crap. He made one remark too many. One took it to HR and brought two others with her. It was goodbye, Steven Parker. Or Parker Stevens." His entire body joined in the laugh.

Jeffrey changed course. "At the time of his death, he was writing a book about the murder of a young girl named Jeanne Holman. Do you know anything about that?"

"I haven't talked to him in a couple of years, so I wasn't aware he was still working on it, but I sure as hell recall the case."

"Tell me about it," Jeffrey said.

"She was thirteen." Karol Novak sat at Lydia's kitchen counter, a notepad before him. "I was a beat cop and took the call. Two kids, six and four, found her body."

He stared into the cup of coffee she'd poured him and turned it in a circle as a thought crossed his mind. She couldn't recall when he'd seemed more agitated. "They called to their nanny, who didn't believe them at first. When she spotted the corpse, she backed away screaming then scooped up the kids and sought help from nearby homes. She was Black, and few opened their door to her. Those who did thought she was hysterical and turned her away.

"She stepped into Highland Avenue, directly in front of a bus, waving her arms. The driver stopped, listened to her story, and called it in. I was in the vicinity when I got the call, so I arrived first."

He sighed and took a sip of his coffee, now lukewarm. "It was a frightful thing to behold. Our daughter Mariel had just had her seventh birthday. Although this girl was twice her age, I couldn't look ..." He shivered. "Nearly nude. Her blouse tied around her neck. Her face blue. Blood down ... where he'd raped her. Read the details in my report if you can stomach it. It's all there."

He described detectives arriving on the scene, followed by the coroner. "I helped them secure the inner perimeter then the outer ring, which was the west half of Highland Park. People who'd refused to come to the door when the caregiver needed them now crowded around the area." He shook his head and hissed with such vehemence a torrent of spray spewed from his mouth. He wiped it away with the back of his hand. "A detective took charge, Rolf Peterson. He was intimidating, over six feet, muscular, blond short-cropped hair, in his mid-thirties. This becomes important later."

Novak had always been a linear thinker. Point A led to point B then C. Today, he jumped around, piecing the story together as it came to him. "The victim matched the description of a missing girl. Peterson had me drive down to Shadyside to collect the father. He kept asking me questions from the back of the cruiser. Was I sure it was their daughter? How had she died? Did she suffer? Who did this to her? I kept silent. I didn't know most of the answers, and those I knew weren't mine to say.

"I parked alongside the other cruisers, blocking the road. But no one was going to come around the other way, were they?" It wasn't like Novak to drag superfluous detail into a story, but he did so now. "I let him out and led him to where the officers and coroner's team were gathered. Peterson pulled back the sheet that covered her. I'll never forget the guy's face. He seemed to melt, like a snowman on a warm day. He started keening. An Irish woman taught me that word."

He said nothing for ten seconds or more. "You got any more of this?"

She refilled his cup. "Peterson had us go house to house questioning neighbors about anything they might have seen. No one came to the door at half of them. Those who did expressed ignorance. When we returned, two people in the crowd recalled seeing a young man and woman riding a motorbike up Highland Avenue the afternoon before. One who'd been walking her dog saw the bike headed toward Negley Avenue a half-hour later with only the young man aboard. Peterson had his suspect."

Novak drank the coffee as he continued the story. He'd had no further involvement at that point but had followed what happened in the following days. Based on the description, police spoke to students at Taylor Allderdice High School. One told them a fifteen-year-old boy named Dwight Truesdale had been riding his brother's motorbike earlier in the afternoon, talking to neighborhood girls. When questioned, the young man admitted to having talked Jeanne into going on a ride with him. He said he'd taken her to the park and that they'd walked around for a bit. When it came time to leave, she'd grown frightened. He'd driven too fast, she told him. There wasn't enough room for her on the back seat. She'd walk home. It wasn't that far.

Her parents didn't buy the story. Jeanne, they said, was a wild, adventurous girl. Once on the bike, she wouldn't have refused to remount it. Under questioning, Truesdale broke down. He admitted that once they reached Highland Park, they'd taken the path along the reservoir. When he tried to kiss her, she refused then decided to walk home to Shadyside, only two miles away.

He hadn't reported this to the police after the search for Jeanne became public because he wasn't supposed to be using his brother's bike. After her body was discovered, he feared he'd be blamed. "The kid was overweight and had a terrible complexion," Novak said. "Peterson read a lot into that. He'd tried to get girls his own age to go for a joyride but struck out. Jeanne, he figured, was impressed when this older boy showed an interest in her. At the park, he forced himself on her and, when she refused, overpowered her, raped her, then got scared and strangled her. They found no physical evidence linking him to the crime. He had no marks or bruises, despite indications she'd fought back. But Peterson had his man. This was before DNA evidence came into use."

Novak clenched the empty cup in his hands. For the first time, he referred to his notes.

"A Black youth named Jabari Jackson had been seen in the area during the day. He lived in East Liberty, a mile down the hill. Jackson had been in and out of trouble with the police throughout his seventeen years for dealing marijuana. Peterson brought him in for questioning and without notifying his parents kept him for two days. The kid finally told him what he wanted to hear, that he'd been in the park that afternoon and saw Truesdale attack a white girl. Being Black, he left on the double and returned home, saying nothing to anyone. Given the positive ID, Peterson charged Dwight with rape and homicide. He was tried as an adult, convicted, and sentenced to life in prison."

"But you don't think he was guilty," she said.

"His family never gave up trying to win his release. In 2003, an attorney working pro bono got the court to order a DNA test, using samples from Jeanne's clothing. His did not match that of the attacker. Under questioning, Jabari Jackson confessed he'd lied at the trial but claimed he'd acted under police duress."

"What became of Truesdale?"

"That's the only positive news out of this affair. It took two more years, but his parents won his release. He moved to New York State, got married, and now works as a youth counselor. I kept up with him for a while. The last I heard, he was doing well."

"The girl's killer was never caught, was he?"

Novak shook his head but said not a word.

"That's what Parker Stevens was working on, what he claimed to have solved," she said. "What about Peterson?"

"He'd been accused in the past of falsifying evidence and intimidating witnesses to get a conviction, but he always explained his way out of it. The Jeanne Holman case was the final straw. He was fired. The police union tried to fight it, but the arbitrator, for once, supported the city."

Lydia let out a long sigh and hung her head. "This is quite a story."

"It's why I became a detective," he said. "What some beast did to an innocent young girl and the fact he remains free haunts me like nothing else I've ever worked on."

She had never heard him speak with such passion. He was normally a by-the-book cop, holding firm to his convictions but never making a show of it. "Read the case file. I have a strong opinion about how it was handled, but I was close to it. I'd value your take."

She had one more question for him. "Someone with the initials MJ told Parker, 'He is capable of it.' Does that mean anything to you?"

She watched as he searched his memory, which they both knew was not the best. "Nothing. Do me a favor. Keep me informed."

Lydia promised. Novak might be a source of further information if she found the keys to unlock what he'd seen and heard three decades ago.

***

The security guard examined Jeffrey's ID, dialed the PR agency on the sixteenth floor, and announced his presence. The detective stood in the lobby, tapping his notebook against his free hand as he studied the glass palace that surrounded him. Designed by architects Philip Johnson and John Burgee, PPG Place comprised six buildings of matching design containing nearly 20,000 sheets of glass, topped by 231 transparent spires. Known as Pittsburgh's Crown Jewel, on sunny days, such as this one, the panes' reflections sparkled like diamonds.

A woman stepped from the elevator and walked toward him, looking from her left to her right as though fearful of being discovered. She wore a white blouse, a linen open-front blazer in bright blue, and a gray calf-length skirt. Her blonde hair, light-brown at the roots, was bound in a bun at her neck.

The only exceptions to her conservative look were a gold necklace and a ring with a solitary diamond that rose from its base like one of the glass towers. He fixed his eyes on her long fingers, which trembled as she extended her hand, and the polished nails that extended behind them. Jeffrey, who typed using nothing but his two index fingers, wondered how she did so.

"Detective?" she said in a low voice as she drew him away from the guard. "I'm Susan Nance. I've been expecting you, but I wish we could meet elsewhere."

Jeffrey gave his standard response, that every hour that passed made finding the perpetrator more difficult, and asked if there was a place they could speak.

"There's a coffee shop a block from here."

"Somewhere private," he said. "Or we can go to the courthouse."

She blinked as though a reflection from an adjoining tower blinded her. "All right."

She led him to the elevator and scanned her pass for the upper floor. They stepped into a paneled lobby, and Susan asked the woman at the front desk for a conference room. She did not introduce her guest, nor did Jeffrey expect her to do so. Assigned a small space off the reception area, she closed the door, directing him to a seat with his back to the glass wall.

"I'd offer you coffee, but—"

"I've had my fill," he said. "As I'm sure you know, I'm here about the death of Steven Parker."

"Steven," she repeated, biting her lip. "I know nothing about it."

"But you knew him."

"I'm sure you've figured that out, or you wouldn't be here."

"You had an affair," he prompted. "When did it start and how long did it last?"

"We met in 2011. I was a junior reporter at the *Herald*. He was a columnist there and took an interest in me. In a professional way," she added.

"He offered to help your career."

"No. I know what you're implying, but it wasn't like that. He didn't groom me."

"What then?"

"I was assigned to city hall. He had contacts there. Hell, he had contacts everywhere," she said, chewing over the thought. "He took me on a tour, introduced me to aides to council members, and explained which were the actual powers behind the public facades their bosses put forward. He vouched for me, I got some exclusives, and ..."

She smiled, recalling better times when, he supposed, her editors had been impressed by her ingenuity. "We grew close. He kept bringing stories my way. We'd sometimes have lunch together and soon began sharing personal frustrations."

"Such as?"

"I don't care to get into it." When Jeffrey continued to wait for an answer, she emitted a long sigh. "I suppose I opened the door. My husband—ex-husband, now—had anger management issues. The slightest thing would set him off. Where's this? Where's that? Why was I late? We'd started off fine, but as I became more successful at the paper, he grew resentful. He felt like Mr. Susan Nance, if you know what I mean."

"We'll get back to him in a moment. I take it Parker shared his own complaints."

"Yes. He never criticized his wife in so many words. He just said that they'd drifted apart after two decades of marriage. They didn't share any common interests, and with their two kids growing older and more independent, they'd become bored with each other."

She leaned an elbow on the table and rested her mouth on her knuckles. Jeffrey waited. "One day, he said, 'I wish I'd waited and married someone more like you. Someone successful in her own right.' But then he said that given the difference in our age, we wouldn't have even known each other."

Jeffrey noted how he'd maneuvered the conversation from the theoretical to the concrete. He could have predicted how she'd responded.

"I told him his age didn't matter to me, that he respected me for who I was, and that was all that mattered."

Bingo! Jeffrey thought. "And so you began an affair. How long were you together?"

"For two years, the first time."

"You separated but got back together again? How did that work?"

"How did it work?" she said, examining her fingernails while she considered her answer. "My husband found out about us. It was my fault. I was always saying Steven this and Steven that. Steven threw me another story today. He grew suspicious and started spying on me. He was a web designer and worked from home, so his time was his own. One day, he followed us from the paper and saw us having lunch. By then, we were pretty obvious about our feelings for one another. A few days later, he saw us check into a hotel. The *Herald* kept a couple of rooms there for visiting correspondents. We had reporters in New York, Washington, even London." The corners of her mouth turned down. "Things have changed a lot since then. I don't think they have a full-time reporter at the courthouse these days."

"How did your husband react?" He had no patience for her reverie. She described Ted Nance storming up to her desk, screaming at her.

She shivered as she recalled the scene. "It scared the hell out of me. I had no idea what he was about to do. He turned on Parker and threatened him."

"Threatened him how?"

"To a fist fight. In the middle of the newsroom. Like they were a couple of kids on a playground."

"How did Parker react?"

She snorted and let a smile play across her face. "He sat at his desk with this stoic expression, like he was an observer and was watching this thing play out. He knew how it would end."

"How did it end?"

"They brought in security and hauled him out of the building. But I lost my job."

"What happened to him?"

"Steven or Ted? Nothing," she said when he'd clarified his question. "He was too big a shot." She laughed at her wordplay. "You know how it was until recently. Man and woman have an office affair, it upsets the balance, and one of them has to go. It's never the man."

"Did you resent it?"

She threw her arm over the back of her chair. "Let me tell you something. Steven Parker was many things, but disloyalty was not among them." She seemed to have forgotten the unfaithfulness to his wife, but he let it go.

"He found me this job. More money and more responsibility. They hired me as a copywriter. I'm now an account executive, handling some of our bigger clients. I expect to make partner in a few years. Steven did that for me, and I've never looked back."

"Is that why you got back together?" Jeffrey said.

"Ted called Steven's wife and ratted us out. He was forced to break it off. But we ran into each other at a civic dinner a few years later and renewed our acquaintance." She punctuated this with a wry smile, meant only for herself. "That went on until I met Brad, my husband. I broke it off. Steven was very understanding. I think ..."

"Go on," he said.

"I suspect he'd met someone else. He usually called me, suggesting we meet. I hadn't heard from him for a few months, so I figured he'd moved on."

Jeffrey posed a few more questions about their relationship, but this well had run dry. "Your ex-husband, Ted. Is he capable of killing someone?"

"When I heard about Steven's murder, I wondered." She rubbed her forehead while she considered it. "Yes, I think he is, though why he'd wait over a decade is beyond me."

"And where were you Saturday afternoon?"

She giggled, her fear of him gone. "Right here. We had a client presentation Monday morning, and their marketing director had asked for a last-minute change. I was here with an artist, copywriter, web designer, and digital supervisor.

We worked until eight that night. I'll give you their names and contact info if I must, but I'd prefer you didn't. I've lost one job over Steven and don't intend to lose this one."

"I'll hold off unless other evidence compels me to do so."

"Thank you. I'll tell you one thing though. I loved the guy. Even after we went our separate ways, I kept a place for him here." She tapped her chest over her heart. "I hope you catch whoever did this to him and lock him away forever."

HAVING DIVIDED up the list of authors whose tables flanked that of the victim, Nadine Foster wasted no time locating them. She was struck by how quickly Detective Barnwell had put her to work but knew not to let it get to her head. It was an opportunity to show what she could do, and if she did poorly, there might be few others.

They had met while investigating a body found in a drainage ditch in North Fayette when Nadine served as a patrol officer. She had been first on the scene, and something about the way she'd handled herself when Barnwell arrived had impressed her. She had added her to her team, which in the end involved not one but two murders. Eight months later, here she was again, this time a recruit on the county force and pressed into service by the young detective. She would not fail her.

David Marcos lived in a two-story brick house on a side street above Dormont Park. He studied her ID and welcomed her in, trailing through the disorganized house to his office, a small space in the lower level.

"This is where the magic happens," he said, spreading

his arm as though it were a spacious parlor rather than an eight-by-ten room with a bookcase on one wall, a standing desk at the second, and entrances to the garage and laundry room on the other two.

He pulled a folding bench out of the garage and set it up alongside his wheeled chair. "So this is about the crime writer," he said. "Terrible thing, although I was glad to see the back of him when the day was over."

"Why is that?" she asked.

"He had all these fans. I write fishing guidebooks. I didn't sell enough to make it worth my while," he said. "Six hours of my time produced six sales. After expenses, that works out to eight bucks per hour. I should have stayed home and written. Or gone fishing. All because the organizers put me next to him."

"Why did that present a problem?"

"He was so popular that no one could get near my table. People crowded around trying to talk to him and get him to sign his books. No one could see me or my table."

She asked if he'd noticed anyone paying particular attention to him. Everyone, he said. Anyone acting strangely, as though they were homing in on him? They all were, he said. The man could talk a mile a minute. He kept regaling them with stories.

"He'd start a tale, get them interested, then say it was all in this or that book. They thought he was entertaining them, but he was using the stories as bait, feeding out line, hooking them, and reeling them in."

After a half hour of conversation, Nadine left, having attained nothing more than a sense of how the event had been organized.

Her next stop was a ranch-style home in suburban Bethel Park. A woman with a narrow face and a body to match answered her ring. She wore a cotton jumpsuit over a gray knit turtleneck sweater and a necklace of silver disks. Unlike the angler, Doris Kearney brought her into her living room rather than her office and offered her coffee. Nadine accepted it, hoping to strike a congenial tone.

Before she launched into her questions, she made a mistake asking Kearney what sort of books she wrote. "Space opera," she said. "Do you know what that is?" Nadine did not and had no interest in learning about it, but she listened as the woman sketched the history of the genre. She began in the nineteenth century and had reached 1920 when Nadine brought an end to the lesson. "Pardon me, but did you pay much attention to Mr. Parker?"

"Parker?" she said.

Nadine explained she meant Steven Parker, that Parker Stevens was a pen name. This led her down another rabbit hole as the woman told the various names under which she worked. She also wrote horror novels. Nadine, feeling less cordial by the minute, interjected herself between a ghoul and a zombie.

"Did you notice anyone hanging around his table who seemed to take an unusual interest in him?"

"They all were. Everyone was clamoring to speak to him."

"What about a person who didn't approach him, perhaps an individual who hung back eavesdropping?"

"You mean the older man with the green bag?"

Nadine decided she probably did. "Tell me about him."

"Like you said, he was standing about eight feet back from his table, lurking. I've always liked that word." She leaned forward and wrote it on a scrap of paper. "He never approached him. He didn't come near any of us. But he was focused on Mr. Parker. Do you think he had anything to do with his death?"

"Can you describe him?"

"I can do better than that." She reached for her phone. "I take pictures of people all the time. I use their descriptions in my stories. Let's see now. Here he is."

Nadine left ten minutes later, having forwarded the image to her own phone and feeling as though she'd won the lottery.

***

Barnwell turned away from her computer as Jeffrey entered the bullpen. "I've had quite a day," he said.

"As have I," she replied. "Novak filled me in on what's become a cold case. It's scarred him."

Without a word, Jeffrey stepped into the kitchen and filled his mug, emblazoned with the ACPD logo and reading, "To Serve with Honor." He continued through the bullpen toward the row of interview rooms. Lydia followed, carrying her water bottle and notepad. After months of working together, neither needed to tell the other it was time for a conference.

"I need to make this quick," he said between slugs of what had to be his sixth cup of the day. "Ullrich is interviewing the book fair witnesses. I'm supposed to help him." He was hooked on caffeine. Whenever he cut back, headaches assaulted him until he gave in. Every cop saw daily evidence of the corrosive effects of drugs and alcohol on society. "You first."

Lydia summarized what Novak had told her three hours before. "There were aspects of the case he wouldn't discuss. He directed me to his written report. I've requested it." The county now digitized all evidence but kept paper records for only ten years, after which they were stored at a warehouse.

"What's your theory?" Jeffrey said.

"That Parker delved into Jeanne Holman's murder and found something we missed. He was about to name the killer. Whoever it was silenced him."

"Someone at the book fair?"

"Not necessarily. His suspect could have been in the crowd that day and followed him home. It also could be a coincidence. It was no secret Parker was at the event. The library featured him on all its promotional materials. Jeanne's killer could have waited at his house for his return and ambushed him." She beat one fist on her open palm. "I wish Ross could get into his computer. Once we read what's he's written…"

"He's working on it. My turn." He recounted what Brian Ransom, the retired managing editor, had told him. "Parker loved the ladies. He stalked the younger reporters, impressing them with his reputation and flair."

"The man was still on the prowl," she said. "Remember how Brandy found his wedding ring in his pocket?"

Jeffrey turned to his interview with Susan Nance. "She denied he'd been grooming her, but his approach had all the hallmarks of the process, reaching out to a young co-worker, helping her find her feet at the courthouse, even though there was no reason for him to do so."

He described how her husband had burst into the newsroom. "She thinks he's capable of killing Parker. That's the direction I'm taking, although the ten-year gap between the end of the affair and his murder makes little sense."

"We've seen cases where someone's resentment eats away at them until they explode," she said. "Anger and frustration can lead to mental illness."

"Point taken," he said. He finished his coffee, which was now cold, and rose to refill it. She couldn't believe the man's hands weren't shaking.

While he was gone, she opened her phone and read a message from Nadine. "That recruit I had assigned to us found something." She turned her screen toward him. "One writer spotted this man hanging back from Parker's table. She took his photo."

Jeffrey mounted reading glasses on his face and stared at the image for a moment. "Forward that to me. I'll share it with Ullrich. If any of these tipsters mention someone matching his description, we'll show it to them."

She had already done so.

"We have two lines of inquiry that have no obvious connection. Let's pursue them separately. You take the cold case, and I'll follow up with Susan Nance's husband and any other women with whom he was involved. We'll check in each day until we decide which branch of the river to navigate."

Scott Ullrich's day had been fruitless. Five book fair attendees had responded to the request for information about anyone whose behavior had struck them as peculiar. Ullrich had interviewed three of them, two of whom appeared to be attention-seekers. The third had seen an older man dressed in a wool coat, which was odd given the mild temperature of the day, but he couldn't provide a more complete description. He was now on his fourth when Jeffrey joined him, apologizing for his lateness.

Ullrich knew the detective had been following other leads. He'd just started questioning the woman. "This may be nothing," she said, "but I saw John Shumway reporting your request on KDKA, and that got me thinking."

"Yes?" Ulrich prompted.

"I don't mean to be nebby," she said, using the colloquial term for nosy.

"What did you see?" Jeffrey interjected, having experienced enough dancing around from others he'd interviewed.

"There was this man," she said. "He stood at the rear of the crowd listening to Mr. Stevens. I was in the back row, so I patted a seat next to me. He looked at me and returned his attention to the writer."

There didn't seem to be much to her story, but Ullrich said, "Can you describe him?"

"He wore a heavy coat—too heavy for the day. Like he was sick or something."

Ullrich sat forward. It was the second time someone had mentioned a man in a warm coat.

"And he carried a tote bag. It was heavy, but when I'd seen him earlier, he didn't buy anything. It was like he'd brought it with him and was carrying it around."

"What color was the bag?" Jeffrey asked. Ullrich turned his head to catch the reason for the question, but Jeffrey gave no hint.

"Green," she said. "I think it was from a market of some sort. Maybe a farmer's market."

Jeffrey reached in his pocket and pulled out his phone. "Does he look anything like this?"

"That's him. See the coat and that scraggly mane of hair? That's the fellow. He hung on to everything Mr. Stevens said."

CHAPTER FIVE

LYDIA POURED Calvin half the contents of the Moka pot, topped it with steamed milk, and shoved a half bagel with cream cheese and salmon his way. "And a good morning to you," he said with a grin, noting the pleasant change from oatmeal. "Is this a special occasion?"

"Sort of," she said. She turned down the volume on the small TV on the counter and slid into a seat alongside him. "I want to thank you for your parents."

"It wasn't my doing," he said. "I was just around for the ride."

He waited for an explanation and, when none came, said, "I take it you and Dad had a talk."

"We did. I spoke to him, and he opened up about his life. I appreciate your advice." Calvin could have explained his father's reticence. Instead, he'd asked her a question. Have you tried speaking to him? He'd made it her idea, so when she did so, it came out naturally rather than forced.

"I was referring more to your mother," she said. He raised his eyebrows in an unspoken question. "You've heard my family situation more than you probably care to. No

mother. Distant father. The closest thing to an orphan."
She'd had a procession of maternal figures, from the wives
of other officers on the many bases where she'd been trun-
dled, to Barbara Novak, Karol's wife, who'd asked the right
questions as her relationship with David Kimrey soured.

"She senses how—" Lydia interrupted herself. "Some of
my resistance to a church wedding is that I'm on my own. I
don't have anyone to help me. Your mother's taking me on
as a project."

"You've never wanted a big to-do. A few friends and
Chief Novak officiating. That's what you said."

"But Ruth does," she replied, "and I want her to
have it."

He covered her hand with his. There was no need to say
anything.

"What's that?" she said. She turned and raised the
sound on the television as the image of the man Nadine
Foster had found flashed across the screen. "...are asking
anyone with information on this person to contact county
police at 412..."

"Who's that?"

"That's who may allow us to solve this case."

***

AFTER TWO WEEKS OF BRIGHT, warm fall days,
temperatures plunged on Wednesday morning. The
sparkling colors were muted a dull gray, and a wind from
the northwest tore at trees, stripping their leaves into piles
that clogged gutters. Pittsburgh's weather had reasserted
itself, a declaration that winter would not be long in coming.

Barnwell stepped from a cruiser as a squall flooded the
parking lot at Parkway Center, drenching everyone and

everything in it. She ran the four dozen steps toward the building, but not soon enough to avoid her curls catching every drop they encountered.

Rain was not the only thing to inundate her five days after the murder. A box of evidence and files awaited her in a conference room, a trickle of tips had come in responding to the photo of the man shown on morning newscasts, and Ross Sutton had asked to speak to both detectives once they arrived. She didn't know where to begin, but Jeffrey, passing behind her with his omnipresent coffee mug in hand, settled the matter.

"Sutton has news," he said. "Bring your bottle." She followed him across the hall into the darkened offices where the digital magus and his minions worked their magic.

"What've you got?" Jeffrey asked.

"This wasn't easy," he proclaimed in his booming voice. "We got into his phone. He used an encrypted email client. We've thrown everything at it and haven't broken in, but we're working on it. He didn't encrypt his notes though, so you'll find some terse memos, phone numbers, that sort of thing. We also have his calendar, but he used a kind of shorthand for some of his appointments."

Sutton's flair for the dramatic took hold as he proclaimed, "Now to his computer." He was incapable of explaining how to start a fire without first describing how to forge an ax. For three minutes, he described the system that threw passwords at an electronic device until it disgorged its contents. Parker's password had been complex, a combination of initials, numbers, and symbols that may have had some meaning to him. "Monograms, dates, some of it backward, I suspect. It ran to sixteen characters. Tough to key in, but he didn't have to. He used his thumbprint, but the coroner failed to provide his thumb."

He paused and smiled at his witticism, waiting for them to react. Jeffrey chuckled, but Lydia waited for the rest of the story. *Get on with it.*

Once they got in, he said, they encountered the same roadblock to his emails. "But we haven't given up. We had better luck with his word processing files. Some are open, but I saw nothing of consequence. Others, he protected with passwords, but they aren't as convoluted as the key that unlocks his computer. I've preserved the encoded originals so they're admissible, but I've posted uncoded copies to the file.

Finally, she thought, *the coda.*

Jeffrey praised the giant for his hard work to keep him fed. Lydia muttered something similar, and the two returned to the bullpen.

"When it rains, it pours," she said, describing the case file from Jeanne Holman's slaying awaiting her in the secure conference room. "I spoke with Jeffrey's cardiologist on the way in. He was treating him for the heart condition, but that wasn't what most concerned him."

"Which was?"

"His drinking. He'd been troubled by results of the liver enzyme test and had advised him to back off, but Jeffrey couldn't stop. He'd always been a heavy drinker, but the doc says it had increased since he'd lost his job. He told me it was reaching a crescendo, that he risked serious problems if he didn't quit."

"Sounds as though something else was eating at him. I wonder what it was."

"We'll keep digging," she said. "The man may have had a secret."

"Why don't you start on his file? I'll go through his notes. But first, I want to question Susan Nance's hot-headed ex-husband." And they needed to track down the tips they'd received on the person who stalked Parker at the event. Four days of small drips of evidence now became a deluge.

———

THE FILES on Jeanne Holman's murder filled an accordion folder with file folders, each labeled with their contents, and plastic bags with physical evidence. The folder's cover contained a record of who had checked it out and when. Lydia scanned the list, seeing names unknown to her, but one stood out. Karol Novak had been the most recent person to examine the file, ten years before. His name was listed three times before that, the first in 2003, when Dwight Truesdale had been exonerated. Here was confirmation of how much the case had gnawed at him. His years of searching had turned up nothing new. Was she wasting her time now?

Whether online or on paper, a case file was dry and technical, including not just photos and interviews with suspects but every form and court filing associated with the investigation and prosecution. Anyone expecting some revelation to burst forth would be disappointed. She cast the folder containing photographs aside. Although she was inured to violent images, she could not endure Jeanne's rape and strangulation.

The earliest record in the case was a transcript of the 911 call from the bus driver. "A woman says she's found a body in Highland Park. She stepped in front of my bus. I almost ran over her. You need to send someone." The operator told him to hold at his location until police arrived, but he protested that he'd be suspended if he didn't stick to his route. All reports were filled with such minutiae.

Next was the statement Novak had written, detailing his arrival at the park as the woman lead him to the body while her two charges scampered on playground equipment. He described the condition of the corpse and his call for investigators. In precise handwriting, he detailed securing the murder scene, a thatch of weeds concealed behind a tree, and the surrounding area, including the swings and slides.

This was followed by the report of Rolf Peterson, the detective who'd assumed command of the investigation. In dry prose, he listed the steps he'd taken on his arrival, his supervision of the crime scene investigators, since this was before the office of county medical examiner had been established, and his assignment of Novak and his fellow foot soldiers to question neighbors in the immediate area for any suspicious activity they'd noticed. While they'd uncovered nothing, Peterson himself had found an onlooker who recalled seeing two teenagers charging up Highland Avenue the afternoon before and witnessing the driver return alone on Negley Avenue forty minutes later.

For reasons not stated in the report, attention shifted to students from the nearest public high school, Taylor Allderdice in Shadyside. Peterson and his partner had interviewed several teenagers. One girl said they spent the first weekday afternoon of summer vacation at nearby Frick Park, where a fellow student, Dwight Truesdale, tried to strike up a conversation with her and two girlfriends. "He had this Yamaha," she'd told the detectives, "and kept trying to take us for a ride. I turned him down. I didn't like the idea in the first place, but I don't like him. He's fat and has acne all over his face."

Another of the girls confirmed the story. "Dwight wouldn't take no for an answer. He was so insistent, almost whining. We wanted nothing to do with him. He went away, but we could tell he wasn't happy."

They questioned the young man, who finally admitted he'd seen Jeanne Holman walking alone along Fifth Avenue and asked her to come for a ride. "She was real excited," he told them. "She'd never been on a motorbike before." Though neither wore helmets, he drove north on Shady Avenue then zoomed up Highland. He parked the bike and suggested they walk along the footpath above the reservoir. She then decided to walk back. "She said I'd driven too fast. I promised to take it slow, but she'd made up her mind."

Peterson asked if she wasn't more afraid to walk alone through East Liberty. "I pointed that out," he said, "but she told me she had friends there and wasn't worried." They hammered at him. Why would Jeanne have been willing to come with him if she feared riding on the bike? Why wouldn't she have returned with him once he promised to drive more slowly? Only when they accused him of raping her did he admit he'd tried to kiss her, but she'd refused. This, he said, was why she'd returned on her own. The detective wasn't buying it, but nothing could shake his story.

She scanned the transcripts of two subsequent interrogations. He admitted he'd tried "messing with her," by which he meant grabbing her breasts, but he refused to confess to the crime. "She was mad, and I was afraid she'd tell my mother, putting me in a jam. But she was okay when I left her.

"It's my brother's bike, and I wasn't supposed to touch it. He had a summer job in Oakland and was due home at five. I had to return it before he showed up, so I came back on my own." According to the transcript, he began weeping, said he regretted taking the bike and picking her up. He was sorry for what had happened to her but swore he hadn't harmed her.

Enter Jabari Jackson, a seventeen-year-old Black youth who lived on Stanton Avenue, the dividing line between the Highland Park and East Liberty neighborhoods. Peterson's report stated that Jackson had been near the park on the afternoon of June 7th and seen a boy lying atop a girl younger than he was. She was crying, insisting he get off of her. He'd torn her blouse off. She continued to resist but had gone quiet. "I saw him humping her," his statement read. "Then he tied up the blouse and looped it around her neck."

Why hadn't he helped the girl? "Someone would have blamed me for raping her. They do it all the time to us." Jackson picked Truesdale out of a line-up, initiating a prosecution that ended with his conviction and sentence to life imprisonment.

Lydia took a break, checking messages before returning to the file. Something was missing. Jackson's signed statement was in the file, along with Peterson's report on the interrogation, but there was no transcript. How had he found this key witness? Had he come in on his own? She sipped at her water bottle as she tried reconstructing the Pittsburgh of the early nineties. Would a Black youth have volunteered this testimony if he feared being accused of the rape and murder himself? Had he told his story to a friend who reported this to the police? Novak had said he'd been seen in the area. By whom? The report answered none of these questions. Jackson had appeared out of nowhere.

Police work was seldom fun, but Lyle pictured his partner enjoying herself as she poked around in the old files. Some of her brightest moments had come from investigating cold cases. For his part, Jeffrey was not looking forward to his session with Ted Nance. The change in weather had cost him a night's sleep and left him in a foul mood. When he'd spoken to the man by phone, he'd given him a lot of lip, demanding to know on whose authority Jeffrey was questioning him. He thus invited Nance to headquarters, "inviting" being a euphemism. "You can come here or I'll visit your business." Nance didn't question what this was about. Parker's murder had led the newscasts on all Pittsburgh stations since Sunday.

He asked if he needed an attorney, to which Jeffrey replied, "It's up to you. We haven't charged you with anything."

Nance came alone, as Jeffrey had suspected, since public records suggested he couldn't afford an attorney. He brought along a bagful of arrogance, however, saying to the detective as he admitted him from the sealed entry area into headquarters, "Let's get this over with. I'm a busy man." Jeffrey expected to encounter a flood of deflections and obfuscations.

With Barnwell shaking off dusty records in a nearby room, Jeffrey enlisted Scott Ulrich to join him. Before they even started the recording, Nance said, "I was with my girlfriend on Saturday afternoon. We'd driven out to Ligonier. She'll tell you the same. Can I go now?"

Jeffrey ignored him, began the interview by asking for his name, date of birth, and place of employment. "You know that, or you wouldn't have called me there. It's Wyatt and Associates, a marketing company. We handle things like web design and social media management for small companies." In one step, he'd gone from evading every question to providing a sales pitch.

"You were acquainted with Steven Parker?" he asked.

"Yeah, but you know that too. He screwed my wife and ended our marriage. Ruined my business." While still married, he'd been self-employed, but he'd since gone to work for someone else. Jeffrey had intended to ask why, but Nance saved him the trouble. "The divorce cost me my income and my house, even though it wasn't my fault. Damned courts. They always side with the woman. I couldn't afford to scratch out a living, going from client to client, especially when I was operating out of a one-bedroom apartment. Bitch!"

The detective did a quick translation. He'd depended on his wife's income, augmenting it with work he brought in. When she left, he had to find steady employment.

"When was the last time you spoke to him?"

"In 2013. He issued a stay-away order. If I'd violated it, he'd have put me in jail."

"And since it expired? You haven't contacted him?"

"Why would I?"

"Answer the question." His exasperation was on full display.

"I haven't seen or heard from the bastard since the day I confronted him in the *Herald* newsroom. I'm sure she told you all about that."

"And your ex-wife. When did you last speak with her?"

"We talked through our lawyers. Cost me a ton, and I got nothing out of it." He dropped his crossed arms and leaned forward. "He used his status to get my wife into bed with him. Sure, I went after him. Wouldn't you have done the same?"

Jeffrey ignored the question, and from the way he

rushed on, Nance didn't expect an answer. "I had it out with him just that once. He came after me through the courts, pinned my ass to the wall. Then Susan divorced me, as though I'd been the one hopping from bed to bed."

"So you hated him?"

"Sure. I know you want me to tell you I've gotten over it after ten years, but I haven't. Someone gave him what he deserved. I wish I'd had the guts to do it, but I didn't. I was over an hour away when he was killed. Katrina—that's my girlfriend—wanted to see the old fort out there. Fascinated by American history. Here's her number." He slid his phone across the table. "She's afraid of cops. She's Russian, so you can't blame her. But she'll confirm we were nowhere around when he got what was coming to him."

Jeffrey had one last question for him, though he knew it was useless. "Do you know anyone who might have killed him?"

"I didn't know him, so how am I supposed to answer that? Whoever did, pin a medal on him, will you?"

As Lydia munched on her tuna salad sandwich, she considered what she'd learned. Novak had told her Jabari Jackson, who claimed to have witnessed the rape, had been in trouble over dealing marijuana, but she'd checked before taking her break and found no record of it—neither a conviction nor even a prosecution. She suspected what that might mean but would have to confirm it. She put her meal aside and ran her hand through her curls as she considered the situation. Did this detail matter? Her task was to identify Steven Parker's killer, not to right an old wrong. Parker thought he'd solved Jeanne Holman's murder. Wasn't that where her focus should be, not on musty three-decade-old records?

She would read the crime writer's work in progress, but she owed it to herself to examine the original record to learn what else the detective had uncovered. She dropped the unfinished sandwich in the trash, refilled her water bottle, and returned to the conference room.

After more than an hour, she had more questions than answers. Without a transcript of his interrogation, she couldn't tell how Jackson had witnessed Jeanne's assault. How did he get close enough to identify Truesdale without being observed himself? As a Black youth in what was by then a white neighborhood (never mind that Billy Strayhorn had been born and raised there), he would have stood out. Had a third person reported seeing him? Was that how the detective had located him? If so, why hadn't that person been interviewed? Wouldn't that individual have also seen the attack?

Leafing through the folder, she found other things missing. Unless Peterson had failed to document it, he'd investigated no other suspects. One and done. That wasn't how good police work was conducted. Apart from the canvas of neighbors Novak and other beat cops had conducted in the hour after the body was discovered, she found no evidence Peterson had conducted a more in-depth search.

No wonder Novak was troubled by the investigation. It had been shambolic. Unless significant portions of the file had been lost over the years, a defense attorney should have been able to get the case dismissed. She made a note to learn who had represented the young man, if he or she were still alive.

Lydia's last act was to read the postmortem examination. As Novak had hinted, it was stomach-turning. The girl had been attacked, and she'd fought back. Traces of skin and blood were found beneath her fingernails. Dirt on her sandals and heels showed she'd been dragged from wherever she was accosted to the relative cover of the vegetation behind the tree. Her shorts and underpants had been pulled down, her blouse and bra ripped from her body, and she'd been brutally raped. Someone much larger than her had penetrated the youngster, breaking her hymen and causing significant bleeding. Either before or after raping her, the assailant had knotted her blouse, yanking it behind her while kneeling on her back. The garrote broke her hyoid bone and crushed her larynx, asphyxiating her.

She leaned back in her chair, replaying the scene in her mind. A young girl, enjoying nature on a bright day, caught unaware as someone grabbed from behind and threw her to the ground. She heard Jeanne protest, plead, then scream. One hand to her mouth, silencing her, as the other tore at her clothes. Her heart pounding. The pain as he entered her.

Lydia shielded her eyes. Her heart raced, and her breathing came in quick gasps. She stumbled to the restroom, splashed water on her face, and peered at her drawn features in the mirror until she regained control. Returning to her desk, she glanced around to satisfy herself that no one had witnessed her panic attack. This case felt too close to home.

HENRY ZIEGLER LIVED in an apartment on Mount Lebanon Boulevard, blocks from the borough's library. Not sure what to expect, Jeffrey had brought not only Detective Ullrich but a patrol officer. He opened the door as a woman who appeared to be in her eighties made her way out of the entry, steadying herself with a cane. Spotting the uniformed officer, she brightened.

"You're here to see Henry, aren't you? I'm sure he'll be helpful."

He did not reply, opening her umbrella, since the cane made it difficult for her to manage, but Ullrich said, "We hope so." Jeffrey shot him a withering glance, unwilling to announce who they were there for or why. They took the stairs to the third floor and knocked at 304. A pear-shaped man with shaggy salt and pepper hair answered and smiled at them.

"You're here about my story," he said.

That seemed an odd way to put it, but Jeffrey asked him to identify himself and for permission to come in. "Of course," he said. "Let me get it for you."

What "it" was became apparent when Ziegler grabbed a green bag from behind the door. Ullrich reached inside his coat, ready to withdraw his weapon, but some instinct caused Jeffrey to enforce calm with a downward motion of his hand.

"Sit down. Please," Ziegler added as a plea. He deposited the bag on the coffee table. "I can't let you take it, but you can read it here."

"Mr. Ziegler…"

"Henry," he said. "I'm just Henry."

"Henry." He introduced both of them.

The man's face brightened. "Oh, you're here about Mr. Parker. It's terrible what they did to him. Do you think it's because of his book?"

Jeffrey gave a slight nod, catching the man's drift. "And this is yours," he said, placing his hand on the bag.

"My memoir. I've worked years on it. The writers group

at the library is helping me." When Jeffrey didn't interrupt, Ziegler explained how a dozen authors met monthly to review each other's works in progress. "I get to present three times a year. They're very thoughtful. At first, they had a lot of suggestions, but now they mostly listen. One of them, a mystery writer, keeps saying my writing has improved."

"Is that why you attended the book fair this weekend?" Jeffrey asked.

"It's almost finished," he said. "I hoped someone would read a bit of it and help me find an agent."

"That's why you approached Parker Stevens," Jeffrey said, using the victim's pen name.

"I didn't approach him." His tone suggested Jeffrey had accused him of something.

"But you hoped to?"

He shook his head with fierce determination. "Only if he had a moment. I didn't want to disturb him. But so many people wanted to speak to him, particularly after what he said about his next book."

Turning to Ullrich, Jeffrey said, "Send the uni on his way. Let him dry off." Ullrich made a small sound of protest but did as he was told. "You heard Parker tell the audience he'd solved a case?"

"Yes, I asked the question." Sensing Jeffrey's confusion, he said, "He'd finished speaking. I called out to him, asking what he was working on next. That's when he said he'd solved a murder from years ago."

"Did someone ask you to pose that question?"

"No." His answer was swift and indignant. "I asked it because I wanted to know." Before Jeffrey could follow up, he said in a quieter voice, "Okay, I thought if I shouted it out, he'd remember how I'd helped him and do the same for me. I never got the chance. People mobbed him. I waited my turn, but it never came."

"When he told the audience about solving the case, did you notice anyone paying particular attention? Someone who reacted in a way you didn't expect?"

Ziegler uttered a small sound behind closed lips that sounded a bit like "huh-uh."

"How about those gathered around his table? Did anyone display unusual interest?"

Again, he rocked his head from side-to-side. "I don't pick up on things like that."

"You don't?"

"That's what they tell me. I don't understand it myself, but they say I don't read people's responses the way most folks do. But I'm lucky. Some have it worse than I do."

"I see," Jeffrey said, and he did. "That's what your memoir is about, isn't it?"

Ziegler brightened. "Yes, it's about how I've overcome this..."

"Autism," Jeffrey prompted.

"Being on the spectrum. That's the polite term."

"I apologize."

"It tells how I've made a life for myself despite all this. I'm showing others they can make it, if they try."

"Good for you," Jeffrey said.

"Would you like to read it?" Ziegler's face glowed like that of a child anticipating a day at Kennywood.

"I would," he said, rising, "but right now I don't have the time. I'm trying to catch the man who killed Parker Stevens."

"I hope you do," he said. "I admired him."

It had been months since Lydia Barnwell had curled up with a good book. If that moment ever came, it wouldn't be with this one. Not that there was anything wrong with Parker's story. It just wasn't what she would read if she had the time. Too much like real life. Nor could she be described as having curled up, anchored as she was to a rolling chair in the middle of the busy bullpen.

It opened with a preface that laid the story out and teased what made it more than the recounting of a heinous crime.

On a sunny morning in June 1993, two children playing in a wooded park in Pittsburgh's east end discovered the body of a young girl. She had been brutally raped and strangled. Within hours, police identified the nude corpse as that of thirteen-year-old Jeanne Holman, who had been missing from her home since the previous evening. It took only hours for Pittsburgh police to identify a suspect, fifteen-year-old Dwight Truesdale. The youth admitted to giving her a ride on his brother's motorbike the afternoon before but said she'd refused to return with him.

As they questioned him, his story changed. After first saying he'd reached out to kiss her, he now admitted he'd fondled her, and that it was for this reason she'd insisted on walking home through a troubled neighborhood. While he'd tried to conceal his actions, one aspect of his story remained unchanged, as it would through the next decade. He insisted that when he'd left, she'd been alive and well.

When detectives brought forward an African-American youth who swore he'd witnessed the attack and identified Truesdale as the killer, they had their man. The youth was arrested, tried as an adult, convicted, and sentenced to life in prison.

In 2003, genetic testing, not yet admissible at the time of the trial, showed Truesdale was innocent. It took two years before he was pardoned and released, still maintaining his innocence. Only in 2007 was his conviction overturned.

This left open the question of who had killed Jeanne Holman. The case remains unsolved. In this book, I reveal how a Pittsburgh detective, in a rush to judgment, concocted evidence to convict the young man while overlooking a far more likely suspect hiding in plain sight. This man remains at large and has never been charged with the crime.

I will name him, present the case against him, and indict a system that continues to protect him while bullying a defenseless teenager.

The rest of the preface was a biography of sorts, reviewing the writer's career in journalism, the books he'd written since what he called "my retirement," and recounting several cases in which he claimed to have aided police investigations. Wrapping up, he wrote, "After years of studying this case, I hope to bring closure to the family of little Jeanne Holman by bringing her killer to justice."

Before she could begin the first chapter, Jeffrey slid into his chair alongside her, wiping raindrops off his face and wearing a frown as gloomy as the weather. She raised her eyebrows in inquiry. "You ever been shushed by a librarian?" he asked.

"Not since I was in high school. You?"

"Five minutes ago. Henry Ziegler, who so many people thought was acting suspiciously at the book fair, said he has nothing to do with Steven Parker's murder. I believe him, and the Mt. Lebanon librarian wants to make sure I do. She left a message demanding to know why I'm harassing a man who wouldn't hurt a fly."

***

Tommy Molnar stood on her front steps as Lydia returned home. Holding his umbrella over her, he exchanged the leashes for Howie and his dog, Ginger, with her bag of groceries. "You didn't have to do that, Tommy," she said as he carried them into the house.

"I'm happy to."

"Your Cub Scout good deed for the day?"

He gave her a broad grin. "I'm just doing it. And I'm a Boy Scout now."

She stepped back, realizing how much he'd grown over the summer. He now topped Anna by an inch, and there'd be no turning back. "How's your mom?" she asked.

"She's good. Did she tell you she's getting a promotion?" Anna worked as a licensed practical nurse in a retirement home. "They're training her to become a diabetes counselor."

Lydia set the dinner ingredients on the counter as they talked. "When did this happen?" Anne hadn't mentioned it Sunday evening when she and Ruth prepared the meal.

"Yesterday. Her employer's paying for it. The last one left, so Mom will replace her."

She told Tommy to send her congratulations and paid him for his week of dog walking. She recalled the time when he'd refused payment, in part because of a racial incident a classmate had goaded him into committing when Calvin had first moved in with her. Now he pocketed the bills and left without complaint. *He is grow-ing up.*

She sautéed mushrooms, garlic, and shallots, deglazed the pan with Marsala wine, chopped the mixture in a food processor, and added mascarpone, ricotta, and Parmesan cheese. Calvin came through the front door. "Don't drip on the floor."

"I shook my raincoat out on the porch. I stopped drip-ping when I was three."

She smiled but didn't laugh. He kissed her on the neck, but she didn't respond. Without a word, she placed a large pot of water on the flame and spooned the mushroom mixture onto strips of pasta dough with a cookie scoop. At one time, she would have made the *sfoglia* by hand, but as her work ate into her waking hours, she now settled for sheets purchased at the store.

Calvin watched as she folded the strip over itself and sealed the individual squares of ravioli. "You're quiet tonight," he said.

She looked up as though seeing him for the first time. Folding her hands, she buried her face in her knuckles and shook her head from side to side. "This case…"

"Want to tell me about it?"

"No, but I will."

He tossed a salad while she cut strips of sage and tossed them into bubbling butter. She lowered half the ravioli into the pot, waited until they floated to the surface, spooned them into individual bowls, and topped them with the herb mixture. She placed the uncooked ones in the refrigerator, making a mental note to freeze them for later use.

They ate in silence, sipping a Tuscan vernaccia. He knew enough not to interrupt the meal with whatever both-ered her. Only after they had finished did she describe her day of slogging through the case file and the crime writer's unfinished book. "What he did to that girl," she said. "I think of myself when I was her age, developing, feeling uncomfortable with the secrets my body was delivering. To be torn apart by some monster... I can't get the image out of my head."

"Put it aside for the evening. Let's catch a movie on TV. Have a second glass of wine. Maybe a third." Rare was the occasion when she had more than one drink, and only with dinner.

"I can't. Parker thought he was on to something, but he hasn't revealed what it is. I need to log on and continue reading."

"Don't." It was an order, not a suggestion. "Drop it, or you'll never get to sleep."

They began a series on Apple TV called *Slow Horses*, not the sort of thing to make her forget she was a cop. In the morning, she would recall nothing about the plot except that the portrayal of the characters had made her laugh for a moment.

When she turned in, she couldn't put Jeanne Holman's ordeal out of her mind. Whenever she dosed off, panic forced her awake.

CHAPTER SIX

"YOU LOOK like you slept in the rain," Jeffrey said as he collapsed into his chair, a geyser of coffee erupting from the lip of his mug.

"Thanks," she said. She had started her day by driving through Highland Park. Much had changed in three decades. After a century of use, the park had fallen into decay. Ten years after Jeanne's murder, a local group had restored the Entry Garden then created pools along the boulevard bordering the acreage. She'd stood at the spot where she believed the attack had occurred, stepped back onto the roadway, and tried to envision what anyone standing there might have observed.

Instead of revealing this to Jeffrey, she said, "Jeanne Holman cried out to me in my sleep."

"You know cops," he said as he wiped his hands on his slacks. "They're so jaded, they never let a case get to them."

"Right," she said. Both knew this public perception was untrue. While they handled most cases without getting emotionally involved, some stuck with them, not for a day or a week but for the rest of their lives. Deaths of children topped the list, but any crime involving a vulnerable individual might trigger a reaction.

Jeffrey was haunted by the case of a homeless woman sleeping in a county park who'd been set afire by a couple of teenaged youths. He'd lost sleep not only for the plight of the woman, who'd endured agony for two days before succumbing, but for the boys who were the same age as his older son. What had made them do such an evil thing to a fellow human being? He'd reacted by increasing the time he spent with his family, even when it meant letting a case slide for a few hours. Barnwell covered for him when he attended Mass or one of his children's sporting events, and he appreciated it. His former partner had been less accommodating.

They reviewed their plans for the day. Lydia would finish Parker's book, searching for the uncharged suspect to which he alluded. Jeffrey would check out Ted Nance's alibi, although he suspected it would hold up. "If so, I'm at a dead end."

Something she'd observed tugged at Lydia's memory, but she was too tired to dredge it up. It would come to her, just as she would shout out something like "The Cranberries" long after she'd forgotten the group's name in a conversation. She refilled her water flask, opened a bag of mixed nuts, and resumed reading.

The first chapter recounted the day Jeanne disappeared and was told from the perspective of her parents. Though rich in detail, the narrative shed no light on what Stevens had uncovered. It did provide background on the family that was missing from the dry reports found in the case file. The girl's father, Mathew, was an accountant at US Steel. Ellen, her mother, clerked at Kaufman's Department Store a few blocks from his office in the Steel Building. She'd worked at Gimble's before she had children and dropped out to raise them. Now that Jeanne and her older brother, Charlie, were teenagers, she had rejoined the workforce. The couple commuted to and from work each day. Stevens depicted them as a close-knit family. The chapter described their initial lack of concern when they returned home Monday evening to find neither child at home. Charlie had baseball practice, and Jeanne loved to hang out with friends. It was the first day of summer vacation. The Holmans would have been more surprised had they found them there.

Lydia read on as the hours went by and the parents' anxiety increased, culminating in their call to police at sunset. The chapter ended with a foretaste of what was to come. "Little did they suspect that a man living not two miles from them had just upended their lives ... and ended that of their daughter." He provided no clue who this mysterious person might be.

She skimmed through the next chapter, which recounted the discovery of the body the following morning. She barreled through the description of the corpse. Again, the chapter ended by hinting at the existence of an unnamed stranger: "Jeanne's killer lived within walking distance of the park. He might have been present in the crowd that gathered at the scene. But Detective Rolf Peterson was about to turn his attention to another suspect, in the process derailing the investigation and postponing justice for the murdered girl."

"Get to the damn point," Lydia said to no one in partic- ular. Jeffrey had left to question Nance's girlfriend and tie up two loose ends. Other detectives were bent over their monitors or on the phone. She took a break, refilled her bottle, and returned to Parker's document. The third chapter described the investigation and arrest of young Dwight Truesdale. Like the first two, Stevens concluded it with another teaser, but provided no hint of his suspect's identity. In the fourth chapter, he described the ten-year battle his parents had waged to free him. As she read, she found sections outlined but unwritten. "Parents' backgrounds," read one. "Financial effect on family."

He hadn't finished the manuscript. She rested her mouse on the scroll bar to her right and saw that it was three-quarters of the way down the screen. Was this all he'd written? She paged down and, instead of copy, found blank chapters filled with cryptic notes.

- Introduce BV
- Trouble childhood and prior arrests
- Peterson questions
- Sister's alibi
- MJ's suspicion
- Question JJ
- Distance from MD
- Never pursued

MJ again. She recalled the words the medical examiner's team had recovered from the notepad she'd found on Parker's desk. "MJ- 'He is capable of it.'"

He'd named another chapter "Justice Denied." His notes suggested he intended to indict Detective Rolf Peterson, referring to a subsequent case and his removal from the force. Then two more notes, "BV Never Charged" and "Day of Judgment," from which she imagined he intended to conclude his book with a demand that police or the DA reopen the case and investigate this BV.

Was that it? Had she spent all this time only to hit a brick wall? In one chapter, he'd entered "MaryJo ex" and a ten-digit sequence that began 724, the area code for the region surrounding Pittsburgh. Was this MJ? Did "ex" mean former wife? If this was a cell phone number, she might be anywhere today, but she hoped the woman still lived in the region. She also found the name Sheila, the notation "cover for him," and a number with the 303 area code, which might be anywhere in Maryland.

She recorded when she'd learned.

> Steven Parker, a/k/a Parker Stevens, suspected someone with the initials BV. He lived near Shadyside or Highland Park. He'd had a troubled childhood (run-ins with police?) and been arrested, possibly serving time. Sister (Sheila?) provided him with an alibi, but Parker questioned it. Detective never pursued. MJ (ex-wife?) thought him capable of murder.

It wasn't much, but it was something. She picked up the phone and dialed the first number but cut off before completing the call. How was she going to approach a woman whose relationship to the case was unclear? Ask her why her number had been found in the murdered writer's file? What if she said she didn't know? What then?

Barnwell wanted to give this some thought before diving in. She messaged Ross Sutton and asked him to identify the holders of both numbers. Meanwhile, someone might short circuit the process. She dialed Novak's cell phone. He picked up almost immediately.

"I can't talk now," he said. "We're at the hospital. I'll call back soon as I can." He disconnected without waiting for a response.

What was he doing at the hospital? Had someone been hurt? This was another question she couldn't answer on her own. She'd have to do the one thing she hated most, wait.

Her name was Katrina Makarova. She was nearly six feet tall and slender. In her shapeless lounge outfit, he might have taken her for a man. Tight dark curls danced across her forehead as she gave him a shy smile, but Jeffrey noticed her hands trembling. He introduced himself, and she swept her arm toward the interior of the apartment, inviting him in.

She asked if he'd care for a cup of tea. Against his normal rules of non-engagement, he told her he welcomed it. While the kettle bubbled in the kitchen, he looked around the small flat. Its plain furniture was enlivened by bursts of color, reflective of sunsets, maple trees, eggplant, limes, and lemons on a profusion of blankets, throw pillows, and table coverings. It was like entering a Van Gogh painting.

One glance told him she lived alone, that Ted Nance might be a part of her life but didn't occupy it. She returned with two cups and saucers, placed them in gaps on the fiery tablecloth, which appeared as though it had been dropped there when he suspected she had folded it with care.

"So what can I do for the police?" she said. Her consonants were clipped and her vowels softer than American English, particularly when compared to Pittsburghese.

He posed a few introductory questions to put her at ease, but when he asked about what part of Russia she hailed from and how long she'd been in the country, she crossed her arms and shifted her body weight. What was he to say? That he was not from the border patrol?

"Welcome," he said, "though I sense you've lived here many years."

"I applied for citizenship. I'm waiting. It takes a long time," she said.

"Good for you." He sipped at his tea, wishing he could flash a reassuring smile behind the rim of the cup. "I have a few simple questions. Where were you Saturday afternoon?"

"My friend drove me to a town in what they call the Highlands. We visited a fort there."

"Your friend being..."

"Nance. Ted."

"And what brought you there?"

"I study American history. I aspire to be a part of this country. Fort Ligonier was built by the British against the French and their native allies." She launched into a description of how the British had extended their control beyond the Alleghenies, using it as a launching point to attack Fort Duquesne at what is now Pittsburgh. "Your George Washington was an officer then, long before your war with the English."

Jeffrey knew all this but was fascinated to hear a Russian woman giving him a lesson in US history of which many Americans were unaware. Or ignorant. He let her finish her answer, making appropriate sounds at certain points to keep her going.

"I'm impressed by how well you know this," he said.

"To become a citizen, you have to learn a lot about America."

"Do you recall what time you left here on Saturday?"

"In the morning sometime. Maybe ten." Which would have put them in Ligonier at around 11:30. "And when did you return?"

"It was getting dark. The sunset made it hard for him to drive. After six."

They'd spent the day at the fort, she said, only leaving when they closed the gates at five. She had packed a lunch, so they hadn't gone to a restaurant. The pair returned to her apartment, she said, and ordered a pizza. "And did he stay here?"

"All night, you mean?" She wrinkled her nose, and dark clouds came over her features. "No, it's not like that. He is my friend, not my lover."

Had Nance suggested there was something more to the relationship? Jeffrey was sure of it.

Novak returned the call thirty minutes later and apologized for making her wait. "That's okay," she said. "Why are you at the hospital?"

"We couldn't awaken Izabela this morning and called an ambulance." Isabela was Novak's mother, a Slovakian immigrant whose life story could have made a movie. "They've taken her to Presby. They suspect she's suffered a heart attack."

"I'm sorry. I hope she'll recover." She recalled her many visits to the Novak home, always dominated by the TV blaring from wherever Izabela watched it. On her most recent visit months ago, the house had been still. She hadn't considered the implications until now. Had she been ill even then?

"We don't know a thing yet. She's in the ICU, and they're poking and prodding her." His voice was subdued, as though others were within range. She replied that what she needed would hold, that she understood he was preoccupied. "No, go ahead. It's going to be a long wait. I need the diversion."

"I've read the file," she began.

"All of it?" She told him she'd skimmed the court documents but studied the reports. "What did you think?" he asked.

She gave the matter some thought before venturing an opinion. Novak didn't reach conclusions until all the facts were in. "It doesn't appear they looked very hard after they identified a suspect."

"Go on," he said.

"I don't understand how they didn't challenge Jabari Jackson's testimony. I drove to the park this morning. There's no way he could have witnessed the attack unobserved."

"And you conclude…"

"That Detective Peterson put him up to it."

"You're familiar with the federal investigation of the police force in 1997?" he asked. Without waiting for a response, he told of the lawsuit filed by a pair of civil rights organizations after two Black men died while in custody. The Department of Justice joined the suit, forcing the city to submit to a consent decree. "Until then," he said, "officers did as they pleased. JJ—that's what he called himself— claimed Peterson threatened to arrest him on trumped-up charges unless he agreed to testify.

"How had a fifteen-year-old boy discovered how to fashion a garrote?" she asked. "It's not the sort of knowledge you walk around with. And to do so on the spur of the moment—"

"Boys younger than that shoot each other in schools and on the street."

"Yes, but this was thirty years ago. Did his attorney even make that case before the jury?"

Novak did not answer the question. Had it not been for the sounds of paging in the background, she would have thought he'd disconnected the call. "I don't know how far you want to delve into this, but if you're interested, I'll ask Dwight if he'll speak to you."

"He's still around?"

"Not here, but nearby. He's changed his name, married, and has a family. They've spent two decades trying to erase the past. I don't know if he's willing to dredge all this up again, but I can approach him."

"I'd appreciate it," she said.

"It might have little bearing on your case, but Parker may have spoken to him."

"We have nothing else," she said. "The only suspects appear to have alibis. We have no physical evidence. No fingerprints in the garage of anyone who shouldn't have been there. The only thread I have is his book, but he didn't get very far with it."

Again, Novak paused, as though he was considering something. "I'll ask him and get back to you."

She told him about the contacts and phone numbers in Parker's unfinished manuscript. Neither meant anything to him. When she asked for advice on how to open a conversation with either of them, he chuckled. "You're the detective. I'm an old retired guy with too much time on his hands. But if it were me, I'd say that I found their number in the notes of a murdered man and ask what they'd discussed. They just paged us. Gotta go."

She thanked him, but he'd already dropped the connection.

<hr>

WHAT JEFFREY CALLED loose ends were two stories he had to check. Recalling Ron Schuster's alcoholic insolence on the day of the murder, he barged into his insurance agency unannounced and demanded to speak to him. The man who invited the detective into his office was cooperative and subdued. He surmised the alcohol had been talking.

"What can I do for you?" he said, gesturing toward a conference table and offering to make him a coffee from the machine near his desk.

He passed it up. He wasn't here to make friends or chitchat. "We found your fingerprints in Parker's garage," he said. "I'm wondering why."

"Steven and I often golfed together with two other friends. Parker has a big SUV and hauled all of us around in it, along with our equipment. I've been in and out of that garage dozens of times."

"When was the last time you played together?"

"A week ago yesterday. I frequently have to open the office on Saturdays, so I take Wednesday afternoons off, leaving my assistant in charge. She knows how to reach me if anything urgent comes up."

"We also found a restaurant receipt belonging to you on the garage floor. It's dated three days before the murder."

"So? I told you I met him on Wednesday afternoon to play a round. I must have fished it out of my pocket when I reached for something."

Jeffrey made a show of writing in his notebook. "Look," he said, his voice rising, "Joanne and I agreed to have our prints taken. We didn't raise a fuss or call our attorney. Neither of us has anything to hide. We've been friends with both Steve and Lois for years. He and I played together. The girls shopped and had their nails done, that sort of thing. It would have been strange if you hadn't found our prints."

"Okay," Jeffrey said, snapping his notebook shut.

"That's it?"

"You've had time to think about it. Do you have an idea of who might have had it in for him?"

"It's like I told you Saturday. He kept his private life to himself. I can't imagine who would have done such a thing, unless it was something he wrote. All I can say is that I hope you catch the bastard who did this."

"We will," Jeffrey said. "You can depend on it."

SUTTON HAD TRACED the numbers found in Parker's notes. Both were cell phones. The 724 number was listed to someone named MaryJo Keller, who lived in Beaver County, near the Ohio line. The name meant nothing to her, apart from the reference to an MJ. She searched the National Crime Information Center. She didn't have a record.

The 303 number belonged to Sheila Remsen of Cumberland, Maryland. Under her maiden name, Sheila Vogt, she'd been arrested for shoplifting from a Pittsburgh department store in 1995. After making restitution, she'd been placed on probation.

Who were these people? Was Sheila the sister Parker had mentioned in his notes? She dialed the Cumberland number, and it went to voicemail. She did not leave a message. Whatever role she played in the writer's investigation, Lydia didn't want to alert her.

When she dialed the first number, a soft voice answered. Barnwell identified herself. "I found your name in a file belonging to a local writer, Parker Stevens. I'm calling to ask what the two of you discussed."

She waited and heard rapid breathing at the other end.

"I can't recall," she said in a heavy Pittsburgh accent. "It were a wrong number."

"He'd written your name and number. MaryJo. He must have had a reason to call you."

"It were a mistake. He got my name from somewhere, but it wasn't me he was after."

"Do you know the name Parker Stevens or Steven Parker?"

Once more, Barnwell could have played the chorus of a Taylor Swift song before the woman answered. "I don't think so."

"He was a crime writer. Someone murdered him on Saturday. The story's been all over the TV."

"I don't watch the news."

"He was writing a book about a young girl who was murdered years ago. Jeanne Holman. Does the name mean anything to you?"

"I don't know no one by that name."

Lydia asked a few more questions, but she was not forthcoming. "Look," she said, "my Max will be home in a few minutes. I been baking n'at. I gotta red up the kitchen."

A real yinzer, Lydia thought.

The conversation was going nowhere. Lydia thanked her and ended the call. Despite her denials, MaryJo Keller had told her a great deal. She'd hesitated before answering each question. Rather than giving direct answers, she'd evaded them, saying she knew no one named Jeanne Holman and had never met Steven Parker when that wasn't what Lydia had asked.

Had she been involved in Jeanne Holman's murder somehow, or was she frightened? Lydia didn't have enough information to tell which was true. Perhaps both were.

She did not redial the Maryland number. She would

study the backgrounds of both these women before making
her next move.

JENNIFER TILLMAN, Bill Parker's assistant at the theater,
said she'd meet Jeffrey at Point Perk, the university's coffee
shop on Wood Street downtown. He entered the glass front
to find over a dozen young people reading books or tapping
at the keyboards of laptops. Two classmates sat on a series of
polished wooden pews that cascaded up one wall, facing the
brick interior. A willowy raven-haired woman rose as he
stood in the doorway, waving her hand as though he'd called
her name. He walked toward her table at the back of the
room, took the seat across from her, and flashed his ID,
which she appeared to study.

"How long have you been a cop?"

"Since before you were born, I suspect." The answer
seemed to satisfy her.

He looked from side to side, trying to gauge if anyone
could overhear him.

"Don't worry," she said. "They're all listening to music."

Except for the young men engaged in conversation,
everyone else had plugged their ears with electronics of
some sort. A woman at the next table bounced in her chair
in time to some unheard music. (If what she was hearing
could be described as music—Jeffrey couldn't abide his
teenage son's tastes.) How anything she was reading penetrated the distraction was a mystery.

He asked Jennifer a few preliminary questions. She was
from Charleston, West Virginia, as her slight accent
affirmed, in her senior year at Point Park University,
majoring in drama. She told her story with her hands,

moving them before her as though shifting items on the table. As a child, she'd put on plays in her family's basement, building set pieces out of cardboard, developing the plots, and corralling friends from her church to serve as supporting players to her starring roles. She'd acted in elementary and middle school productions and hit her stride in high school, appearing as extras in TV and movie productions shot in the state.

"And now, here I am," she said, raising both arms in a flourish.

"Here you are," he echoed. In the future, he'd see the young woman on the stage, screen, or TV. He was sure of it. "Tell me about your role at Janus."

"I help Bill—Mr. Parker—raise money for the theater. I write fundraising appeals and grant applications, keep the donor list up-to-date, and send out thank-you letters to our angels. Whatever he needs."

"Does this sort of work interest you?"

"Being in the back instead of out front, you mean?" She fluttered her hands. "Not really, but it comes with a paycheck." Her smile disappeared. "This is a tough business. It's thirty percent talent, fifty percent luck, and the rest ... Well, let's call it personal relationships."

Jeffrey suspected what that phrase entailed.

"If I don't make it, I'll still want to be involved in theater work, so it helps to establish a different skill set and pad your resume." As she said this, her hands typed at an imaginary keyboard.

"How did you land this job?"

"Bill posted a notice at Point Park, and I answered the call." Her smile returned, and Jeffrey sensed she'd treated him to a bit of theater jargon. "That was two years ago. I've been here ever since."

"You were scheduled to have a donor reception on Saturday. What happened?"

"When he found his father murdered, we had to cancel it. We're short-staffed here. It couldn't go on without him."

"How did you hear about it?"

"He told me."

"How?"

Her hands ceased their endless migration. "Is Bill going to be okay?"

"Why would you ask that?"

"Because he found the body. Don't you always suspect the person who's found a murder victim?"

It was Lois Parker, not her son, who had discovered her husband dead, but Jeffrey didn't correct the record. "With any crime, we question everyone connected to it and check their stories. That's what I'm doing here. Again, how did he notify you of what had happened?"

"He called my cell phone."

"Where were you at the time?"

"My apartment. It's on Boulevard of the Allies."

"What did he say?"

"He asked me to go to the theater and email the donors we'd invited that night, canceling the event. He explained his father had been killed."

"How did he seem?"

She held out both hands as though expecting a gift. "How would anyone react? He was upset."

"How upset?"

"His voice was trembling. I could tell."

"Did he argue with you?" When she didn't seem to understand, he said, "Become angry when you didn't respond fast enough?"

She paused, as though not wanting to speak ill of her boss. "He didn't mean it. It was the shock of the thing."

He asked what time he'd reached her. Late afternoon was all she recalled. "The email blast I sent out will list the time. I can forward it to you."

"Do that," he said, handing over his card with his email attached.

He thanked her and closed his notebook, about to hoist himself out of his chair.

"So I've been helpful?" she asked. "He'll be all right?"

She teared up, and he settled back in. "You two are close, aren't you?"

She nodded her head without speaking. "I understand. If it's any consolation, your story matches what he told us." It was, he thought as he returned to his cruiser, not unlike the professor who used his authority to initiate affairs with his students. Everyone had a secret.

***

Brocton, New York, was a small village on the shore of Lake Erie, twenty miles from the Pennsylvania border. While in the state's wine-growing region, its claim to fame was a minimum security prison with a boot camp approach to rehabilitation. It took Barnwell over two hours to drive there from ACPD headquarters. Had Novak's call come fifteen minutes later, it would have added at least thirty minutes to her trip, but she'd avoided rush-hour traffic by the narrowest of margins. She signed out for the day and headed north without telling her partner where she was going or why.

Dwight Truesdale, who'd since adopted his mother's maiden name, Sawyer, lived a mile from the village on the outskirts of an even smaller community, Portland. Wind bent the trees in front of the two-story brick home. Soon, winter would come, and the house, street, and community would be buried under a foot or more of snow coming in off the lake.

She mounted the front steps. Before she rang the bell, a boy of about twelve pulled the door open. A man stood behind him and nudged him away, telling him to finish his studies. He was met with a whine. "Ah, Dad." But he wandered off. Whether to do as he was told or bury his head in a tablet, she couldn't tell.

Barnwell introduced herself, but he cut her off. "We've been expecting you." He led her through a hallway that bypassed a living room and into the kitchen, where a woman in her mid-forties was about to shove a casserole dish into the oven. "This is Becky," he said.

Lydia extended her hand, which she took after a moment's hesitation. "I hope you're not reopening all this," she said. "We've built a life here. We don't want it turned upside down."

"I'll try not to. The case I'm working on doesn't directly involve your husband."

"Then why are you here?" She planted her hands on her hips.

"It's okay," Dwight told her. "Mr. Novak vouched for her."

She shook her head and wiped a rag across the work surface. Lydia was glad he'd rescued her, because she couldn't explain why she'd come all this way just to speak to a man who'd been unjustly accused and jailed. He led her into a room that had been added onto the back of the house and served as an office. It lacked heat, and she wondered how he worked here in the winter then spotted a space heater under the desk. He unfolded one of two chairs resting against a wall and settled into his. She opened her notebook, taking in this man who was no longer overweight but muscular. This often happened to men in prison. His complexion, whatever it had been, was concealed by a light-brown beard, clipped to a respectable length.

"Mr. Novak explained you're investigating the death of the writer who was looking into Jeanne Holman's murder," he said. "For the record, he found me and asked for an interview. I declined. As Becky said, I'm not eager to get my name out in public again. And before you ask, I was at the prison Saturday afternoon. I counsel younger first-time offenders. We don't house juveniles there, but there are men eighteen and up who are still kids."

"And your wife?"

"Becky teaches children with special needs."

"You dedicate yourselves to changing lives."

"Something like that. I spent ten years in prison for a crime I didn't commit. Becky's brother had Down syndrome. We bring experience to our jobs."

She asked him to describe what had happened the day he was arrested. He told her the same story she'd read in Peterson's reports and the writer's unfinished story. He'd borrowed his brother's motorbike without permission and tried to get one of his classmates to hop on the back. When they refused, he rode around the park until he found a younger group of girls. He invited them to go for a ride, and Jeanne Holman had accepted.

"We didn't know each other, but I'd seen her around and vice versa, so it wasn't like she was going off with a stranger."

He rode up Shady Avenue and then roared up Highland to the park. "I was showing off to impress her." They'd walked around the reservoir at the top of the hill, and he'd tried to kiss her. "She seemed like she was enjoying herself. I thought she liked me. I grabbed her, and ... you know..."

"Tried to feel her up," Barnwell supplied.

He flinched at her use of the term, but said, "Yeah, it was a stupid move. I don't know why I did it. I had ten years to figure that out and never did." The girl slapped and screamed at him, told him to leave, that she would make her own way back. "I apologized and begged her to let me drive her to her house. Walking through East Liberty was too dangerous, but she insisted. I had to return the bike before my brother got home, so I gave up and left her there."

He looked down and pulled at the hair beneath his lower lip. "I wish I hadn't. I wish I'd never picked her up. But as I tell the kids I work with, wishing changes nothing. Every day, life gives you choices, and each one has some effect on you. It's like the Robert Frost poem about two roads diverging in a wood. You have to think before you decide which way to go."

"It ruined your life."

He seemed to consider the question. "No, it changed it in ways I couldn't have foreseen. I'm married with three terrific kids, and both of us have fulfilling careers. I wasn't going anywhere back then. Things might have turned out worse. Who knows?"

"Still, you must harbor resentment against those who took ten years out of your life. The witness who swore he saw you ..."

"JJ," he said. "No, he was also a victim. Have you spoken to him? I have. After he reversed his testimony, he looked me up and apologized. He explained how the detective put the screws to him. It affected his life too. I work with these kids. They tell you stories about being set up.

Most prison guards don't believe them. I do. Not all of them, but many. Talk to JJ. It will make you a better cop."

"Okay," she said, "I'll do that."

"I'll tell you who came out of this worse than I did. My mother. She and my dad fought for me and got me released, but once they did, it was like they had nothing holding them together. Mom was bitter about what they'd done to me. Dad tried to get her to move past it, but she couldn't let it drop. It created a rift that destroyed their marriage. He found someone else. I don't approve of his choice, but I understand it. The divorce broke her. When I changed my identity, I chose her name as a kind of tribute."

The attorney who'd mishandled his case was long gone. "He was a friend of the family and charged us less than a first-rate lawyer would have cost. You get what you pay for."

He gave her the name of the warden at the Lakeview correctional facility, forced it on her when she assured him she believed him. "I want to remove any lingering question," he said. "When the writer reached me once by phone, I told him I had no interest in reliving the case. I never spoke to him again. I only go to Pittsburgh to see Mom. She's in a nursing facility, not doing well."

Lydia returned home with gray clouds turning dark then retreating into blackness. She drove through the night haunted by what one wrong choice had done to all of them: Jeanne Holman, Dwight Truesdale, his parents, and Jabari Jackson.

Yes, she would speak to the man who'd been forced to bear false witness. She'd promised Dwight she would, and the system owed him that much. To make her a better police officer, he'd said.

CHAPTER SEVEN

LYDIA AROSE BEFORE CALVIN, grabbed a piece of toast, and left him a note. She emerged from the Fort Pitt Tunnel as dawn painted the city in an orange glow. The site never failed to impress her. You drove beneath Mount Washington for two-thirds of a mile, an illuminated tube two lanes wide, and emerged, day or night, with Pittsburgh's skyscrapers arrayed before you along the Monongahela River.

She took I-376 to Forbes Avenue and wound up into the Hill District before traffic thickened. She parked before a narrow two-story townhome on Erin Avenue, which unlike other such structures in the neighborhood, was flanked by grassy lots. A slender Black woman opened the door, her hair held back by a red and green scarf.

"You better come in," she told the detective. "JJ has to leave for his shift soon."

She entered a great room that looked out on the street through a pair of windows. The woman introduced herself as Millie. "You want coffee?"

"I'd love a cup." She sat Lydia at a small dining table in

a corner of the room and called up the stairs for her husband. Jabari Jackson came down a moment later, cinching a belt around his waist. His blue shirt bore an EMS emblem. He held out his hand and took his place alongside her at the head of the table as his wife slid mugs of coffee before them.

"Not what you expected, right?" he said. "I'm sure you've been to the Hill many times. We have our own little enclave here."

She didn't mention when last she'd been here, when a young Black man named Theo Mosely had been shot and killed by a Pittsburgh cop after Mosely had tried to run him over in a stolen car. "You're aware of the history?" he asked.

"It's the center of the Black community."

"Used to be," he said. "This was a thriving neighborhood. Restaurants, grocery stores, small businesses, and jazz clubs. You know how many great artists came out of this town? Mary Lou Williams? Earl Hines? Ahmad Jamal? Billy Eckstein? Erroll Garner? The list goes on."

Barnwell hid her impatience. She had little time with this man who'd testified against Dwight Truesdale at his trial. If listening to local history was the price she had to hear his story, she'd do so.

"You ever heard of 'negro removal?' Some call it urban renewal, but our name fits better. When they built that big ice rink they called Civic Arena, they demolished our heritage. They moved Bethel AME, the center of the Civil Rights Movement, but by some miracle spared St. Benedict's Catholic, one block away. Amazing, isn't it?"

As she was often forced to do, she resisted the temptation to mention that her fiancé was Black. She'd tried that once during a similar conversation and been put in her place. "But you didn't come here about that," he said. "I'm just showing you how things are."

"I've painfully aware of it," she said, noting his use of the present tense. "I see it every day."

He regarded her for a moment then nodded. "You're asking why I testified against Dwight. Here's how it went down. This prick cop Peterson hauls me off the street in East Liberty and takes me downtown. He grills me all day, throws me in a cell overnight, and starts in on me again the next morning. My parents don't know where I am. Peterson and one other guy hammer me. They say someone saw me at the park two days before when that girl got herself killed. I tell them I wasn't there. They insist I was spotted. I can see they're putting me in the frame. He says I musta seen a guy raping the girl. I tell him I didn't see nothing, that I didn't go near the place. 'Oh yes you did,' he says. This goes on and on."

JJ's wife interrupted the flow. "You better leave. You don't want to be late."

He told her he still had a few minutes. "I can always tell them I'm helping the police in their investigation."

She snorted. "Have it your way, but I have to go." She leaned over and kissed him, and he returned it. Warning him again not to take too long, she grabbed a jacket and left through the kitchen door.

Lydia didn't have to urge him on. JJ had gone on autopilot. "I dealt a bit of dope back then. Just grass, nothing hard, and only to friends. I was in it for the status, not the money. Anyway, they knew this. Peterson says they found heroin on me when they pulled me in. I didn't go near the stuff and told him so, but he produced a bag and said they'd found it in the lining of my jacket. Said they knew I was dealing."

He sneered and rolled his eyes. "He'd set me up and left

me to think about that for a while. That's five years in prison, and once they have you, they'll run you in on everything they can find for the rest of your life. Sorry," he said, "but that's the way it is."

"Go on."

"When Peterson returns, he offers me a deal. He'll ignore the smack if I say I saw this guy raping the girl. They haven't even told me his name at this point, just call him a guy. 'He did it,' he says. 'You're only confirming what we already know. By telling the court what you saw, you'll bring Jeanne's killer to justice.'

"He insists they had the right man. Says he's a white guy, not a brother, so I have no reason to protect him. I wasn't putting anyone's neck in a noose who didn't deserve it, he says. I weigh the pros and cons and take the deal."

"Ten years later, you recanted."

JJ hung his head and halted his recitation. "One day, his attorney asks to see me. He says Dwight didn't commit the crime, and DNA proves it. He spends a lot of time convincing me he's innocent." In a voice so low it was almost a growl, he said, "I see they used me to get at him. They framed me so I could frame him. I talk it over with Milly, and she says I have to do what's right. She's like that. Got a great sense of justice, that woman. Without her, I'm not sure I would have done so."

He described how, at considerable risk, he withdrew the testimony he'd given at Truesdale's trial. "I'm scared they'll slap me in jail on that phony heroin charge. Still, I tell the judge what happened, just as I told you. That, plus the DNA, got him off."

"And you reached out to him," she said.

"Yeah. I waited until he was released, which took a couple of years. If you're innocent, they should release you, right? But they had to go through a lot of red tape with the state. Even the governor got involved. Soon as he got out, I jacked up the courage, called, and apologized. He suggested we get together. I was suspicious at first, but he reassured me. Even told me prison had done him some good, that he was leaving Pittsburgh and building a new life. I'd done the same, so I could relate. We met, compared what Peterson did to us, and realized we'd both been his victims."

He checked his watch. "You have to leave," she suggested.

"I've got time. Milly was giving me an excuse. She doesn't like me going into all this, particularly now that someone killed that writer."

"Steven Parker? Did you ever speak to him?"

"Yeah. He found me about three months ago. I didn't want to talk to him at first, but he kept after me. Even showed up at Medic 5 where I'm stationed. I finally caved, told him what I've told you, and sent him on his way."

"Parker thought he'd solved Jeanne Holman's murder. Did he tell you who he suspected?"

He scratched his cheek. "Not directly, but he asked if I knew a pervert in the neighborhood, someone who preyed on kids. He gave me a name. It meant nothing to me."

She tried to stoke his memory, but the man couldn't recall it. "One last question," she said.

"At work," he said, and she frowned, not understanding his response. "You want to know where I was last Saturday afternoon when the writer got killed. I was on duty at the fire station up on Aliquippa, above Presby. You can check with them. We had two accidents and a fire with injuries that afternoon. Besides," he said, "why would I want to kill him?"

Perhaps to prevent the exhumation of his betrayal of

Dwight Truesdale, she thought, but she smiled and thanked him, convinced he was telling the truth.

———

"Where have you been?" Jeffrey asked as she slid behind her desk. She normally reported in before he did, sometimes by half an hour or more. She explained she'd met with the man who'd testified against Dwight Truesdale at his 1993 trial. "Do you think he had something to do with Parker's murder?"

"No, he's in the clear. I asked if Parker had talked to him. He did, even confronted him at his work."

"How did you get on to him?"

"Truesdale asked me to talk to him. They see themselves as fellow victims of Peterson's *investigation*." She rolled the word around in her mouth to convey her contempt.

"You spoke to Truesdale? Why? What does he have to do with Parker's murder?"

"I hoped Parker had spoken with him and dropped hints about the identity of his suspect. Truesdale refused to meet with him, but he asked me to hear JJ's story, so I did."

Jeffrey made a show of stacking loose papers then took a mouthful of coffee without looking at her. "Something wrong?" she said.

"I don't want us to get sidetracked. We're after Steven Parker's killer, not the Holman girl's."

The mild rebuke stung, the first time in their partnership he'd questioned her approach to a case. "I'm glad I took the time," she replied. "Parker asked JJ if he knew of a known pedophile living in the neighborhood. He didn't, but it's our first lead on who he suspected of the murder."

Jeffrey seemed to accept that. "I want to keep our eyes on the doughnut, not the hole. We're in red on the Baltimore Board." He referred to a long, double-paneled white board that listed all homicides the division had investigated over the year, color-coded to show which were open and which closed. The name came from *The Wire*, a television series that featured a similar means of tracking case. A fellow detective had spotted the device while watching the program and recommended it to the chief. The board now dominated the bullpen, honoring success in green and blaring urgency in red.

"I'm glad you have something," he said, "because I'm stuck." He rewound his interviews with Susan and Ted Nance, describing the newsroom confrontation that triggered the divorce. "He had reason to kill Parker, and she believes him capable of it, but his girlfriend, or whatever she is to him, confirms they were miles away all Saturday."

Lydia tented her hands, trying to recall a thought that had raced through her mind the day before. "Susan told you Parker had found someone else?"

"After they got together a second time, he stopped calling her. She got the impression he had moved on. Why?"

She tapped her keyboard and opened notes she'd taken. "When we interviewed the Schusters Saturday evening, two things stood out to me. One," she said, ticking off the points on her fingers, "Joanne's reaction. She was visibly upset, weeping when we arrived at the house, clutching a tissue in her hand."

"They're friends," he said. "I'd expect her to be upset."

"Right, but hold on a minute. When we first arrived on the scene, Lois Parker was composed, stoic even, but Joanne was upset."

Jeffrey's eyes danced as he recalled the scene.

"When I returned to the house to go through Parker's records the next day, she was there and still upset. 'We're in mourning,' she said. Not she, we."

"Hmm," he said.

"Recall her husband's reaction." She leaned toward the monitor, studying her report of the interview. "Joanne tells us they've been friends with the Parkers for a dozen years, and what does Ron say? 'The closest.' She tells him to put the wine bottle down and makes an excuse for him. You asked him if he and Parker were friends. He said, 'Very close.' Joanne steps in to say they played golf together and urges her husband to confirm this. 'Tell him,' she orders."

By now, Jeffrey made uh-huh noises as he tracked where she was headed. "So while Ron played golf, Parker hit a hole-in-one."

"No need to get crude," she said as she stifled a chuckle.

"Perhaps we've been heading in the wrong direction."

"You go your way, and I'll continue mine," she said.

"All right, but Sutton uploaded Parker's emails and phone messages. We have a court order for his banking records and should get them in a day or so."

They were about to get a firehose of information, so much they risked drowning in it. "I'll work it with you, but I have to follow the lead JJ gave me. I'm also trying to reach the two women Parker mentioned in his notes." When he raised his eyebrows, she said, "I have to, Lyle."

He acquiesced. For the first time since they'd become partners, Lydia no longer followed his lead. She'd taken charge.

As soon as Jeffrey left, she dialed Sheila Remsen's number. It again went to voicemail. Did she spend all her time on the phone or leave it off? This time, she left a message, identifying herself and asking the woman to return the call. Since her shoplifting arrest had been in Pittsburgh, she searched court records and learned Sheila Vogt had married an Arne Remsen in 1998. She hunted for any social media accounts the woman might have but found none. Parker had identified his suspect as BV. In his computer notes, he'd listed "sister's alibi."

She followed the same electronic trail for MaryJo Keller. She had no arrest record, and her Facebook page contained nothing but photos of baked goods and reposts of cat videos. The Allegheny County clerk's database had no information on her, but when she logged on to the Beaver County site, she hit pay dirt. MaryJo had married Max Keller in 1982, changing her name from MaryJo Vogt.

Digging back through court records, Lydia learned she had won a divorce from Bruno Andrew Vogt two years before, although they'd been separated since 1976 after only two years of marriage. MaryJo had lied to her. While she would visit her to demand a reason, her more important discovery was the identity of BV. The NCIC revealed a Bruno Vogt had been arrested for indecent exposure to a group of teenage girls at Frick Park in 1987. Because the girls were under sixteen years of age, he'd been convicted of a 1st degree misdemeanor and sentenced to five years in prison. After serving only three of those years, he'd been placed on probation and ordered to remain in Allegheny County.

Lydia drained her water bottle while she reviewed what she'd learned. Steven Parker had discovered that three years before Jeanne Holman was murdered, a convicted pedophile, just released from prison, lived nearby. He'd decided to write a book about the case, made a public announcement about it, and been slain two hours later.

Why had his former wife denied speaking to Parker? What role did Vogt's sister play? Why did Detective Peterson's record contain no reference to Bruno? Had he even investigated him?

As was often the case, she had unearthed more questions, but she understood her task: to answer them and bring Parker's killer to justice.

JOANNE SCHUSTER ANSWERED THE DOOR, wearing a look of surprise. "Ron's at work."

"I'm not here to see your husband. I have a few more questions for you."

"Can't this wait?" she said. "I'm about to leave." Her leggings and baggy sweater were not what a woman in this neighborhood wore to lunch or shop with friends.

"This will only take a few minutes." He used the technique of advancing as though to enter. As expected, she fell back.

"Can I get you something? Coffee?"

"Aren't you in a hurry?" He made it more a statement than a question, enough to keep her off guard. "Where can we sit? Living room? Kitchen?"

"Let's go to the dining table." As she led the way, she said, "I don't know what more I can tell you. We were home all afternoon..."

"I'll get to that," he said. "I'm here to discuss your relationship with Steven Parker."

She responded to what could have been taken as an

innocent question with flared eyes and clenched hands. "Our relationship?"

"Yes." Her reaction confirmed Barnwell's suspicions. He didn't expand on his question, awaiting her next move.

"Who told you that?"

"When did it start?"

She leaned on the table, combing her hair off her forehead with her hand. "Four, maybe five years ago. Ron and I were having problems. I'd mentioned it to Lois. She must have told him. He came over one afternoon, 'just to talk,' he said. He was a good listener, gave me a little advice, and that was that. A couple of weeks later, he stopped by again, 'just to check how things are going.' I was still miserable and ... one thing led to another."

"How long did it last?"

"Ron found out last spring. I don't know how. He didn't discover us together, but he'd somehow worked out what was going on. He came at me like you just did. Didn't ask me if we were having an affair. Just said, 'How long has my best friend been fucking my wife?'"

She lifted her head and crossed her arms, tears welling in her eyes. "I don't know why it shocked me. What did I think would happen? Eventually, one of us would make a mistake and there'd be a blow-up. I didn't deny it. I asked him the same question you asked, 'How did you find out?' He said it didn't matter. He never has told me."

"What did you do?"

"I told him it had started when we'd been drifting apart, that I hadn't been able to get through to him and had turned to Lois and then to Steven. I said he was just someone who'd listen to me but that it got out of hand. He was hurt, angry, all the emotions you'd expect. He asked me, 'Do you love him?' Would you believe this had never occurred to me?"

She sighed as though recognizing her foolishness. "I told him no. For several days, we lived in the same house but avoided each other. Whenever I'd start a conversation, he'd look through me. I don't know if he was punishing me or trying to decide what to do. I put up with his silence for a few days, then asked him what he intended to do."

Hugging herself, she looked away for a moment, rocking from side to side. "He gave me a choice: either end it or he'd file for divorce. He made it clear he'd make it rough for me if he did so. The business is in his name. If he chose to play hardball, I'd be left with little. All the while, I kept repeating it was over between us."

"Did you inform Steven your husband knew?"

"Of course."

"How did he react?"

"He nodded, like he already knew."

"And Lois?"

"No." Asked if she was sure, she said, "I warned Ron not to say a word, and Steven certainly wouldn't. She's never acted differently toward me, and if she knew..."

Jeffrey looked over her head as though seeking divine guidance. The conversation could go in one of two directions. He picked the first. "How have you maintained your friendship with her? Whenever you enter that house, you must wonder if she knows what you've done to her."

She hesitated for so long he wondered if she'd heard the question. "Toward the end, she told me Steven had once had an affair with a co-worker and almost lost his job over it. She said she'd told no one but her daughter."

"And Bill?" he asked.

"If she told him, she didn't say. I tried not to show much

interest, so I didn't pursue it. You can imagine how uncomfortable I was. Why was she telling me this? Did she know? But she made no accusation, just confided in me. That's why I'm sure she hasn't learned about it. I saw how hurt she was. 'Embittered' is a better word. I think she hated him."

She grimaced. "When Ron confronted me, I'd already pulled away from Steven, making excuses, being too busy. I couldn't completely break it off though." She snorted. "He had a way with me. I see that now."

"Are you telling me you kept up the affair after your husband discovered it?"

She shook her head in denial. "No, it was over between us."

"But you maintained your relationship with Lois."

She drew back as though he'd attacked her. "What was I supposed to do? She was my friend. My neighbor. I couldn't ignore her. She'd have wondered why. Besides, she needed me."

Some friend, Jeffrey thought.

"I told Ron not to say a word of this to either of them. Let's pretend this never happened. We will repair our marriage and hope they can do the same."

"How did he maintain his relationship with Parker?"

"I don't know. You'll have to ask him."

"He had to be angry with him."

"He was more upset with me."

Jeffrey didn't accept her story but would take it up with her husband. He shifted to his other line of questioning. "Where was he Saturday afternoon?"

Once again, she crossed her arms. "I already told you. We were together."

"Where?"

"Here at home."

"On a beautiful fall day, the two of you just sat around," he said.

"We're Penn State grads. We watched their game against Ohio State." A sullen look crossed her face. "They beat us twenty to twelve, knocked us out of championship contention."

"It was over around 4:40," he said. He'd finished watching the same game when the dispatcher called him.

With her nostrils flaring, she barked her response. "I was watching the game, not the clock. They did interviews afterward."

"Can anyone corroborate that?"

"It was on Fox. Ask them."

He stared at her for several seconds. In the twenty minutes they'd been speaking, she'd gone from dismay to defiance. "This is not a joke. Someone murdered Steven Parker. No one has a better motive than your husband. I'll ask again. Did anyone else see him between four and five on Saturday afternoon?"

She clasped her arms around herself again, her balloon of anger deflated. "I guess not."

Returning to his cruiser, Jeffrey texted his partner a message, "You had it right, Barnwell. Nice work."

Rolf Peterson lived in a small, two-story wooden structure fronted by a brick porch on Rossmore Avenue in Brookline. Lydia had called in advance, and the former detective was at first reluctant to see her. She had been vague, saying only that she was working on a cold case and hoped he could be of help.

Looking at the house from across the street, she

wondered if he had been born and raised there. A line of colored light bulbs dangled from the gutter. She suspected they'd been there since the previous Christmas, perhaps even the one before that. Ignoring the rain that spattered her windshield, she drew her jacket around her and mounted steps at the right end of a long porch shared by a small wooden table and two chairs.

A burly man with receding gray hair, close-cropped in military style, answered her knock. The creases on his face looked like a relief map of a canyon. "Barnwell?" he said through closed lips, as though he was concealing dental issues.

She flashed her ID, which he waved away. He followed her into a small living room in which a couch and over-stuffed chair faced a TV screen. The acrid smell of tobacco smoke filled her lungs. She pulled a tissue from her pocket and dabbed her eyes. Peterson lowered himself into the chair. He didn't invite her to take the sofa, but she did so anyway, opening her notebook on a wrought-iron table with a glass top on which a filled ashtray rested.

"What is it you're working on?" he said.

"The Steven Parker murder."

"You said this was a cold case."

"He was investigating an unsolved murder from years before. Did he speak with you about it?"

"Which case was this?"

"He must have told you when he called."

He gave her a long stare, sighed, and fished in his pocket for a pack of cigarettes.

"Could you hold off until we've finished?" she asked. "I'm allergic."

"It's my house, and you're on my time." He lit up with a flourish.

"When did you speak with Parker?" she repeated.

"Never, other than to tell him I wasn't interested in helping him."

"His notes suggest otherwise."

"We spoke once," he said, taking a deep drag off the cigarette and blowing a cloud of smoke her way. "He said he was writing a story about an old case I'd handled and wanted to interview me. I refused. He called three or four times after that. I didn't answer. I even blocked his number."

She turned a page in her notebook and wrote, "Blocked Call."

"The one time you spoke, did he mention what he was working on?"

"I don't recall."

"The Jeanne Holman murder?"

His frown, which he'd worn from the moment he opened the door, deepened into a scowl. "Yeah, he may have mentioned it. I worked a lot of cases. This one? Maybe he did."

He took another puff, expecting her next question, but she waited. "Has something new come up? We didn't have DNA back then."

He already had his excuses lined up, and there was more to come. "From your report, it appears you zeroed in on Dwight Truesdale from the beginning."

"Of course we did. It wasn't just me. My partner looked at the facts and reached the same conclusion. A kid picks up a thirteen-year-old girl, gives her a ride to a park, tries to mess with her, and leaves without her. Who are you going to look at first? The postman?" He stubbed out the cigarette and reached for another but didn't light it.

"Did you investigate any other suspects?"

"There weren't any."

"Were you aware a convicted pedophile lived in the neighborhood?"

"I don't think so."

"Bruno Vogt?" she prompted.

"Never heard of the guy. Has he confessed now?" He tapped the cigarette against his thumbnail, preparing to fire it up.

"Doesn't it seem odd to you that a man who'd done time for exposing himself to teenagers and pre-teens wasn't even questioned when a girl of the same age was raped and murdered?

He lowered his head and glowered at her. "I'm not on trial here. You had to be there. The newspapers were full of this story. TV news had it on every night. Mothers were scared to let their girls outdoors. If school had been in session, they would have kept them home. My higher-ups pushed for an arrest. The lieutenant demanded to know why we'd question others when this kid was so obviously guilty and a witness swore to it."

He lit the coffin nail while she blew her nose. Her handset chirped that she had a message. She glanced at it and checked her watch. "The witness being Jabari Jackson," she said.

"Was that his name? I don't recall. Kid was no good. I remember that all right."

"He says you threatened him and forced him to finger Truesdale."

"That's a lie."

"It cost you your job."

He rose from the chair and stood over her. "I've had enough of this. I did as I was told. The DA won the conviction. Talk to them. Everyone wanted this case closed, but when the kid got off, guess who was the fall guy. So get out of my face."

Jeffrey had summoned her to headquarters, and she couldn't take more time with the man. She didn't want him to get the last word however. "I'll be back."

"If you do, bring a man with you. They're letting too many girls play cop." He slammed the door after her.

———

Jeffrey allowed Ron Schuster to stew in the interview room while he briefed Barnwell on his wife's revelations. She recalled Joanne's concern about his drinking when they'd first spoken the night of the murder. Then, they'd thought she was trying to curb his belligerence. It now appeared she feared the wine would loosen his tongue and blurt out their secret.

"I brought him here rather than questioning him on his own turf. It will show we mean business."

"He'll be more subdued in either location without a bottle to boost his courage."

They outlined a strategy then joined Schuster, who twisted as he tried to get comfortable in the Spartan witness chair. Jeffrey turned on the recording device, announced the date and time, and listed those present. "I spoke to your wife an hour ago. She gave me quite a story."

"I know. She called me as soon as you left and told me I'd be next."

"How did you discover she and Parker were bedmates?"

"Something he said. I don't recall what it was." Schuster cleared his throat, stared at his folded hands, then jerked his head to dislodge the memory. "I have a book on my night-stand signed by Arnold Palmer. He asked where I'd found it. I'd never mentioned it to him. He would only have one-upped me." He sneered, as though this was Parker's common practice.

"The only way he could have seen it was if he'd been in our bedroom. That set off an alarm and made me notice other things: glances, remarks between them. Once, when we were having dinner with them, we started talking about music, bands we'd grown up with, concerts we'd attended. Joanne mentioned his not liking The Eagles. He shot her a warning look, a slight shake of the head, as though he'd shared this during a … private moment."

"So you confronted her," Jeffrey said.

"I was sure by then but wanted to see whether she'd lie to me. Her face gave her away, and she confessed."

They took him through the aftermath, which was as Joanne had described it, her seeking forgiveness, taking the blame on herself, and insisting they continue their friendship with the Parkers as though nothing had happened.

"That must have been hard for you," Lydia said, speaking for the first time.

"Of course it was." His response hinted at the aggressiveness he'd shown Saturday evening, but it fizzled out. "Very," he said in a subdued tone.

"You must have confronted Parker," Jeffrey said.

"Not really. He came to the house while Joanne was out. She must have arranged it. I didn't want to speak to him at first, but he insisted, said he wanted to explain what had happened."

"And?" he prompted

Schuster took a deep breath and looked at the ceiling. "He said Joanne had come to him while we were having some disagreements, wanting a shoulder to lean on."

"What sort of disagreements?"

"Hmm." He rubbed his hands together and looked down. "I honestly don't recall. Just things, like married couples often do. Anyway, they started spending a lot of time together, he said, and one day she began crying and said she needed him to comfort her."

Lydia suppressed the urge to say that Parker had done a great deal of comforting during his time on Earth. Jeffrey's lips turned up in contempt. Was he thinking the same thing or reacting to how cleverly Parker shifted blame? "And you accepted that?"

"She wanted to maintain the friendship. To protect Lois, she said."

"Did you consider divorce?" she asked.

He kneaded his hands together. "I had a little dalliance of my own early on. Joanne never found out, so far as I know. I'm not a hypocrite. I made a mistake, so did she. After twenty-eight years of marriage, you learn forgiveness." This was a far cry from how he'd spoken when fueled by the wine six nights before.

"You must have been angry at him," she said.

"No, I understood what had happened."

She had teed up Jeffrey response, and he swung at it. "C'mon, Ron. Your best friend has a months-long affair with your wife, sleeping with her in your home ... in your bed. You just shrug and walk away? I'm not buying what you're selling."

"I don't know how to make you understand—"

"You can't."

"But Joanne insisted we put this behind us, work on our marriage, and move on."

"And the way you do so is to play rounds of golf, attend baseball games, and have dinner with the man who cuckolded you?"

Jeffrey paused, waiting for a response that didn't come. "Here's what happened. For five months, you kept up the pretense, acting like nothing was amiss and all four of you were best buds. All the while, your resentment built, not only over what he'd done to you but at having to maintain appearances. After a couple of beers last Saturday, you saw Parker arrive home."

This was impossible from where the garage was located, but Jeffrey forged on. "You walked down the street to have it out with him, saw him with his back turned as he removed books from his car, and snapped. You pulled a pair of gloves from your pocket. The restaurant receipt flew out without you noticing it. You picked up a shovel and brought it down on him with all the rage you'd stored up. Then you shut the garage and returned to watch the rest of the Penn State game."

"No, no." Throughout this recitation, Schuster had been yelling out denials, half rising from his chair. "I was home all that time. You can ask her."

"I'm sure she'll cover for you, as you have for her all these months. We can't have this scandal getting out among the neighbors, can we?"

Schuster had seemed to sink under the weight of the relentless interrogation. Now, his hands clenched, the cords in his neck threatened to burst his collar, and he roared like a caged animal. "I've had enough of this. You can't question me without my attorney. Either arrest me or let me go."

"WHAT DO YOU THINK?" she asked after Schuster stormed out of headquarters.

"The man knows his rights." As she started to follow up, Jeffrey said, "I get what you're asking. He's guilty, but …"

"We don't have enough evidence to take to the DA."

Jeffrey leaned back and combed his hair with his hands. "He has a motive and the means, but if his wife sticks to her story, his ass was planted in front of the TV at 4:13 with a beer in his hand." He kicked a table leg in frustration. "All we have is that damn receipt, and he's explaining that away. We need more."

She reminded him—and herself—that Ross Sutton had dumped a ton of email and message traffic into the file the night before. "Why don't you sort through it?"

"Why me?"

"I still want to follow the Jeanne Holman angle. Parker thought he'd found something the police missed. I now know what it was." She told him what she'd learned about the convicted pedophile and her conversation with the former detective. "If Peterson is to be believed—a big if—he never questioned Bruno Vogt. I've tried to reach his sister without success. I'm driving to Cumberland in the morning to talk to her."

"You'd better alert the police." She needed no reminding that, when operating on someone else's turf, you needed to let them know. "I think it's a long shot."

"You always tell me we have to follow every lead, not do as Rolf Peterson did and focus on only one suspect."

"Point taken. You're right."

Her personal cell phone chimed. She glanced at the screen and answered it. "Yeah, Chief."

Lydia listened for a moment, her face deepening into a frown as she peppered Novak with questions in a low monotone. "I'm so sorry," she said. "If there's anything Calvin and I can do …"

Jeffrey studied her expression as she issued more condolences and ended the call. "Karol Novak's mother died."

"So I gathered. How old was she?" Lydia answered and gave him a thumbnail sketch of the woman's remarkable life.

Bringing the conversation back to the present, he summarized what they'd decided. "You'll pursue this Vogt angle while I wade through Parker's communications."

He studied her for a moment while she awaited whatever else was on his mind. "This Jeanne Holman case. It's important to you, isn't it?"

She didn't return his gaze, pretending to study her notes as she responded. "Parker was attacked two hours after proclaiming to an audience he'd solved a murder. I don't believe in coincidences." Although, during their brief time as partners, they'd seen a few.

"All right," he said, dropping the subject. "I'm equally obsessed with the Schusters. She has an affair with her friend's husband, who's also his best friend. When it's discovered, they go about their merry lives as though nothing's happened. I can't understand it. I've never seen a more fucked-up family situation."

"Yes, you have," she said.

He gave a sarcastic chuckle. "We both have."

CHAPTER EIGHT

THE FASTEST ROUTE to Cumberland was over the Pennsylvania Turnpike to Somerset in the Laurel Highlands then south via two US highways into Maryland's northwest corner. This Saturday, one week after Steven Parker's murder, dawned with a crystalline morning and a temperature in the high forties. Most of the trees had lost their color, fading to a lifeless umber, but some stands in lower valleys hinted at the blaze of yellows and oranges with which they had painted the countryside two weeks before.

Before leaving headquarters Friday evening, Lydia dialed Sheila Remsen again, only to reach her voicemail. She'd left another message then shared her frustration with Ross Sutton, asking if he knew a way to interrupt her conversation. As she'd suspected, he couldn't do so without a warrant. "If you've tried that many times and it keeps going direct to a recording, chances are she's blocked the call."

"Why would she do that? The first time I called, I didn't leave a message."

Sutton smiled as he often did when he was about to give a lecture. "She may have blocked the area code." Barnwell was unaware you could do such a thing and made the mistake of saying so. This led to a ten-minute dissertation and demonstration. She'd thanked him and settled for the two-hour drive. She'd called the sheriff of Allegany County to inform him of her plan. After listening to the reason for her call, he assigned her an officer "in case something goes south."

As she drove, she reviewed her conversation with Chief Novak the night before. She and Calvin had taken a meal to the family only to find that everyone in their borough had done the same. "You might as well stay," he'd told them. "I don't like food to go to waste."

She listened as Barbara outlined plans for Izabela's funeral. They'd had three days to think about it and were wasting no time in planning her ceremony. He'd questioned her about the progress of the investigation. "We have no physical evidence," she told him. "The killer seems to have worn gloves, so there's nothing on the handle of the shovel. We have one partial shoe print but no shoe with which to compare it. And the only prints we've found at the murder scene are those that belong there—his wife, son, and the two neighbors, all of whom have alibis. I think it's a blind alley. I hope to find a link to Jeanne Holman's slaying."

Novak grew silent for a moment. He frowned as he chased a thought. She didn't press him. The traumatic brain injury that had forced his retirement from the Pittsburgh Police Bureau years before often left him trying to put pieces together. If he sussed out something she'd missed, he'd tell her.

She passed through the Cumberland Narrows, the canyon that gave pioneers access to the Appalachian

Plateau and the Ohio River Valley beyond it. Though she longed to take it in, she drove on. *Another day, another time,* she thought, as the sun glinted off Wills Creek below her. When she neared Cumberland, the Allegany County seat and once the northern terminus of the Underground Railroad, she asked herself if this was a fool's errand. If a known pedophile living in the neighborhood had murdered a girl in her early teens, wouldn't someone have made the connection?

Then she recalled Jeffrey reminding her they'd been assigned to solve a more recent murder. The immediate issue was not whether Bruno Vogt had killed Jeanne Holman but whether he'd silenced the man who was about to expose him.

Still, she couldn't let it drop. Detectives weren't supposed to let personal matters interfere with an investigation, but if she could bring the girl's killer to justice after all these years, she was compelled to do so.

JEFFREY ENTERED the cafe and spotted two men seated at a table for four. Both looked up, one signaling him to join them. "Bryce Combs," he said. "This is Scott Mattingly."

A server brought coffee, and the detective took a sip before he began. "You two played golf with Steven Parker three days before he was killed."

"With Ron Schuster," Combs replied. "We play every Wednesday afternoon. Or did."

"How long have you known them?"

The pair looked at each other. "Ron, since grade school," Mattingly said. "He introduced us to Parker a few years back, after he left the paper."

"He didn't have time to play while he was working," Combs said. "We had another partner back then, but he passed away. I guess we bring bad luck." They chuckled at the dark humor. Neither looked like candidates for the grim reaper.

Jeffrey led them through a few more introductory questions while they ordered breakfast. Over pancakes and sausage, he got down to business. "The two of them, did they seem to get along?"

They looked at each other. Mattingly shrugged. "Yeah," Combs said. "Ron knew Steve before he brought him in."

He looked up at his friend as though seeking confirmation, and the detective caught the signal. "Until last May," Jeffrey suggested, making it a statement rather than a question.

Again, they shared a look. "I know he's spoken to the two of you, told you what to say. Right? That's why I had such a tough time getting you to sit down with me."

Mattingly peered into his omelet, foraging for mushrooms. "But you're not helping him by hiding things. It only makes me probe deeper. If Ron is innocent, the delay makes it harder for me to find Parker's killer. So let's cut the crap. Something changed between them in late spring. Tell me about it."

Combs was the one to cave. "He never told us what had gone on between them, but when we got together right after Memorial Day, he had us switch carts. The two of them always rode together, but this day, he told Scott to take Steve, and he'd ride with me."

"The two of them scarcely spoke," Mattingly said, joining the party. "This was unusual. They usually chattered to each other through every hole. Drove me nuts, to tell you the truth. On that day, they said not a word."

"It stayed that way," Combs said. "From that day forward, it was Scott and Steve in one cart, and Ron and I in the other. After a few weeks, they resumed speaking, but it was all about golf. No more back and forth about weekend plans with the wives and that sort of thing."

"Did Ron ever tell you what had come between them?"

"Nuh-uh," both said in unison.

"Did you ask?" He got the same response.

"This began in late May and went on through the summer. How about recently? Did you see any other signs of discord?"

This time, Mattingly spoke up. "Yeah, the last few times we were out, it got so tense I wanted to break up the quartet. Nothing said, mind you. It was just heavy. I don't know any other way to explain it."

Combs said nothing but dipped his head in agreement.

"You've been friends for a long time, and I know you don't want to get him in trouble, but what do you think was going on between them?"

They shared another moment of silent communication. "Woman trouble is what I thought," Mattingly said. "Isn't that always the case?"

"Or politics," Combs said. "We made it a rule never to touch that topic, but maybe they did."

"I'll tell you one thing," Mattingly said. "I'm glad it's over. Not that I'm happy Parker's dead. I don't mean that. But I won't have to play around all that tension any longer. It was spoiling my game."

Barnwell parked before the sheriff's office, separated from the Potomac River by railway tracks from the B&O

Railroad. Long gone now, it had been the first rail system in the country. She entered the station and announced her arrival over the lobby phone. Deputy Jake Pollard opened the glass door, introduced himself, and signed her in.

"Sheriff Walker wants me to look after you," he said.

"Do I look like I need looking after?" She accompanied it with a smile.

"We'll see." He offered her coffee, which she refused. She made a pit stop, and minutes later they launched into the countryside in the deputy's cruiser.

They were headed to North Branch, he explained, a community along the towpath of the C&O Canal, which followed the Potomac all the way to Washington, DC. The old barge canal now hosted a bicycle and hiking trail into the heart of the nation's capital.

"That's West Virginia," he said, nodding toward the opposite shore. He turned off Pittsburgh Plate Glass Highway, named for a factory long since closed, and halted before a rustic cabin with a broken lawnmower in the front yard and a rusted-out Chevy in a lean-to.

Leading the way, he knocked at the door. A woman in late middle age answered, staring at the officer as though he were a Jehovah's Witness. She was a big person, not only overweight but hefty, wearing a pair of jeans and a short-sleeve shirt bearing the logo of a local trucking firm. "What do you want, Jake?"

"This detective has come from Pittsburgh to talk to you."

The woman scowled and looked Lydia up and down. "About what?" she said.

"If we can come in, I'll explain why I'm here."

"Not sure I want to do that."

"Now, Sheila," the officer said, "she's here on an important matter. Either talk to us here, or the sheriff will invite you into town."

She considered that, sniffed, then backed into a room that served as the living and dining areas. A pullman's kitchen was off to one side. Lydia figured the closed door led to a bedroom. The smell of urine assailed her, making her wish she'd asked her questions on the front stoop.

Sheila Remsen didn't invite them to sit, but the officers settled onto a divan. Its tan fabric had been shredded by a cat that, Lydia's allergies told her, was hiding close by. The woman collapsed into an old recliner, the loose flesh on her upper arms shaking like gelatin.

"Well?" she said.

"I tried calling in advance," Lydia began.

"If you called from Pittsburgh, I've blocked it."

"Why is that?"

"Someone keeps calling, a person I don't want to talk to."

Lydia buried her face in her handkerchief and blew her nose. "Who was it?" she managed to ask.

Her nostrils flared about narrowed eyes. "He sent you, didn't he?"

"No one sent me. I'm investigating a murder."

She leaned on the armrest to shift her bulk from one hip to the other. "I told him I don't know nothing about that."

"Who did you tell?" Lydia kept her voice flat but insistent, giving nothing away as she probed to see how much Sheila Remsen knew.

"That writer. Something Stevens."

Lydia's eyes watered as she supplied the full name. The woman acknowledged it. "It's his murder I'm investigating."

"He's dead?" she said. "Good. Who did it? Let me bake

'em a cake." Her face fell slack. "You think I had something to do with it? That's why you're here?"

"Steven Parker," she said, switching to the pen name he seemed to have given her, "was struck by a blunt object and killed in the garage of his home last Saturday, hours after he announced he'd solved the murder of a girl who'd been raped and strangled in 1993. We believe he was about to name your brother."

"It couldn't have been," she said. "He was living with me back then. You folks drove him out of Pittsburgh. Called him a pervert and put him on a list, all for making one stupid mistake. He'd served his time, his probation was over, but you wouldn't let him alone."

"He lived here in June 1993? He didn't drive up to Pittsburgh, maybe to see old friends?"

"Why would he go back? He had a record. He couldn't live anywhere around children. That's why I took him in. Didn't want to, but he had no place else to go."

Lydia took in the room. Cozy didn't describe what it must have been like for the two of them to share this one-bedroom shack. She sneezed again. "Where was he last Saturday?"

"How the hell would I know?"

"You're not in contact with him?"

She turned to Deputy Pollard. "You want to tell her?" Pollard returned her stare with a confused look. "Yeah, you're too young and dumb to remember. When the sheriff learned about his record, he put him on another list and forced him out again."

"Where is he now?"

She nodded to the left. "Over there. West Virginia," she added when the detective's face made it clear she didn't understand. "Down in Short Gap."

"Did you tell Parker this?"

"I didn't say nothin' except what I told you. My brother was here in 1993. He never left. Had no reason to."

"Have you spoken with him in the last week or so?"

She folded her hands and looked at a point between them. "No," she said after a moment's hesitation. "I'm glad to be rid of him. He's got a temper when he drinks, and he drinks too much. I'll tell you one thing though. He didn't kill that girl. Couldn't have. He was here all along."

"One last question," Lydia said. "Where were you last Saturday afternoon?"

The woman laughed, showing the absence of two teeth on the right side of her lower jaw. "I work at the Dollar Store on weekends. It's the only thing left around here. You can follow me and ask if you don't believe me."

Lydia snapped her notebook shut and rose.

"Whoever killed that writer, I'm glad he did so. Did I tell you he stalked me? Not just calling, day after day. He came down here. I wouldn't let him in, so he waylaid me while I was at the laundromat. I tried to get away from him, but I couldn't leave. They'll steal your clothes."

She retreated to the car, grateful to be back in fresh air. "Short Gap?" she asked the deputy

"Across the river in Mineral County. Ten miles, if that."

"And you have no authority there?"

"No, but Sheriff Walker's on good terms with Sheriff Brinson. He'll set it up." He looked ahead at the road without turning his head. "I'd like to tag along, if it's okay."

"Got you hooked, did I? Welcome aboard."

AT FORTY-SEVEN, Lyle Jeffrey wasn't anyone's definition of old, certainly not his own. But he could remember back when police work required more shoe leather than time spent with your ass in a chair staring at a screen.

Yet here he was on a Saturday morning, when he should have been watching his son's baseball practice, opening files Ross Sutton had unearthed from the dead man's phone and computer records. Inspector Morris was fond of saying science now solved eighty percent of criminal cases, not a ringing endorsement of the hard work and long hours he and his fellow detectives put in.

He wished his partner were here. She excelled at this, part of the generation that had grown up in a world in which the solution to every problem was in bits and bytes, rather than the dribs and drabs of his era. But she was not around this morning, chasing what she saw as a more promising lead, leaving him to sort through the avalanche of data the digital forensics team had sent cascading toward him.

He turned first to Parker's bank records, which Sutton had secured through a search warrant. They stretched back for three years. Lacking time to go through all of them, he focused on the past few months. He found nothing but routine purchases, food, clothing, and gasoline. The only extravagance was his greens fees. He was surprised by how little the couple spent, as if they were on a tight budget. Given that Parker had been unemployed for four years, this might well have been the case. He spotted transfers from a savings account, which Parker had all but emptied. Left barely enough to keep it open, he suspected. Sutton's message said he was seeking financial additional records but didn't mention the source.

Jeffrey turned to the dead man's email traffic. This was

also overwhelming, so he limited his search to the past three months, sorting the inbox by sender. Most meant nothing to him. Looking at the headings, he ignored the ads and charitable appeals, the alerts and summaries from news sites, and the plethora of offers to make his books into instant best sellers or film adaptations. He also passed over those related to speaking engagements or the writers' group in which he took part.

Two credit card companies and a sporting goods company had sent dunning notices, and a collection agency demanded immediate payment of $1,376 for unpaid bills to a department store. Here was more evidence of financial troubles.

Of the personal messages, many were from golf buddies. A few were responses from law officers from whom he'd asked technical questions on topics from weapons to drugs. The detective picked through these, seeking anything dealing with the Jeanne Holman case. While he found nothing, he might be missing earlier exchanges on the topic. He'd have to return to this later.

An email from his agent ten days before his death advised him to submit a working title and synopsis. "You know how this works," Jerry Ransom wrote. "I can't make a sale based only on hints and assurances." Beneath it was Parker's original message, "My investigation is incurring costs I can't afford to pay out of current income. Can you find a publisher willing to provide an advance for a crime story that will have Americans on the edges of their seats?"

Had he even begun working on a synopsis? Barnwell hadn't mentioned it. He reflected on what Parker's cardiologist had told her about the man's alcohol intake. Was that why he'd made little progress on his manuscript? Was he falling apart?

Jeffrey read two emails from Parker's son, one reminding him to buy a present for his wife's birthday and a second headed, "Trust." It simply read, "When do you expect to settle up? Luv." Did this relate to the dunning notes from creditors? He made a note to question Bill.

He found fewer emails in the man's sent folder. His original appeal to his agent was there, along with four to Rolf Peterson, the disgraced former detective who'd investigated Jeanne Holman's murder. None had been returned, unless Parker had erased them. Many were questions he put to former police officers. Jeffrey had already read the responses.

Parker had also written to two publishers, seeking their interest in a book about the unsolved murder of a Pittsburgh girl years before. The letters were identical except for their recipients and declared, "I have solved this case and will name the killer. Readers will be shocked to learn how an incompetent police investigation by a corrupt detective has allowed this heinous crime to go unsolved for decades." The letter continued to seek an advance "to enable me to complete work on this riveting crime story."

Jeffrey had seen no replies. He made another note to ask Jerry Yarborough if he was aware his client was going around him. The agent had suggested Parker was paranoid, worrying that someone else would get to the story first, yet here he was dropping hints about the murder of a teenaged girl. Had one of the two publishers assigned a more established writer to the story?

He turned to the exchanges Sutton had found in Parker's messaging app. Some were with his wife, concerning items to be picked up at the grocery story and her schedule with girlfriends. Two were to his son, one assuring him he had Lois's birthday covered, the other saying, "I expect this book to be the crowning achievement of my career. It will change everything. I wish I could give you more details, but I have told no one. Another writer or one of those cold case TV show might steal it from me before I can finish."

Interspersed among them were message to a contact he listed as JS. He read the first, checked the date when he'd sent it, and emitted a drawn out, "Holy shit!" He read a second, then a third.

> SC: Lois lunching with friends today. Can
> you get away?

> JS: Ron with clients. Will be fun.

> SC: Leaving garage open. Be careful.

> JS: No worries. Luv u.

He closed the file, wishing he could see Barnwell's reaction. After everything they'd put their spouses through, Parker and Joanne Schuster were still at it. This explained why she had insisted they maintain appearances. And it made Ron Schuster suspect number one.

***

After Pollard related the situation over his radio, Sheriff Walker agreed to contact his West Virginia counterpart. Ten minutes later, the deputy retraced part of his route and turned south on Canal Parkway, crossing over the Potomac to State Road 28. Along the way, he kept up a steady stream of information, none of which Barnwell had requested. Pointing toward the water on his right, he said, "That's Maryland again. The North Branch wanders back and forth through this region. When you fly out of here, you leave West Virginia for Maryland and back again."

She muttered an acknowledgment, but her mind was focused on what Vogt's sister had told her. Parker not only called her, he came to Cumberland to see her. When she refused, he followed her to a laundromat and cornered her.

"This was coal country," Pollard rattled on, explaining that, because of its location along the Allegheny Front, Mineral County now maintained its role in the energy industry through wind farming. "It doesn't employ as many people, but it brings money in."

She ignored him as she recalled something else Sheila Remsen had told her, that Bruno Vogt had never returned to Pittsburgh. This was unlikely. He would have had to return to...

"You should come down here sometime when you're not working." His eyes were on her, rather than the road.

"Got you hooked?" she'd asked. He had, but it was not the murder case that intrigued him.

"That's a great idea. My fiancé would love taking that Western Maryland Scenic Train trip into the mountains." This ended the conversation and allowed her to think.

She opened her cell phone but had no signal. Continuing to fumble with it until two bars lit up, she dialed Jeffrey. "I need you to check something for me."

"Okay, but wait until you hear this."

"I don't have time. We have weak coverage here, and I'm afraid I'll lose you." Without waiting for his response, she told him what she needed. "It's urgent. I'm on my way to question him. Hello?" The signal faded out again. She hoped he'd received enough of the message to follow through.

When they arrived at the sheriff's office, a deputy told them Sheriff Brinson was on his way and wanted to talk to them before they questioned Vogt. She used the time to redial Jeffrey's number, but he didn't answer. She hoped that meant he was working on her request.

The sheriff, a lanky man with a full head of gray hair, came into headquarters and led both of them into his office. "Fred tells me you're questioning Bruno Vogt in a murder investigation." His gravelly voice suggested a life misspent with smoking. "He hasn't been in any trouble here, but we monitor him to make sure he doesn't hang around schools or playgrounds. What's he done?"

"Maybe nothing," she said. "That's what I'm here to find out." She outlined the case, backtracking from Parker's murder the week before to the reason for his interest in Vogt.

"Your theory is he drove to Pittsburgh and killed this writer to prevent him from publishing this story about him?"

"That's it."

"Are you here to arrest him? If so, I'd better go along so his attorney can't claim you were operating out of your juris-diction."

"Not yet. I don't have enough evidence. Still—"

Her phone chimed. She held up a finger to excuse herself and answered. She listened to Jeffrey for half a minute, asked him a few questions, and thanked him. He continued to speak, but she said she'd talk to him later.

"That's an excellent suggestion," she told Brinson.

JEFFREY SCOWLED at the dead phone in his hand. "C'mon, Barnwell, you need to hear this."

As he slid his phone back into his pocket, a voice behind him said, "Something wrong?"

He turned to find Chief of Detectives Glen Carpenter. "No, I think I've had a breakthrough on the Steven Parker murder, but Barnwell's working on another angle."

"The murder of that young girl?" he asked. When Jeffrey confirmed it, Carpenter said, "Where is she?"

"Somewhere in West Virginia. She drove to Cumberland this morning, but the suspect, a convicted pedophile named Bruno Vogt, has moved."

Carpenter invited him into his office and had him lay out where the investigation stood. As he did so, he began drumming his desk with his pencil, something he did whenever he was annoyed or impatient. "It looks as though Schuster's our man then. He had an obvious motive and only his wife to vouch for him. We need to devote all our resources into building the case against him. Let's get her back here."

"She and the local sheriff left to question Vogt. I'll contact her as soon as they return."

Carpenter halted his drumming and leaned toward him. "Her theory is that Parker was about to name him as the Holman girl's killer, Vogt found out about it, and drove all the way to Pittsburgh to silence him. Is that about it?"

Jeffrey confirmed it and added a few details. "What physical evidence does she have?" Carpenter demanded. "Were his prints found in the garage? Has anyone seen him in the area? It's a thin reed, isn't it?"

"She makes a valid point, Glen. Jeanne Holman's killer has been free all these years because the detective in charge focused on one suspect to the exclusion of all others."

Picking up a second pencil, Carpenter tapped out a paradiddle. "Isn't that what she's doing? Parker's murder's a week old. The trail gets colder by the day. Reporters keep asking where things stand, and I don't have an answer. I want to meet with both of you first thing tomorrow. Let's get this investigation back on track."

"After Mass, okay?"

Carpenter eyed him in a silent challenge then gave up. "I guess a few hours more won't kill us. One o'clock. Make sure she's there."

"Yes, sir."

"Lyle," he said, "we recruited Barnwell. She's our protégé, and she's done an outstanding job so far. We don't want to see her getting ahead of herself. You're the senior detective. Keep her focused."

THEY APPROACHED the shotgun shack in two cruisers, Sheriff Brinson and a uniformed officer leading the way, with Lydia and Pollard following. The structure, if it could be called that, was on a side road off Rocket Center, named for the Second World War ballistics factory that now housed a company manufacturing composite materials for military aircraft. The house stood alone, forlorn and out of place. An apple orchard ran behind it.

Vogt lived out in the country, the sheriff had explained, because everything in Short Gap was within sight of Frankfort High School. "We can't have him hanging around young girls." He stepped out of the cruiser and waited for them to emerge, standing back as they approached the house. Both he and his deputy held their hands near their holsters, waiting to draw if the need arose.

Barnwell approached the door with Deputy Pollard flanking her. She knocked and listened as a chair shuffled across a bare floor inside. Behind her, the sheriff called out, "Open up, Vogt. We're here to talk to you." She realized he had peered out the one window at the front of the narrow structure and seen Brinson, who he recognized.

"What is it?" the voice answered. "What do you want?"

"We have a few questions for you," he replied. "Open up so I don't have to do it for you."

The door inched open, and a puffy, unshaven face emerged, blinking at her in the sudden burst of sunlight. He hitched up a single suspender over his shoulder and said, "Why are you here? I ain't done nothing."

Barnwell introduced herself.

"Allegany County?" he said. "My sister send you? I paid her back a long time ago."

"The other Allegheny," she said. "Pittsburgh." His eyes narrowed. He looked her up and down then took in the deputy standing alongside her and the sheriff and his officer in the yard.

"May we come in?"

"There's not enough room for all of you."

"We'll wait out here," the sheriff called. "Let her in and leave the door open."

Vogt backed into what served as living room, dining room, library, and parlor. A wood stove rested on stone tiles against one wall, a kitchenette stood behind it, and a narrow hallway led to a back entrance. It was called a shotgun shack because you could fire a shotgun through the front door and out the back without hitting anything.

Vogt collapsed into a chair, the cushion sagging to within inches of the floor. Lydia drew out one of the two wooden chairs from the kitchen table while Pollard stood. "Do you know a man named Steven Parker?" she said. "He also goes by Parker Stevens."

"Never heard of either of them."

"He was trying to get in touch with you. Are you certain he didn't call you? Visit you?"

"No."

"That's curious, because he was quite interested in you. He was a crime writer working on a book in which you play an important role." She waited for him to ask why, but he kept silent, staring at her chest. "How about Jeanne Holman? Have you ever heard that name?"

"Nope." He lowered his eyes and scratched his chin.

"Are you sure? She was a thirteen-year-old girl who lived in Shadyside. Another teenager gave her a ride up to Highland Park on the afternoon of June 7th, 1993. He returned alone, leaving her to walk home. She never made it."

She fixed her blue eyes on him, waiting for him to ask a question. He tried to return her gaze but could not. "Don't you want to know why?"

"It has nothing to do with me."

"Steven Parker thought it did. A couple of kids found her body in the park the following morning. She'd been raped and strangled. The young man who brought her there was convicted of her murder and sentenced to life in prison. He insisted he didn't do it, and his parents fought to free him. It

took them ten years, but they found the evidence to clear him. He didn't kill Jeanne Holman, so someone else did."

An innocent man would have expressed some curiosity, but Vogt sat in stolid silence. "In his book, Steven Parker intended to name you as the girl's killer."

He rubbed his hands together and hunched his back. "I didn't have nothing to do with it. I was nowhere near Pittsburgh by then. My sister must have told you that. I was staying at her place."

"I don't believe I mentioned speaking with your sister." She glanced at Pollard. "Did I say anything about his sister?"

"No, ma'am."

"So she called me and told me you were looking for me," he said. "There's no law against that."

"Did she also tell you she'd given you an alibi for June 1993?

Vogt sneered. "She didn't give me nothing. I was living with her back then."

"Where were you last Saturday?"

"What?" He seemed confused by the sudden change in subject. "I was bowling with some buddies up in Cumberland."

Hiding her disappointment, she said, "Names?"

He reeled off three names and provided their phone numbers. "Why'd you ask?"

Now we're interested, she thought. "Because someone murdered Steven Parker at about this time last weekend. That makes you our chief suspect."

"It wasn't me. I was here. You can ask them." He nodded toward her notebook.

"I will. And you're certain he never contacted you about little Jeanne's murder?"

"Uh-huh."

"Did he mention he was recording your conversation?" His hand halted in midair as it sought the stubble on his chin. "He didn't have to. West Virginia is a one-party consent state. If you spoke in Maryland, he would have had to get your permission. Not that it makes much difference with him dead."

Her prattle was designed only to reinforce her bluff. She had no recording, and Parker had not mentioned a conversation in his notes.

"All right," he said. "He came to my door about three weeks ago, just like you did. I didn't know him from Adam, but he talked his way in."

"What did he ask you?"

Vogt went back to tugging at the saplings of hair on his face. "Same thing you did."

She pretended to study her notes. "He seemed to do more accusing than asking."

He shifted his weight and muttered to himself. "Yeah, he had it in his mind I'd done something to that girl. I got arrested years back. Bunch of girls said I flashed them at a playground. Weren't true, but you know the courts when females make a complaint against a man."

Lydia knew all too well, though not with the conclusion Vogt wanted her to reach.

"I did time for something I didn't do. Then they put a big sticker on my back, 'This guy's a pervert. Don't let him live near you.' I couldn't land a job and had no place to live. Still can't be near a school, even though my parole's been over for years.

"Anyway, this Parker fellow found that out, added two and two and came up with eight. As in eight ball, with me behind it. I told him I didn't know a thing about any girl being murdered. I said I had been nowhere near Pittsburgh at the time."

"And then you called your sister to confirm it?"

"What?"

She spoke slowly, as though to a child. "Once you'd told him you'd been in Cumberland on that date, you had your sister tell the same story."

"I didn't need to. She knew where I was. Bitch kept complaining there wasn't room for both of us."

Lydia turned a page in her notebook. "It's one thing to lie to a writer, but she told me the same story two hours ago. She lied to an officer of the law. She's in big trouble."

He hesitated two beats before responding. "She didn't lie to you. I was there."

"Not according to the report your parole officer filed. You were required to check in twice a year. You arrived at his office at 8:30 a.m., Tuesday, June 8th. Since you weren't allowed to leave the state, you listed the address of your ex-wife as your own. If he'd caught this lie, he could have revoked your probation then and there. This puts you in Pittsburgh on the day Jeanne Holman was murdered."

Vogt sprung from his chair like a jack-in-the-box. Deputy Pollard, who stood between him and the back door, tried to block his way, but Vogt crashed into him like a defensive tackle. As Pollard fell back, striking his head on the stove, Vogt bolted out the rear entrance.

Barnwell followed as the man raced into the orchard with the sheriff and his deputy pursuing both of them. "Stop!" she ordered. Vogt continued running, but he had at least four decades on her, and she knew she'd get the better of him.

Behind her, she heard a voice shout, "Stop or I'll shoot!"

"Don't fire," she replied. "I want him alive."

Vogt stumbled as he dodged between trees, and as she drew nearer, she saw him look down as though searching for something. This made it even easier for her to close the gap. "On the ground with your hands behind you!" she ordered.

He turned to face her, a broken limb in his hand. She halted beyond his reach while a voice behind her ordered him, once again, to stop. Couldn't they see he already had?

Lydia advanced on him, and he swung the branch at her. The eight-foot length of wood arced past her, then she closed on him, gripping his shoulder and allowing his momentum to carry him to the ground. As the two men behind her grabbed his arms, she said, "You're under arrest for assaulting a police officer."

"You have the right to remain silent ..." Sheriff Brinson began.

"The obligatory chase scene," she muttered as she rose and brushed herself off. "What a stupid move. But now I'll get his DNA."

THE SMELLS OF TOMATO, garlic, and onion enveloped her as she stepped through the front door. She danced into the kitchen and threw her arms around Calvin, who stood before the oven wearing an apron emblazoned with, "A man's place is in the kitchen."

"Almost done," he said. An open bottle of zinfandel was on the counter alongside a bowl of salad. He'd told her to message him as soon as she'd deposited Vogt's DNA swabs in the evidence locker. Sliding a baker's peel under the pizza, he eased it onto a cutting board. Green and red roasted peppers and mushrooms shared the surface with the tomatoes and onion, which poked above the bubbling Parmesan and provolone cheese.

"Where's yours?"

"I can get by without pepperoni for one night."

She took her seat at the kitchen table as he served her. "What's the occasion?"

"None. You've had a rough day."

"Not as bad as a sheriff's deputy." Between bites, she

took him through her day, ending with the chase that had left Deputy Pollard in the hospital with a gash at the back of his skull and a concussion. "Vogt is in a holding cell at the Mineral County Courthouse. He'll be arraigned Monday morning."

"Will you bring him here for Parker's murder?"

She lifted her wineglass to her lips but held it there, recalling how calmly he'd responded to her questions about his whereabouts the previous Saturday but bolted when she challenged his alibi for June 1993. "He claims he was bowling with friends. The sheriff is questioning them. I'm not sure that will stick."

"But..." he said, responding to her emphasis.

Her cell phone postponed the rest of her thought. She glanced at the screen and answered the call, peppering the conversation with monosyllabic questions: What? Why? When? "Okay. See you then."

Calvin questioned her with his eyebrows.

"Lieutenant wants to see us tomorrow afternoon to go over the case."

"Fair enough," he said. She grew silent and let the rest of her pizza grow cold. "Something wrong?"

Lydia shook her head, as she did when there was something on her mind she wasn't ready to discuss. She helped clean up, still close-lipped.

"By the way," he said, "Mom called. She wants to talk to us."

Lydia told him to put her on the phone. They sat at the table sipping their wine—a rare second glass for her—while he put Ruth on speakerphone. "I spoke to the reverend yesterday about wedding arrangements. Did you have a date in mind?"

"Whatever works for you," she said.

"Are you looking at spring or summer?"

"Mom, it doesn't matter. I care, but I'm not fixed on a particular time. Soon, I hope."

"It's too late for fall," Ruth said, "and the weather is so unpredictable in winter. We'll have a lot of family coming from Ohio and Michigan, and the roads—"

"I agree."

That meant spring, she said, and the church was booked in June. Lydia listened with only half an ear as she went through reasons this month and that would present difficulties. "What about May?" she said. "The weather will be warmer, and it's too late for an early spring blizzard. What do you think?"

"That's perfect." She grinned at Calvin as his mother tiptoed around the arrangements on which she'd already decided.

Ruth asked if she needed to check the date with her father. Lydia assured her he'd be okay with it, even though she hadn't spoken to him and wasn't sure he'd attend if the wedding were held blocks from him in San Antonio. As always, the colonel would do whatever he would do.

"I'm still worried you'll feel comfortable at Ebenezer Baptist," she said.

"I'm sure we will."

"Why don't you check it out? I want to make sure it works for you."

In a millisecond, she processed what Jeffrey had told her on the phone, that Carpenter wanted to meet with them first thing, but he'd asked to attend Mass. *What's sauce for the gander*, she thought.

"I'll go there in the morning," she said, catching Calvin's eye to make certain he heard her. "We both will."

CHAPTER NINE

ANYONE EXPECTING a Black church on the Hill to reflect the comparative poverty of the neighborhood, the setting for August Wilson's moving plays, would have been disappointed.

The three-story sanctuary with its brick facade faced Wylie Avenue. The tall glass windows of the entrance, with their decorative wrought iron hinges, reflected a construction site across the street that signaled the slow recovery of the area. Inlaid crosses flanked the twin doors, one of which led to its outreach programs, the food pantry, parent and child learning center, and workplace training program.

Lydia held Calvin's hand as they entered the sanctuary, an unadorned hall with a semi-circle of seats facing the dais. He started toward the front, but she pulled him into a row near the back, hoping she could remain unobserved. As she settled into the padded pew, she reflected on its contrast with the uncomfortably hard benches of her youth, designed to serve as penance.

Eight female singers took the stage, flanking the male leader. "I feel joy," they sang, repeating the words until they finished the line with "for what he's done for me." The congregants joined in as the chant repeated itself.

Only half the pews were filled. Had the epidemic given the church a case of Long COVID?

A young man in dreadlocks sat at a keyboard and led the music for a few minutes. Surrounded by another keyboardist, drummer, and bass guitarist, he sang, "What do you know about Jesus?" The chorus, standing between two silver buckets bursting with red and white carnations, replied, "He's all right."

"All right, all right," the congregation echoed.

"What do you know about Jesus?" the director demanded.

"He's all right." Calvin joined in the refrain, clapping his hands and swaying in time to the music. Lydia became aware of her pale skin, blonde curls, blue eyes, and narrow nose, so unlike those around her. She wished she could melt into the off-white wall behind her, observing but not observed.

"Do you feel joy?" the choir director asked? A chorus of responses greeted him. "Raise your hands if you feel joy."

Lydia complied, beginning to join the swaying. "I feel joy," the leader called, repeating the phrase as those around her echoed the chant. She joined in, feeling the spirit of the moment. "I feel joy," the leader called at the top of his voice, "for what he's done for me."

The singing died out, and the keyboardist turned the melody into a jazzy riff, lowering the volume. As the music faded away, a man on the front pew mounted the dais and opened a notebook computer. Two monitors mounted on the proscenium arches came to life, displaying words from Matthew 26:41, "Watch and pray so that you will not fall into temptation. The spirit is willing, but the flesh is weak."

"I'm late to begin preaching," he said, "but there was church going on." His flock murmured agreement, while a few chuckled.

While Lydia had expected a fire and brimstone sermon, the pastor went through a series of slides on the theme of resisting temptation. "God allows Satan to tempt you, but not to the point that you break. When I claim the blood of Jesus, I surrender to you to lead my life. The Devil is strategic, but God is more strategic. And you must be equally so to resist him."

Looking about her, she saw that the congregation comprised three groups: children, their parents, and the elderly. Missing were the youth who most needed to hear this message. Lydia wished she could take the pastor along to neighborhoods where young men used each other for target practice. But would they listen? It was not as though bereaved parents weren't begging other kids to put down their weapons.

The sermon over, the minister invited those present to come forward. As he prayed over them, a few prostrated themselves on the carpeted steps at his feet. After they returned to their seats, a dozen men advanced, accepted communion, then filed back along the pews, passing trays of bread and grape juice. Not being a member of the church, Lydia wasn't certain whether to take part, but as a tall, handsome man reached her pew, the pastor intoned, "All are invited to attend the Lord's Supper." It was a message meant for her.

A soft hymn followed the sacrament. The minister closed with a benediction, calling for "peace in our world, our nation, and our hearts." As he walked up the center aisle, Lydia grabbed Calvin's hand and made for the door, but the pastor beat her to it. He stuck out his hand, his smile splitting his face like a cake knife. "I'm Derrick Boardman. And who might you be?"

"Lydia Barnwell, Reverend."

"No one calls me reverend. I'm just Derrick. Are you visiting or thinking of joining us?"

"I'm getting married here. This is my fiancé, Calvin Mayfield."

The grin grew wider. "Ruth and Ben's son." He pumped Calvin's hand. "She's been on me all week. It seems this wedding is the most important thing that's happened to her since you were born."

She joined in the laughter. A woman behind her tapped on her shoulder. "We're so glad you've come. Join us in the community center for coffee and cookies." Another chimed in, and Lydia was soon surrounded by a small crowd. She had never experienced such a welcome.

"I wish I could stay," she said, "but my boss has summoned me to a meeting at one."

"On Sunday?"

"I'm afraid so. I'm a police detective, and my work doesn't respect weekends."

"Well, you come next weekend. We want to get to know you."

Calvin helped extricate her. As they left the Hill for downtown, he asked, "Will this work? Do you feel comfortable here?"

"How could I not?" she said. Though she was non-observant, Lydia felt a welcoming presence that was unlike anything in her experience.

"Where've you been?" Jeffrey asked as she slid into her chair.

Lydia stuffed a bite of tuna salad sandwich into her mouth, letting a single word escape the cud. "Church."

"Church?" he repeated. "I thought you were a nonbeliever."

"Lapsed." She looked up at the clock alongside the Baltimore Board. "Where's Carpenter?"

"He'll be along."

Setting the sandwich aside, she opened her screen and scrolled through messages. "Listen, Barnwell, I want you to keep your cool when he meets with us."

"Why wouldn't I?"

"He's going to walk us through the case, and—"

"Hold on a minute." She leaned into her screen and studied the message, which read, "We've spoken to Bruno's playmates. See the attached photo and study the metadata. Call me when you've finished. Brinson."

She opened the attachment. It showed four men hamming it up for the camera, one holding a bowling ball over Vogt's head while he pretended to duck. Behind them she saw the converging paths of the polished lanes. She clicked on the icon above the image. In addition to the file name, it listed a timestamp and a small map showing where the image had been taken.

"Damn," she said.

"Something wrong?"

Lydia leaned back and ran her hands through her curls, which popped stubbornly back into place. She picked up her phone and dialed the sheriff's number. "Conclusive, isn't it?" Brinson rasped. "Vogt was where he said he was that Saturday. He couldn't have been in two places at once."

She massaged the back of her neck with one hand while

cradling the phone with the other. "You still have him on the assault charge, right?"

"Yes, Bruno's not going anywhere except upstairs for his arraignment in the morning."

"How is Deputy Pollard doing?"

"He'll live, but he was pretty banged up. The concussion's the worst of it. When I spoke to the hospital an hour ago, they said he has no memory of what happened. That's not an encouraging sign."

She asked Brinson to convey her best wishes, though from the sound of things, he might not recall who she was. "Meanwhile, I've submitted Vogt's DNA to our lab and asked them to fast-track it."

While it could take weeks for the FBI lab to extract a strand and search through its database for a match, having two known samples was a different matter. Rapid DNA testing could compare the twenty loci types through modern amplification kits in hours, yielding a CODIS-eligible profile admissible in court.

"I sometimes envy the tools you big-city folks have," he said, "but I wouldn't want to deal with the type of cases you get."

"Nor I yours," she replied, knowing the havoc opioid addiction was wreaking on rural communities in his state. She thanked him and disconnected.

"Something wrong?" Jeffrey repeated as though he hadn't overheard her end of the conversation. Before she could answer, the chief of detectives lumbered into the bullpen and motioned them to follow him.

Lieutenant Glen Carpenter, who'd been chief of the detective division for less than a year, said, "Sorry to bring you in on a Sunday."

"We'd be here anyway," Jeffrey replied.

He asked them to review the case. Jeffrey explained they were pursuing two lines of inquiry. "Barnwell is looking for a suspect in the Jeanne Holman murder cases who might have silenced him before he could reveal his identity. I'm pursuing a domestic angle."

"Let's hear your story first," Carpenter said.

Jeffrey described Parker's history of philandering, his pursuit of female reporters, his long-term affair with Susan Nance, and his investigation into Ted Nance. "He has a temper and once attacked Parker in the *Herald* newsroom, so he seemed a likely suspect. His Russian companion confirms they were more than an hour away when Parker was murdered, so he appears to be in the clear."

"Is she lying to cover for him?"

Jeffrey replied that Katrina had produced their Fort Ligonier gate receipts. "She was there with someone that day. I'm inclined to believe her. What's more interesting, however, is Parker's relationship with his neighbor, his wife's close friend."

He explained how Ron Schuster had discovered the affair. "Barnwell had a hunch, and it paid off." Carpenter nodded in her direction. She had the feeling this had been staged, but for what purpose?

"After he confronted her, Joanne insisted the couples maintain their friendship. Ron went along with it, which itself is odd. They cover for each other at the time of Parker's murder, but there's no third party to corroborate their story. I felt we were at a dead end until yesterday."

He described what he'd found in the messages between

Parker and Joanne. "Far from ending the affair, she and the victim shacked up on at least two more occasions. That puts Ron back in the bullseye."

Lydia leaned forward, pondering. Her partner had tried to reveal this to her the day before, but in her rush to her confirm her hunch about Vogt's visits to his probation officer, she hadn't given him a chance.

"We need to find out whether he knew they were still carrying on," he continued. "I think they're lying to protect each other, though why she would cover for him is beyond me."

"Why would he continue to associate with Parker after learning what he was doing to his marriage?" Lydia said. "That also makes no sense."

"None of it does," Jeffrey said.

Turning to Barnwell, Carpenter asked what progress she'd made. She recounted Parker's interest in the 1993 death of the murdered teenager, which he'd followed for years in his newspaper stories and, later, his column. He'd become convinced a local pedophile, Bruno Vogt, was responsible for her death, and he was writing a book about the case. She described the extraordinary steps he'd taken to conceal his investigation from everyone—his family, his agent, and even publishers to whom he'd pitched the idea.

When she learned he'd dropped hints about the case at the book fair, she'd investigated whether someone present might have followed and silenced him. "That turned out to be a false lead, but Parker left enough clues to identify his suspect as a child predator named Bruno Vogt. Yesterday, I tracked him to a small community in West Virginia."

She described how he'd fled during her questioning, injuring a local police officer. "They're holding him on that charge now. At his booking, I got a DNA sample I hope to match with one found years ago on Jeanne Holman's clothing and body."

Carpenter, who knew some of this from what Jeffrey had told him, drummed the pencil on his desk. "Can you tie him to Parker's murder?"

Both men stared at her as she took a deep breath. "No, I spoke with the local sheriff who confirmed he was bowling with friends at a lane in Cumberland last Saturday. He could not have killed Parker. But—"

Carpenter leaned forward and cut her off. "That makes Ron Schuster our prime suspect. I don't have to remind you of the intense public interest in this case. You've eliminated all other avenues of investigation. Focus on this pair and break down their alibis. Bring them both in, put them in separate rooms, and interrogate the hell out of them until one breaks. Try for a breakthrough today."

"Will do," Jeffrey said, closing his notebook as though the conversation was over.

"What about Vogt?" Lydia said. "He may be in the clear on Parker's murder, but not on the Jeanne Holman killing."

"Sheriff Brinson has him under arrest, and you have his DNA sample. If the lab finds a match, we'll file charges against him. Meanwhile, focus on the Schusters."

"I may have more than DNA evidence," she said. "Vogt's ex-wife told me she hadn't seen him since the divorce, but he was using—"

Carpenter pointed both index fingers at her like a pair of horns. "Parker," he said. "That's the priority. I recognize your passion for this cold case, but you're assigned to the murder of Steven Parker. If you don't think you can handle it, I'll assign someone else to the investigation."

Lydia accepted the reprimand. "Of course I will. It will have my full attention."

"Make certain it does. If there are no further questions…"

"No, Chief," Jeffrey said, "we've got the ball."

Lydia left his office and headed toward the women's restroom. She ran cold water over her face and studied her image in the mirror until she stopped shaking. Glen Carpenter had helped recruit her to the county. He'd never spoken to her like this before. If she couldn't handle it … Didn't he understand bringing justice to Jeanne Holman was as important as solving the murder of this disgraced crime writer? More so, in her book.

Back at her desk, she turned toward the computer without meeting her partner's eye. "You okay?" he said.

"Sure. What's our next step?"

"You and I take a couple of unis along, separate the Schusters, and bring them in."

"All right."

Her curt reply concealed the quavering in her voice, but Jeffrey caught the tone. "This is personal for you, isn't it?"

She shook her head. "Parker is the priority. Let's get on with it."

<hr>

RON SCHUSTER PUT up verbal resistance when they arrived at the house and told him they were bringing both in for questioning. Jeffrey advised him he could call his attorney if he wished, but they were within their rights to question him at headquarters. Schuster placed a call but got his voicemail, left a hurried message, and surrendered, heeding Jeffrey's warning they could drag him out the door and charge him with resisting commands if he failed to do so.

Joanne submitted without a fight, almost, Barnwell thought, as though she had expected something of the sort.

A small crowd had gathered, attracted by the squad cars, and watched as they were led out. She saw onlookers exchanging words and imagined they had already convicted them of Parker's murder. This was unfair, but she could do nothing to change it. Their lies had placed them in this position.

The drive to headquarters was a short one, a right turn onto Greentree Road and a straight shot to Parkway Center. Jeffrey's cruiser followed hers. He waited until Lydia had ushered Joanne into the building, giving the pair no chance to coordinate their stories.

She escorted the woman up the stairs and into the first of two interrogation rooms, flipping the switch to show it was in use. She showed her into the uncomfortable chair, took the padded seat across from her, and opened her notebook. The woman shifted, her heavy breathing filling the silence. "What is this all about?" she asked.

"My partner will be along once he gets your husband settled."

"What am I being charged with?"

"All in good time." She sipped her water bottle while studying her notes, knowing how unnerving the wait could be. Joanne looked around the room, but there was nothing to see except the white walls, overhead camera, and microphone between them. Nothing to hear but the droning of the air conditioner.

Ten minutes passed before Jeffrey entered, sharing a smile and a muffled chuckle with his partner. She recognized the act, hinting that Ron had told him something without saying so. Joanne did not, however, wrinkling her brow as she shifted her gaze between them.

He began the recording, stated the date and time, and identified those present, insisting that she speak her name aloud. "Do you know why we brought you here?" he asked.

"No." She gnawed at her lower lip.

"No?" he repeated. "Lying to law enforcement officers is a misdemeanor in the first degree, punishable by up to a year in prison."

"I've told you the truth."

"Joanne Schuster, I'm charging you with lying to a police officer and impeding an investigation. You may remain silent..." As he read out the Miranda warning, she knotted her hands and darted her eyes like a cornered animal.

He closed his notebook as though finished, but Barnwell took over. "You told Detective Jeffrey that once your husband discovered your affair, you broke it off. He put the question to you directly, and you answered, 'No, it was over between us.' Do you remember saying that?"

Continuing to knead her hands, she averted her eyes, first looking past them then settling on the table. "I don't recall."

"You don't recall saying that or don't recall whether you continued to have sexual relations with him?"

She held her breath and arrived at a decision. "If I said that, I only meant I no longer loved him. I'd had an infatuation, but I was over it."

"Despite that, you hopped back into be with him."

"I think we got together once. It was a mistake."

"More than once," Jeffrey said, reopening his notebook. "The first time was on July 18th. Parker texted you that his wife was having lunch with some friends and asked if you were free. You responded your husband was meeting with clients. 'Will be fun.'"

"We didn't have sex. We got together for conversation and coffee."

"So you say." He continued in a flat monotone, as though reading a grocery list. "On August 5th, he wrote you again, but you couldn't get free from your husband. 'I wish I could,' you said. But you had better luck later that month. This time, you initiated it. 'I need you,' you said. 'Can we get together?'"

He closed the notebook again. "That's a lot of scheming for a cup of coffee."

She held her hands to her temples but said nothing.

"I told you lying to law enforcement officers in a homicide investigation is a first-degree misdemeanor. You may think that's no big deal. But continuing to do so raises it to a third degree offense. That's a five-year sentence."

Now her right hand picked at her lower lip.

"Why not be straight with us?" Lydia said. "After your husband confronted you, you carried on as though nothing had happened. You suggested to my partner you'd seen it was a mistake, that Parker was using you, that you considered him a serial philanderer. But that was a mask, wasn't it? You were still in love with him and continued to crawl into his bed every chance you got."

"Parker records four assignations," Jeffrey said, though he knew of only two. "Were there more?"

They watched as she turned from one to the other. In a small voice, she said, "Only three. He must have bragged to someone." She pulled a tissue from her jacket pocket, wiped it over her eyes, then across her nose.

"And the third was…"

"Two weeks ago. You know that."

"How did Ron react when he found out?" Lydia asked.

She returned her attention to Barnwell, wrinkling her forehead. "He didn't. He doesn't know."

"Of course he does. Are you asking me to believe a man who's been cuckolded doesn't watch every step his wife makes? He must have been extremely angry. Not only with you but with Parker. Is that why he left during the game last Saturday? To have it out with him?"

"No." She leaned forward, her hands clutching the arms of the chair. Her eyes reddened and her voice rose half an octave. "He didn't find out and never left. You're suggesting he killed Steven? He did not. He was with me the entire time."

"Ron knew when Parker was due home," Jeffrey said. "He walked to the corner to confront him. Did he plan to kill him, or did things get out of hand?"

"No," she wailed. "You've got it wrong."

"The distinction is important. If he intended to argue with him, that's third-degree murder. Maybe even manslaughter. But if he set out to kill him—"

"He did no such thing," she screamed, leaning over the table toward him, spittle forming around her lips. "He was with me."

"You went with him?" he said. "He didn't tell me that."

"He what?"

Turning to Barnwell, he said, "Let's take a break and talk to him again. This puts a unique spin on things."

THEY LEFT JOANNE TO FRET, entering the adjoining interview room where her husband sat waiting. He raised his eyes as they entered, his face impassive. Lydia recalled his aggressive responses when they questioned the two of them the night of Parker's murder. He displayed none of that now and, unlike his wife, didn't ask why they'd brought him here. Did he know? Fresh from Joanne's insistent denials, she felt her confidence wane.

"Your wife has corrected the record," Jeffrey said. "Perhaps you'd care to do the same."

"About what? What's she told you?"

"In May, you learned Joanne had been having an affair with your neighbor and good friend. At her insistence, you kept up appearances with Parker, acting as though nothing had transpired between them. Is that your story?"

"It's the truth."

"So you say. And you remained friends with him until the day he died." Schuster nodded but did not speak. "You were fine with that. Everything was hunky-dory."

"I was not 'fine' with it. I was hurt. Of course I was. But I did as she asked to save our marriage."

Jeffrey said nothing, and Lydia took his cue. "Even while she carried on the affair?"

"She what?" His body stiffened, his eyes locking onto hers.

She repeated the question. Schuster stared open-mouthed, turning his attention from Barnwell to Jeffrey and back again. She waited while silence hung over the room.

Regaining his composure, Schuster snickered, "I see what you're up to. Sew discord and try to get me to implicate her. It won't work."

It was Barnwell's turn to stare, training her cerulean eyes on him. "They met at least three times after you discovered the affair. We found their messages on Parker's phone. She's admitted to it."

"I don't believe you." But his slump told her he did.

"When did you learn this?"

"I didn't know. I still don't."

"Did Parker let it out?" Jeffrey asked. "He seems to have dropped hints like a horse drops shit, hoping you'd pick up on it. Why? To humiliate you?"

Schuster twisted his head from side to side in silent denial. Tears welled in his eyes.

"He'd told you when he was returning from the book fair," she said. "During the fourth quarter of the Penn State game, you slipped away, wandered down the hill, and accosted him in his garage. Did you argue before you struck him, or did your anger take over?"

"I did no such thing." His voice broke. He spoke so softly she could barely hear him. "I didn't know they... Are you sure about this?"

"Ron," Jeffrey said in a tone that matched his, "why are you pretending you were unaware they were still at it? Once you'd learned of their affair, you must have watched every step she took for anything that sounded off-key. Vagueness when you asked how she'd spent her day. Singing to herself for no reason."

Leaning on his elbow, he covered his mouth, not making eye contact with them.

Snapping her fingers for emphasis, Lydia said, "None of this makes sense. A husband discovers his wife is having sex with his best friend. Not only does he not confront the man, he continues to enjoy his company. 'Pretend nothing has happened,' his wife insists. He goes along with it. That's not a natural response. It's not how human beings react to—let's face it—the greatest act of betrayal."

The tears overflowed, cascading down his cheeks. He looked at the ceiling. "God, help me."

"Only after agreeing to this ruse, you discover your wife and friend are continuing to lie to you, cheating behind your back, making a fool of you. That's enough to make anyone snap. Is that what happened?"

"I did not know," he said, "and I did not kill him. I didn't go near the place. Joanne and I were home together the whole afternoon. Ask her."

"We have," she said, "but she's lied to us, as well as to you. How can we believe her? Do you think a jury will?"

She looked at Jeffrey, who picked up the thread. "Ron, are you protecting her? Did she want to break it off with him but couldn't bring herself to do so? Did she send you to do her dirty work?"

He swung his head back and forth like a pendulum.

"Did she promise to cover for you?" Barnwell said, the two detectives hurling questions to him in rhythm. "'Take care of him, Ron. I'll say you were here with me. Go now, before Lois returns.'"

"Nothing like that happened," he spoke slowly, enunciating each word. "I did not kill Steven Parker. I resented him. No question about it. He was giving her something I could not. She needed someone, and I gave her permission through my silence, all to keep the part of her I could."

Neither detective responded at first, not daring to shoot questioning glances at each other. "Explain," Lydia said.

Schuster wiped his nose with a handkerchief and looked to his side through bleary eyes. "Prostate cancer."

"You're impotent?" she said.

He dropped his face without responding.

"You couldn't have sex with her, but she needed it. The two of you settled on this ... arrangement?"

He sat back and studied the ceiling. "I knew she was seeing someone but didn't know who. I chose not to ask questions. She'd grown morose in the two years following my surgery. I feared she'd leave me. Of course, I noticed the signs. Do you think I'm blind?" He looked from one to the other as though expecting an answer.

"Whoever she was seeing made her happy. We were a couple again. Call me foolish, if you will, but I love her. I've spent thousands of dollars—tens of thousands trying to... But nothing worked. I accepted the situation. It was a heavy price, steeper than all those miracle cures, but it worked."

"And then you discovered she'd turned to your best friend."

"Yes." He didn't immediately follow up, but they waited him out. "Lois seems to have cut him off following an affair. At least, that's how Joanne explained it. She rationalized it. 'We're both getting something we need, and we're not hurting anyone.'"

"But it hurt you?" Jeffrey said. "Playing golf, attending baseball games together, lifting a few beers with friends. You must have wondered if he'd boasted about it, if everyone at the table was laughing behind your back."

"Of course it was humiliating," he said, "but Joanne assured me she'd ended it. Unless we wanted to uproot ourselves and move elsewhere, change churches, find new friends, and everything else it entailed, I had to live with what they'd done."

"Until you learned they hadn't ended it," Lydia said.

"No, no. I didn't. I'm still not sure you're telling me the truth."

She closed her notebook, not meeting his eye.

———

THEY PLAYED table tennis with the pair throughout the afternoon and into the early evening. Apart from Joanne confirming her husband's explanation for her infidelity, neither wavered, insisting they'd watched the entire Penn State game without leaving their living room. Ron maintained he'd been unaware she'd hopped back into Parker's bed—or he into hers—and she insisted he'd given no sign he'd learned of the affair.

Neither had any idea who might have murdered Steven Parker, and Joanne burst into tears whenever the subject was broached, which raised another question. Did she still love her husband, or had she transferred not only her body but her affection to their neighbor?

"It's beyond our remit," she said, affecting a British accent. "We're here to solve the crime."

Catching her tone, Jeffrey said, "I'm sorry Carpenter was so rough on you. He's trying to protect you from going off in the wrong direction."

"I never was. What's your metaphor? I kept my eye on the doughnut, but the hole isn't empty. It's sitting on the shelf where it's been for thirty years." She watched to make certain he'd heard her. "So what do we do now?"

"She lied to us, and I've Mirandized her. We can hold her until her arraignment. Meanwhile, do you still think they're covering for each other?"

"I don't know. If not, they're putting on one hell of an act."

"They've had a week to rehearse it. Would you agree he's still our top suspect? No one has a better motive. Anyone who entered the garage had the means. His prints are all over the place. We have the receipt he dropped on the floor. Barring their continued lies, he had the opportunity."

Lydia agreed, even though a part of her thought they were telling the truth.

"We hold both of them," he said. "We'll speak to the

DA tomorrow. Their attorney will get them released once he returns from wherever he is, but in the meantime they'll have time to consider their stories."

Even as she concurred with the plan, he continued his argument. "They're both lying. We need to prove it."

"Lois," she said. "Let's not forget this wasn't a love triangle but a rectangle. Where's Mrs. Parker in all this?"

He flipped his reading glasses up and down with a finger as he considered it. "Let's take this up in the morning."

"I have an errand to run first thing. Make it ten o'clock or later."

"You're not working this Jeanne Holman murder, are you? Carpenter wants you to await the DNA results."

"I'm doing that," she snapped. "It's a personal matter."

"Okay." He drew it out, making it sound like a question. He waited as she folded her notebook and prepared to leave. "This personal matter ..."

"Is none of your business," she said.

"What's wrong?" Calvin watched as Lydia slumped over the Ahi tuna he'd seared.

"Nothing," she said. "Everything."

"Tell me."

For five minutes, she poured out her heart while he listened. She described her misgivings about the role the Schusters had played in Steven Parker's murder. As she spoke, her discussion morphed into Parker's probe of Jeanne Holman's death.

"I thought Bruno Vogt had killed Parker to shut him up. It turns out he couldn't have. But he raped that poor little girl then strangled her." She clutched herself as she shuddered. "So far, the bastard's gotten away with it. I want to bring him down, but the lieutenant is holding me back." Her voice rose as she finished. "He sees it as a sideshow. It is not."

Calvin watched her breath slow. She speared a piece of tuna only to return it to her plate uneaten. "I haven't seen you this passionate about a case since the disappearance of that child. What was her name?"

"Rosie," she said. Rose Fallon was a toddler whose mother had reported her missing from a thrift store two years before. Lydia was on the borough police force at the time and wasn't assigned to the case, but she'd attached herself to it like a barnacle. As she investigated what appeared to be an abduction, the mother turned to her for support. Something about her story rang a discordant tone. Ultimately, Lydia proved her boyfriend had killed the girl and the woman had staged the abduction to cover for him. This was the first time she'd come to the attention of county detectives, but not the last.

Calvin waited for her to continue, and when she didn't, said, "What is it?"

Lydia shoved her plate away and buried her head in her hands. "I haven't spoken about this in years. I've never told anyone stateside about it, but you need to know." She looked up at him, her eyes brimming with tears. "To understand me, to know why I became a cop."

"It happened to you," he said.

"I was fifteen, living in off-base housing in Spain. An airman, a mechanic, followed me one evening and began talking to me. He seemed nice enough. I was naïve. Without a mother, I didn't know what I didn't know." She folded her hands and said nothing for ten seconds. When she continued, her voice was soft and frail. "I thought he was walking along to protect me. We got to a deserted section, a playground. He turned on me, dragged me into a grove of trees, ripped my clothes off, and—"

She stopped, unable to continue.

"You don't have to tell me more."

"I do," she said, gushing as tears cascaded down her cheeks. "He raped me, Calvin. He took my innocence. And my father—" Again she choked. Her voice dropped an octave as she turned toward him. "He asked what I was doing out alone after dark. My own father."

Calvin poured her a second glass of wine, which she downed as she cried. He scooted his chair alongside hers and wrapped his arm around her. "And you have to bring Jeanne Holman the justice you never received."

She nodded without speaking, her body heaving.

"Do it," he said. "The lieutenant be damned. Do what you must."

CHAPTER TEN

LYDIA AROSE BEFORE DAWN. She left Calvin a note to remind him of Izabela's viewing that evening, made herself an espresso, gobbled a bowl of bran flakes, and merged onto I-376 toward the airport. She passed it and continued another twenty minutes before turning off at the exit to Aliquippa, taking Kennedy Boulevard to Fillmore Street.

Despite her training, she couldn't help gathering impressions of people from phone conversations. MaryJo Keller's home was not what she expected, an attractive white-framed house with an entry covered by an aluminum canopy. The lawn was mowed like golf course greens, and the last of the season's flowers struggled against the waning daylight along both sides of the front steps. A blue Ford-150 was parked in the asphalt driveway to the right. As she emerged from her personal vehicle, a man stepped out of the side entrance and opened the door of the truck. He turned as she approached him.

"Can I help you?" He was in his mid-fifties, tall and

gangly, with a face to match, an elongated shape with long, droopy ears and the trace of a smile.

"Are you Max Keller?"

He nodded. Lydia flashed her badge and identified herself. "I'm here to see your wife."

His brows knitted in concern. "She's just up. What's..." His unasked query hung in the air.

"It's about her former husband. I have to ask her a few questions."

He shook his head as though it was the last thing he wanted to hear. "Are you allowed here? I mean, this is Beaver County."

Lydia had not alerted the local sheriff to her presence, as was the custom when operating in another jurisdiction. "I don't suspect her of anything. This is informal. I need some information." As he continued to stand with the door in his left hand, she said, "This will only take a few minutes. Why don't you stay and listen?"

This seemed to put him at ease. "Wait here. She's not dressed yet."

He disappeared and returned two minutes later, motioning her through the side door. Far from a dumpy lump of pudding Lydia had envisioned, MaryJo Keller was slender with sharp features and half-glasses reminiscent of a schoolteacher. She wore a robe and slippers, and her short, light-brown hair framed a face that was devoid of makeup but did not need it.

She held out a hand and said, "I suspected I'd hear from you again."

"And here I am," Lydia said.

"Watch yourself." She directed her to the round kitchen table. "The floor's slippy. It needs worshed. I was about to."

Lydia avoided a greasy patch near the stove as she took a chair the woman pulled out. Without the luxury of time, she dived into her questions. "I know Steven Parker contacted you. Why did you tell me he hadn't?"

"Why does anyone?" she said. "I didn't want to get involved in whatever Bruno had been up to."

"And Jeanne Holman? You told me you'd never heard of her."

"I didn't say that exactly."

Lydia recalled the woman's exact words "I don't know no one by that name."

"No, you didn't, but you know who she was."

"Yeah,." She motioned to her husband, who poured her a cup of coffee, offered one to Lydia, which she refused, and joined them at the breakfast table. "She's the girl that got herself killed."

Lydia's head screamed, *She didn't get herself killed—someone murdered her!* But she presented the most impassive face she could muster. "And that's why Steven Parker came to see you?"

"Yeah. He didn't call himself that. He had it flipped, but it don't make much difference."

"What did you tell him?"

"That I didn't know nothing about it. Me and him had already split. I got rid of him while he was in prison for showing himself to those little girls. I was only nineteen. We'd been married less than two years. The first time, the cop brought him home and told me what he'd done. Bruno said it weren't so. Like a fool, I believed him. When they caught him at it again though, they charged him and sent him away. I had enough."

Lydia was not surprised to learn Vogt's arrest was not the first time he had exposed himself, nor shocked that a police officer had let him off. Times had changed, but the past hung over many cases she'd investigated.

"You told Parker you knew nothing about the girl's murder, and he went away. Is that it?"

She turned toward her husband, who nodded as though giving her permission. "I said I thought he was capable of it."

"Because…"

Again, she checked with her husband before answering. "Cause of the way he treated me."

Lydia didn't need her to draw a picture. "Was that all you told him?"

"Yeah." She looked into her cup as though something lurked beneath its creamy surface. Barnwell was sure it did, but MaryJo raced on, amplifying her story before Lydia could question it. "I told him I was afraid of him. It was why I came out here once he got out. Found a job at the mill and worked there till it closed. That's where Max and me met."

Barnwell, who'd done her homework, said, "You moved here in 1964. I'm interested in what happened before that, after Vogt was released on probation."

She nudged the handle of her coffee cup with her finger, spinning it halfway around, then looked at her husband for support. "MaryJo, has any law officer questioned you about Jeanne Holman's murder?" She shook her head. "About where Bruno was the week she was killed?"

"Nuh-uh."

"You're certain."

"Not until you came along."

"Then you've never lied to the police. You haven't suppressed evidence. You can't be charged with abetting a felony."

Her face brightened, though she still didn't meet Lydia's eye.

"I'm asking you now, so how you answer is a different matter. Let me tell you what I already know. A condition of Bruno's release was that he remain in Pennsylvania. He couldn't step out of the state without permission. Every six months, he was required to report to his parole officer. He never missed an appointment. Had he done so, he would have been thrown back into prison. He swore he lived at a Pittsburgh address. Yours, MaryJo. My first question is, was he living there?"

"No," she said. "He was with his sister down in Maryland. He'd drive up the night before, sleep on the sofa, make his meeting, and head back."

"He wasn't living with you, but he crashed at your place? He did so every six months? Is that what you're telling me?"

"Yeah," she said. "I didn't want him there. I tried to turn him away, but he'd barge in and ignore me when I said I didn't want to see him."

"Fair enough," Lydia said. "He reported to the parole officer on June 8th, 1993. Did he spend the previous night on your sofa?"

She looked at Max again, who told her to go ahead. "You did nothing wrong, baby. Tell the lady."

"Yeah," she said. "He was there."

"Did you get a sense something was amiss?" She wrinkled her nose to show she didn't understand the question. "Was anything different in the way he appeared or acted?"

"Yeah. He had scratches on his face, blood on his t-shirt, and grass stains on his pants. He wanted me to worsh his stuff, but I didn't want him peeling off his clothes in front of me. I was over him, understand? But he put on my robe and waited while I got his stuff cleaned up."

"Anything else?" The woman shook her head. He'd left for his appointment first thing the next morning, and she didn't see him again for six months. By then, the murder had been front page news for weeks. "Did you suspect he'd killed her?"

Tears welled in her eyes and spilled down her cheeks. Her husband reached out his hand and placed it over hers. "I didn't know nothing. I suspected, like you said."

"Did you ask him about Jeanne's death?"

"Of course not. I was scared shitless of him. He came, he left, and so did I. Came out here where he couldn't find me. Kept a real low profile. Then I met Max, moved in with him, and took his name even before we got married."

"And you haven't seen him since?"

"Never, and I don't want to."

Lydia closed her notebook. "You'll be happy to know he's sitting in a county jail in West Virginia. He attacked a police officer, which means he won't be going anywhere for a while."

For the first time, she allowed herself a smile.

"Except here," Lydia said. "When I confirm one more piece of evidence, which I hope to do today, we'll haul him back to Pennsylvania to stand trial for the murder of that little girl. You'll be called as a witness. I know it will be diffi-cult, but please tell the court what you've just told me. If you do that, you will have nothing else to fear from this man, ever."

Lydia signed in a bit after nine o'clock, with ample time to spare before they left to question Lois Parker. "Everything okay?" Jeffrey asked, towering over her with his coffee mug in hand.

"Perfect," she said, flashing a smile at him.

He returned it. "You have good news?"

She hid a mental frown then got it. "You think I'm pregnant, don't you? No, it wasn't that. It was … something I needed to resolve, and I have. When do we leave?"

Placing the mug on his desk, he reached for his jacket, but Ross Sutton swam into the room like an orca devouring seals. "You're heading out to see the widow?" he said. "First, you need to hear this."

He continued moving, and they followed in his wake. He took his seat at the head of a conference table and shoved spreadsheets beneath their noses. "You looked at his bank records but didn't find any suspicious transactions. His spending exceeded his income, and he was transferring money from his savings accounts and from other sources we couldn't identify. We've found something more."

Flashing them a grin, he waved his paw at the printouts he'd placed before them. She stared at the first page and flipped to the second while Jeffrey did the same. Neither knew what they were seeing, as the drama-loving forensics detective intended.

"Let me summarize it for you." Looking up, Jeffrey winked at her with the eye beyond Sutton's vision. "Page 2. We found three CDs he'd opened years back when he was still with the paper. They held close to a hundred thou. He'd transferred all of them to his PNC accounts.

"Page 3. A brokerage account at Schwab. He emptied that. He took a loss on a few stocks but sold the rest at a nice profit. The capital gains are taxable."

"Did he declare them on his return?" Barnwell asked.

"The IRS granted him an extension, but the deadline came and went three days before his death."

Jeffrey whistled. "Lois is in a heap of trouble."

"I wonder if she even knows," Lydia said.

"That's why I wanted to show you this before you leave. He has retirement funds at Schwab. He may have borrowed on them, but I need her permission to find out. If he did, it was a stupid move, because she'll have to pay a penalty."

"A financial incompetent," she said.

"But wait," Sutton said, imitating a TV infomercial, "there's more. He maxed out nearly all his credit cards. He was making token payments to Visa to keep one card open, but everything else was shut down. Three stores had put him in collections."

"She must have known that much," Lydia said.

"Again, that's something for you to find out. He hadn't paid property taxes. The township, county, and school system have all filed liens against the house."

"No wonder he was drinking," Jeffrey said.

Lydia asked how he could have kept up appearances for so long. "You had me looking for suspicious transactions that might have led someone to have it in for him. We didn't find any. They lived simply compared to others in their neighborhood. No signs of extravagance, unless you count the fact they had two cars. Those, at least, were paid off. But he had nothing coming in. I don't know what he was thinking."

Lydia saw a pattern emerging. His frantic appeals to his agent. Going behind his back to sell to publishers. The man was scrambling for money. The Holman murder case was his only hope, and he was terrified someone would tell the story before he could.

"Thank you for coming, but they've already told me." Lois Parker stood at her front door, hanging onto it.

"I'm sorry," Barnwell replied. "Told you what?"

"The medical examiner is releasing Steven's body." Her slight smile faded. "It's taken him long enough."

"We've come about something else," Lydia said, introducing uniformed officer Nadine Foster. She was not about to get into a discussion of the laborious process of running toxicology tests on a corpse.

"You've found who killed him?" she said, stepping aside.

"I'm afraid not, but we're making progress." Lois led them into the living room, sat in the armchair, and folded her hands, motioning the two law officers toward the sofa. Knowing that Schuster's attorney was working to get the pair released, Jeffrey had enlisted Detective Ullrich to question them while Lydia spoke with Parker's widow.

She fluttered her hands and picked at pilling on the sleeve of her light-blue sweater. Lydia had only met her once, but she appeared to have aged a year for each of the ten days since she'd discovered her husband's body. Worry lines crowded a face that had seemed unbroken then. A line of gray creased the part in her hair.

"Steven will be cremated, but we're holding a celebration of life tomorrow evening at the church. In the community room," she added as though it were an afterthought. "I wish we could afford a larger venue. A lot of his friends from his newspaper days will attend, but there's not enough ..." She broke off and gnawed at the knuckles of her right hand.

"That's one reason we've come. Our forensics team is examining your bank records. It appears your—"

A bonfire lit in her eyes. "Who gave you permission to do that? It's a personal matter. You have no right to pry into our finances."

"Mrs. Parker—Lois—we do this whenever there's an unsolved murder. We're seeking anyone with a motive to kill him. Perhaps he owed money to someone or had made a questionable financial transaction. We're not trying to invade your privacy. It's a routine part of our investigatory process."

The fire burned out. "Then you know."

From somewhere in the house, Lydia heard a clock ticking. "Can I get you something?" Officer Foster asked. "A glass of water?"

"That would be nice. The kitchen..." She pointed.

"I see it."

Lydia remained silent until Nadine returned, bearing both water and a box of tissues. As she regained her seat on the couch, a voice from the upper level shouted, "That bastard! Jesus Christ!"

They looked up, unaware anyone else was in the house. "Bill is trying to piece things together. There's no money. I may have to sell the house, but we had a second mortgage, a line of credit they call it. I'd signed it, but he told me it was only for making repairs." She raised the glass to her lips and gulped it.

Lydia didn't want to pour salt into the wound, but she'd brought a shaker full of it. "Steven had a retirement fund, and we're not allowed to get into it without your—"

"He borrowed on that too. Bill says we'll pay a penalty to the IRS, but we have no way to do so." She kneaded her forehead with both hands. "I don't know what to do. If he'd told me... I haven't worked in years, but I could have found something to do."

Nadine's brown eyes bore into Lydia's. Would she drop the other shoe? She had no choice. "I'm sorry to have to do this, but I have to ask a personal question. Like your financial affairs, I'm searching for a motive."

"All right," she said, clutching a wad of tissues in her hand. "Things can't get much worse."

"When we spoke, you revealed your husband had had an affair with a fellow reporter. When I asked if she was the only one, you said you knew of no others. Are you certain of that?"

She bowed her head and folded her hands as though in prayer. "I'm no longer sure of anything. He had other women?"

"I'm afraid so."

She waited, expecting the detective to explain. For once, Lydia broke the silence. "Did he tell you why he left the *Herald*?"

"They downsized. He took a buyout. It wasn't much, but it gave him the time to write..." She lost steam, meeting Lydia's stare. "That's not what happened?"

"No."

"Woman trouble?"

"Yes," she said, though her late husband, not a woman, who was the source of the problem. "How about more recently? Are you aware of any other women in his life?"

Instead of responding, Lois returned her gaze. Her blank look morphed into a frown. Her eyes widened. "Ron and Joanne left with you yesterday. Why? Where are they?"

"They're helping us with our investigation."

The ticking of the clock was replaced by a footfall on the stairway. Bill Parker entered the room. His hands shook, and his face was florid, but when he spotted the two officers, he nodded toward them and turned to his mother. "What's happened?"

"Are you saying that Joanne... No."

"What about Joanne?" her son asked.

"They think your father was having an affair with her. That's impossible. She's my best friend. She wouldn't do that to me."

"You didn't know?"

"Of course not," Bill said. "That son of a bitch never told her anything. Are you sure? Joanne and Ron? Hiding it right beneath her nose?"

"Were you aware of it?" she asked him.

"Who are you to come here and upset my mother this way? She has enough on her mind. You can't imagine what she's going through."

Lois reached out and grabbed his hand. "They know. Someone at their office has looked through our bank records. They see what a mess he made of things." She patted him on the knee to make sure he'd calmed down. "Tell me one thing. Did Ron know what was going on?"

"He learned last spring."

"And pretended to be Steven's friend? I don't believe this. What's wrong with these people?"

She'd asked a good question, but Lydia had no answer. "This is for the record." She turned to include the young officer, without stating she was her witness. "Did either of you know your husband and your neighbor were having an affair? No? You're sure? You swear?" Even though neither were under oath.

"Thank you for your time," she said, rising. "I'm sorry to

burden you, but this is a murder case. It's my duty to ask the questions that will help solve it."

"Did Joanne?" she began. "Do you think Ron ..."

"We've charged no one. We're continuing to investigate. I hope to have answers for you soon."

"What *is* wrong with people?" Officer Foster repeated as she returned to headquarters.

WHILE LYDIA WAS NO CLOSER to proving who had murdered Steven Parker nine days before, Lyle Jeffrey was even further. He and Detective Ullrich drove to the county jail where they spent half an hour peppering Joanne Schuster with questions, but she turned them all away.

Yes, she'd hidden from her husband the fact she'd continued her affair with Parker after he'd confronted her. But no, neither she nor Ron had left their home during the Penn State game, staying until the end and even watching the post-game interviews. Nothing either detective said could budge the most minute detail of her story.

Ron was as unshakable, insisting he was unaware she was still cheating on him and had played no role in the death of his "friend." As he had the day before, Jeffrey offered Schuster an out: "If you dropped down the hill to talk to him and an argument ensued, that's different from accosting him with intent. The court may accept a plea of manslaughter under these circumstances. That's a maximum of ten years in prison, but you could be out in five."

He was having none of it. Gritting his teeth, he stared at the detective. Enunciating it as though he were speaking to a recalcitrant five-year-old, he said, "I did not kill him. I went nowhere near his home that afternoon. Not until Lois called us."

"You had reason to kill him," Jeffrey said. "Your prints are all over the garage. You knew he propped the shovel inside the door. It's a short walk from your house to his. Why don't you make things easy on yourself and tell me what happened?"

"Nothing happened," he said. "You think you can wear me down and make me confess to something I didn't do? It won't work. You can keep me here all day, and—"

Jeffrey would not hold him for a second longer. The door to the interrogation room opened, and a uniformed officer ushered Attorney Pat Morgan into the room. "Answer no more questions," he said. "Unless you're going to charge my client, he's free to go."

Jeffrey sighed and pushed himself back from the table. "I'm not ready to charge him, but I will."

"That goes for Joanne too."

"We've booked her," Jeffrey shot back. "Lying to law enforcement officers."

"It's a misdemeanor. You can't hold her." He flashed a signed order from a magistrate, ordering her release.

The detective knew when he was outmaneuvered. He watched as both Schusters collected their belongings from the property guard. Glaring at him as she left the jail, Joanne reached for her husband's arm. He shook her off.

"You may think lying to us is nothing," Jeffrey told her, "but you've sidetracked this investigation for days. The court is going to know this."

The attorney, who as yet had no knowledge of what she had concealed from them, said, "Save your argument for the witness stand. We'll be ready for you."

Jeffrey slumped as they drove away. "What do you think?" Ullrich asked.

"He's guilty as hell, and she knows it. I need to figure out how to break him."

"How'd it go?" Lydia lifted her fingers from her keyboard as Jeffrey entered the bullpen. Seeing his spent look, she said, "Not so good, huh?"

Doffing his jacket, he grabbed his mug, retreated to the kitchen, and returned with steam coming from its lip and his ears. "They're both lying. I'm sure of it." He summarized his thwarted efforts. "Of one thing, I am certain. The Schusters' marriage is over."

"What should we do now?"

He ran his hands through his hair. "I don't know. Need to think about it." He sipped his coffee and muttered obscenities under his breath. "What about you?"

She described her meeting with Lois Parker, the increasing depth of her financial problems, and Bill's anger at his father. "She claims to have known nothing about the affair."

"Do you believe her?"

Leaning back from her keyboard, she laced her fingers and stretched. "She seemed dumfounded, though how she remained blind for so long escapes me."

"You writing your report?" he asked.

"Yes." She hung her head for a moment. "Finished it, actually. I'm working on something else."

"Okay," he said when she didn't elaborate.

They sat in silence while she typed. He refilled his mug, took a tour of the bullpen, and stared at the red entry on the Baltimore Board, showing their case remained unsolved. "Let's take it to the DA and see if she'll file charges."

Lydia finished typing and closed the file. "Do we have enough? That's what you always ask me."

Cradling the mug in his hand, he leaned back so far in his chair she feared he'd topple over and anoint himself. "Let's let Dawkins decide," he said, referring to the assistant district attorney. "Even if she won't go along, she can formalize the charges against Joanne. That may give us some leverage."

His expression showed he doubted it. She silenced her phone by reaching for it and listened, a smile spreading across her face. "You're certain? One hundred percent? Golden, and thank you. Please send me the report."

She rose, smoothed out her slacks, and said, "We have something else to take to the DA."

***

Assistant District Attorney Melissa Dawkins made them wait in her reception area before admitting them to her inner sanctum. "It's her *modus operandi*," Jeffrey said. "She's showing us who's boss."

Not only was he unconcerned that her assistant might overhear him, he stated it for his benefit, since Lydia had been here before and knew the drill. Unlike some prosecutors, who were eager to file charges against anyone the police brought them, Dawkins was a tough customer. She didn't merely listen to your case; she cross-examined you. When she'd first encountered her, Lydia thought her nit-picking reflected a commitment to justice and admired her for it. Carpenter had set her straight. "She doesn't bring a charge unless she's sure she can win in court. She's after his job."

Which was how many on the team looked at their jobs, but Dawkins was a woman, which made her ambition something to be resented rather than respected.

She appeared at the door and motioned them to follow her. "Only a fifteen minute wait," Jeffrey muttered as they trailed her, "a record." Lydia wondered if it was a positive sign.

Dawkins directed them to seats at her round table. "I understand you're bringing me two cases. Who goes first?"

Lydia glanced at Jeffrey, seeking permission to begin, but he plowed ahead. "Steven Parker, a/k/a Parker Stevens, was murdered in the garage of his home a week ago Saturday," he began. Dawkins had to be well aware of this, but his experience had taught him to leave nothing out. He described the physical evidence, which consisted solely of his prints and the receipt to the Mexican restaurant found in the garage, then delved into the tangled relationship between Parker, Joanne Schuster, and her husband.

As he spoke, Dawkins peppered him with questions. "Hold on. You're telling me that after Schuster uncovered the affair, and after his wife promised to end it, they continued to meet."

Jeffrey confirmed the facts.

"The husband insists he knew nothing about this," Dawkins asked. "You don't believe him?"

"Not for a minute," he said.

"What evidence do you have?" she barked. When Jeffrey went blank, she fired questions at him. Had Ron shared his suspicion with anyone else? Sent a text? Removed Joanne's name from bank accounts? "Do you have anything to support your contention?"

Jeffrey countered with "common sense" and "stands to reason," but she said, "That's not proof, Detective. Go on."

"His golfing buddies noticed the tension between them." He repeated the stories he'd dragged out of Combs and Mattingly.

"Not evidence," she said.

Lydia let her attention wander as the assistant DA continued to poke holes in his theory. In most offices, family photos competed with symbols of professional achievement, rafting excursions vying with diplomas, trips to Disney with honors and citations. But not here. On the credenza behind her, the only photo was of Dawkins and a woman Lydia assumed to be her wife, the one concession to any sign of activity outside her calling.

"He was a three-minute walk from the garage at the time Parker was killed," Jeffrey said. "His wife provides his alibi, but she has lied repeatedly. I've charged her with lying to police and impeding an investigation."

"Let's discuss her," the prosecutor said. Jeffrey laid out that element of his case, the twists and turns of Joanne's stories as she'd worked to conceal the reason Ron might have wanted to take Parker's life.

Dawkins made a few notes but gave no sign of how she would come down on the case. She led him back to the case against the husband and let him finish his story without further interruptions. "That's it?" she said when he'd finished.

"Motive, means, and opportunity. Fingerprints at the scene. A restaurant receipt on the floor near the body."

"Which he says he dropped three days before," she reminded him.

He continued as though he hadn't heard her. "A man

twice betrayed by his wife and close friend. It's a classic crime of passion."

She looked at him for a moment and simpered. Was she enjoying herself? "You don't have enough. His attorney will have Joanne Schuster take the stand, prostate herself before the jury by admitting her sins and wallowing in woe, tell them she only lied because she knew the police would try to pin the murder on her husband, to which the lawyer will say that's exactly what happened. He'll put everyone else with whom Parker had an affair on trial and parade his money problems before the jury. He'll tell them they must acquit if they have reasonable doubt as to his guilt, and he'll have created so much doubt they'll do exactly that."

Dawkins let that sink in. Lydia knew she was right. "You need to place him at the scene at the moment he wielded the shovel, if he did." She glanced at her watch. "I have an appointment, so tell me about this other matter and make it quick."

Lydia did her best, stumbling over her words as she rewound from Parker's death, to the teaser he'd presented to the crowd at the book fair, to his investigation of Jeanne Holman's murder. "I won't bother you with how I learned who he suspected," she said, "but—"

"It's no bother," she said. The prosecutor had dropped the pen she'd been sliding between her fingers and leaned toward her. "I remember this case. I was only a child, but we lived in Shadyside. My parents trembled in fear that the same thing could happen to my older sister. Go on."

Lydia slowed down and led her through her investigation, step by step. "When Vogt assaulted the Cumberland deputy, the Mineral County sheriff arrested him, booked him, and took his DNA. I got two of the swabs and submitted them to the ME yesterday. Two hours ago, they matched it to samples taken from Jeanne's body and clothing after her body was found."

Dawkins split her face in a grin.

"I also have a witness statement," Lydia said. Jeffrey's head jerked up, since he'd heard nothing about his partner's early-morning foray to Aliquippa. "Vogt was on probation and was supposed to remain in the state, but he'd moved in with his sister in Cumberland. He used his ex-wife's home as his residence, making the trip to Pittsburgh whenever he had to check in. He reported as scheduled on the morning of June 8th but spent the previous night sleeping on her sofa. When he arrived, she noted scratches on his face, blood on a shirt, and grass stains on his pants."

She closed her notebook and folded her hands. "We can place him here on the afternoon Jeanne Holman was murdered, and we can prove he penetrated her."

"Nice work, Detective."

"Actually, it was Steven Parker who put it together. I—"

"You," she interrupted, "solved a murder that has troubled me all my life. Take a victory lap."

Dawkins promised to make certain West Virginia authorities held on to Bruno Vogt while she built the case, presented it to the grand jury, and arranged for his extradition.

In the cruiser as they returned to headquarters, Jeffrey didn't speak. "At least some good has come of this," she said.

He didn't answer until they'd made their way through the Fort Pitt Tunnel. "Schuster will walk free unless we find a magic bullet. You've been obsessed with this Jeanne Holman murder. I don't know why, though I have an idea. But you've solved it. Good for you."

He parked in front of headquarters, turned off the engine, and placed his hands on the steering wheel. "I need your help on this, Barnwell. I know he's guilty. Help me prove it."

"It's barbaric." Lydia stood at the front door, her arms folded as though blocking an exit.

"You look good in black," Calvin said. "Have I ever seen you in a dress before?"

"This past Sunday," she said.

"Of course, you'd be stunning in a potato sack."

"Don't try to sweet talk me," she said. "Seriously, do you think Neanderthals stood around gaping at the body of a dead person?"

"Probably," he said. "We're doing this for Barbara and the chief. They need someone to keep order."

Lydia climbed into the passenger seat and said nothing as he drove through the rain-soaked streets to the funeral home in Dormont. The lot was full, and he had to park up the street on West Liberty, guiding her past rows of police cruisers. "These folks weren't fools," he said. "I shouldn't have come in our personal vehicle."

They shook themselves out of their raincoats. An attendant pointed them toward a parlor, but there was no need. They could have followed the voices, were not mourners overflowing the room into the hallway. As they entered, Lydia was engulfed in a floral flagrance so overwhelming she was reminded of incense. Her eyes watered, and she grabbed a handful of tissue from one of the boxes placed throughout the parlor.

Between them, Calvin and Lydia knew half those present, some in uniform, the rest in mufti. Hands reached out to them, and they reached for others. Smiles of recognition were muted due to the solemnity of the occasion.

Had this been an Irish wake, voices would have been raised in song, but Slovakians, who made up the bulk of those not in law enforcement, were a more somber lot. As Lydia signed the register for both of them, she heard women speaking in the unfamiliar language. All were old, awaiting their turn to be remembered. Their children, most beyond middle age themselves, held their arms, lending support, conversing to one another in hushed English.

They moved through the receiving line. As she approached Barbara Novak, Lydia spread her arms and embraced her. To Novak, she said, "I'm so sorry for your loss." Stupid words. Empty words. But she didn't know what else to say.

"She had a full life," he replied. She recalled his telling her that when she reached the US after spending either years in Nazi-occupied Czechoslovakia, she refused to leave, even for a weekend trip to Canada. Izabela Novak wore her adopted patriotism like a warm blanket. As Lydia prepared to move on, Novak gripped her elbow. "Come by the house in the morning. We need to talk." She murmured agreement.

Izabela's face and upper torso was in a flower-filled coffin, its lid bearing a cross. Her hair, which she had let go in real life, was done up as though she were about to leave for a party. Her closed eyes were the only natural aspect of her face, which otherwise had been painted an unnatural pink. Mourners knelt at a bench before the casket, crossing themselves and praying. It was the sole aspect of the display that seemed appropriate.

"Do you want to view the deceased?" an older man asked her as he attempted to stand.

"Don't trouble yourself," she said. "I knew her in life." She immediately regretted the reply. She had repaid the man's kindness with what sounded like a rebuke.

He didn't take offense, however, looking up at her through rheumy eyes. "I did too."

After they shared condolences with the Novaks' daughter Mariel and granddaughter Jennifer, who looked as though she would have preferred to be anywhere else, Calvin drifted toward a group of fellow officers. She'd had enough old war stories for one day and eased into a circle of women who proved to be teachers at the middle school where Barbara had been the principal. In hushed tones, they decried some new outrage committed by a member of the school board. Following the district's decision to move a male teacher rather than dismiss him, Barbara had resigned. She had never revealed his offense, but Lydia could use her imagination.

As the evening wore on, they roamed from group to group, looking for a home. They studied two photo albums and marveled at Izabela's wedding pictures and engagement portrait. She had been stunning in her youth. A monitor showed scenes from her life. In one blurry photograph, a dark-haired woman held a small child toward the camera as though making an offering. Izabela as an infant and her mother.

Someone asked Novak to say a few words. He recounted her arrival in New York harbor on a troop ship converted to carry war brides and refugee dependents like herself. They would have to spend one more night aboard the vessel, the captain explained over the loudspeaker, because tomorrow was an American holiday and Ellis Island was closed.

The Slovakian women pressed forward as he spoke, one cupping a hand to her ear. Had she also been on the ship?

At 10 p.m., he said, fireworks had blossomed over the harbor, and terrified women screamed in terror. The captain tried to calm them, but many could not be reassured. Eight-year-old Izabela and her mother made it through the night and the following day, only to gain their independence the day after their adopted country had celebrated its own.

Lydia had heard versions of this story before, and Novak had told it so often he recited it like a monologue from a play. It never failed to inspire, however, and as she and Calvin left, she was glad she'd come.

CHAPTER ELEVEN

IT POURED as Lydia arrived at the Novaks' the following morning. Barbara popped open the door and took her rain jacket, shaking it off on the porch before closing the entrance. She led her into the kitchen and poured a cup of coffee. Knowing it was coming, Lydia had shunned the Americano that usually started her day. They made small talk while waiting for Novak.

As their friendship had grown, Barbara had become something of a second mother, a vital figure since she could scarcely remember her own. Novak came down the stairs, taking them one by one as he always did due to his recurring vertigo. He straddled a bar stool and planted a kiss on her forehead.

"To what do I owe the honor?" she said, noting the unaccustomed display of affection. She could not recall his ever placing a hand on her, other than to shake it, although she suspected he'd hugged her after rescuing her from a crooked police chief's abduction the first year they'd worked together. If so, she'd forgotten it.

"Word has it you've found little Jeanne's killer."

She tried to deflect credit to the slain crime writer, but, like Melissa Dawkins, Novak was having none of it. At his insistence, she reviewed the process by which she'd identified Bruno Vogt, a child predator who had lived in the neighborhood.

"How the hell did I miss that?" he said.

"It wasn't your case."

"Still..." He brooded while Barbara served them egg enchiladas. To break the silence, she finished her story, how she'd confronted Vogt's sister in Cumberland, Maryland, followed him across the state line, and chased him down after he'd assaulted Deputy Pollard. That, she said, gave her access to the DNA that provided the physical evidence.

"Congratulations," he said. "I wish I'd brought him to justice years ago, but at least Jeanne's family will get some closure."

Jeanne's broken family, she thought.

"Where are you on Parker's murder?"

Lydia took a deep breath before giving him her answer. "We're stuck. Jeffrey thinks we've found his killer, but the DA says evidence is insufficient."

"And you?"

"I think he's mistaken, but I don't have an alternate theory."

"Do you want to give me what you have?" he said, draping his enchilada in hot sauce and spooning a helping into his mouth. "No pressure."

Lydia took it from the time she arrived to question Lois, who'd found the body. She described the absence of physical evidence in the garage, Ron Schuster's suspicious behavior during her original questioning, and the revelations of Parker's womanizing.

Novak hunched forward, taking in every detail, while

Barbara cleaned up the kitchen. Normally, Lydia would have pitched in, but she'd told her to stay still. The chief reached for a notepad, his faithful companion since a collision with an opposing soccer player had scrambled his memory. Finally, he looked down at what he'd written.

As she reviewed their interviews with Parker's agent and newspaper editor, he interrupted with occasional questions, making notes to himself. "And his widow says she was unaware of why he'd left the paper?"

"That's her story. I tend to believe her, but without evidence," she said, mocking herself.

She described how Ted Nance had burst into the *Herald* newsroom after discovering Parker was bedding his wife and the alibi his Russian friend had supplied. She turned to the sordid affair Ron Schuster has discovered months before, Ron's passive response when he first learned of it, and that it had continued until the murder. The retelling helped her organize her own thoughts. As she spoke, she tried to poke holes in every suspect they'd discarded but couldn't.

"You can see why Jeffrey is obsessed with them. Ron has a strong motive. Perhaps Joanne does as well. They were within walking distance of the murder scene, but they could be lying to cover for each other. And theirs are the only prints in the garage, other than those of the family."

He jotted a note then circled it, leaned toward her, and pointed a finger inches from her knee. "Focus on the physical evidence. You can see what it suggests." It was a statement, not a question.

She returned his gaze. "Yes," she said, "I get it."

"Welcome," Jeffrey said, studying his watch. He stood before his desk wearing his rain jacket, coffee mug in hand.

"Sorry I'm late," she said, "but Chief Novak wanted me to take him through the case. He asked the right questions and gave me an idea."

"Care to share it?"

Should she tell him what she suspected and risk sending them up another blind alley or pursue it on her own? "Not yet. He's sent me back to the books. I'm going over all the evidence we've gathered, every interview, bank statement, and email. If I find what I'm looking for, I'll send up a flare. Meanwhile?" she said, nodding at his attire.

He placed the now-empty mug on his desk. "The Schusters are lying to protect each other. We both know that, but Dawkins wants solid proof. She's issued a subpoena for their security footage. If I can't find a shot of him on their cameras, I'm going to hit every house on Fairhaven Drive. I wish you were along with me."

Barnwell sensed he felt she was letting him down. "Take Foster with you. She's meticulous. I want to wade into this evidence. If I'm right, I may find something we can present to the DA."

This was an argument he could accept. He called the uniform division and requested that Nadine Foster be assigned to him for the day. Lydia waited until the pair left, refilled her water bottle, and settled into her chair for what she suspected would be a long morning.

Where to start? The king's directive in *Alice in Wonderland* came back to her, "Begin at the beginning." She opened the report she'd made on arriving at the murder scene and reread it. She pictured the scene, the body on the garage tiles, the carton of books overturned behind it, and the bloody shovel lying nearby. The ME's van had filled the driveway. The white-clad crime scene investigator had bent over Parker's form.

She'd taken the inside stairs to the living area, where Lois sat with a couple she'd later identified as Ron and Joanne Schuster, who seemed to console her as she held her hand. *What a hypocrite*, Lydia thought. *Was she comforting herself?* Bill Parker entering the front door, Jeffrey taking him aside to question him, and her insistence that the Schusters leave while she questioned Lois. She'd viewed that as neighborly concern but now saw it in a different light. Were they eavesdropping to hear what she knew? Did they fear what she might say? If Lois suspected Ron had murdered her husband, did they hope their presence would keep her from saying so?

Having banished the pair, she'd questioned Lois, who'd readily answered her questions, even revealing her husband had once been involved with another woman. She closed her eyes, recalling the conversation. Her response had been forthright when Lydia asked whether she and Steven had been a happy couple. An affair in the past, she'd said, as though closing the door on the indiscretion. But Lydia now knew she hadn't overcome it. From that time on, their marriage had been sexless, helping drive her husband into the arms of her best friend. Not that he needed encouragement. Had Lois volunteered these intimate details too readily, feeding it to her to send Lydia down this path?

She went to the restroom and returned to stare out at the cars speeding from the interstate up the parkway, trailing rooster tails in the downpour. She rewound the scene in the living room, considering all the secrets the four of them were concealing. Something bothered her.

Returning to her desk, she dialed a number she now knew by heart. "Timmons," a voice said.

"Brandy, think back on your arrival at Steven Parker's house. Who was present?"

"Only the wife."

"Scott Township had secured the site?"

"Yes, and done a good job of it." They'd taped the immediate scene and restricted access to the property, securing inner and outer perimeters by the book.

"Did anyone else enter the garage after you got there? No neighbors, family members, curious onlookers?"

"No one."

"And after you began your investigation. Who else entered?"

"Until you arrived, we were alone." Once again, Lydia recalled the large white van blocking the crime scene to keep prying eyes away.

She thanked her, called Scott Township police, and asked for Patrol Officer Barry Barnes, the first to respond to the 911 call. He was on an assignment, and it took several minutes before he got back to her. She peppered him with the same questions and got identical answers. Only Lois was home when they arrived. He and fellow officers secured the site, leaving the immediate scene untouched. Neighbors, alerted by the activity, had gathered outside the crime scene tape. One couple asked to be admitted, saying Lois had asked them to come. After confirming their story, he'd shown them into the living room where Lydia and Lyle had found them. Fifteen minutes later, Bill Parker got home, also entering through the front door. No one else had come or gone.

Lydia sent a prayer of silent thanks to Novak. Leave it to a retired cop to show her what was staring her in the face.

ON THE AFTERNOON Parker was murdered, Scott Township police collected videos from residences on McMonagle Avenue, searching for any sign of someone who'd approached the garage. Since none had a view of the murder scene itself, their efforts added nothing to the slim body of evidence. However, they had canvassed homes on Fairhaven Drive, since it was a cul-de-sac.

Jeffrey and Officer Foster set out to close that gap.

Before doing so, they served the search warrant on the Schusters. Ron answered the door, looking up and down the street as though expecting they'd come to arrest him.

"What do you want now?" he said in a tired, resigned tone.

"I have an order for any video you have on your security cameras."

Schuster ran a hand through his thinning hair. He hadn't shaved, and his eyes were bloodshot. "How do I do that?" he said, retreating into the house.

The detective asked him what service he used. When he replied that it was provided by his internet provider, Parker told him to open his computer and log onto the site.

"What are you doing?" a voice screamed as the officers followed Schuster to his office. Joanne appeared at the top of the stairs, dressed in a robe with her hair in curlers. "You can't barge in here. I'm calling our attorney."

"We have a search warrant," Jeffrey said. Ron didn't respond, acting as though he hadn't heard her screech. She retreated, slamming doors and drawers. She was getting dressed or tearing her bedroom apart. Either worked with Jeffrey. He wanted to get what he'd come for and leave.

Jeffrey showed Schuster how to access the file containing videos from the day of the murder. Two external cameras were mounted on the house, one at the front door and another at the back. The split screen allowed them to see both as Schuster scrolled to four o'clock. The officers stood over him, watching as nothing happened. He advanced in thirty-second increments. 4:10. 4:15. 4:20.

Joanne Schuster appeared in the doorway holding a cordless telephone. "Our attorney says you have no right to be here."

Jeffrey took the phone, keeping one eye on the monitor. "We have a warrant for any and all security camera footage over the past two weeks," he said. Schuster had reached 4:25 and kept going.

"Judge Merrill," Jeffrey said, and in response to the next question, added, "No, you can come see for yourself. That's fine. Call her. We'll be here." 4:30.

Jeffrey handed the instrument back to Joanne, who turned and stormed away, muttering maledictions in a voice loud enough to be heard.

4:35. Again, the screen showed no activity at either entrance. "See," Schuster said, "I never left the house."

"Keep going," Jeffrey ordered.

At 4:51, both Schusters exited the front door and hastened out of sight. "That's when Lois called Joanne. We both left to see how we could help." He swung around in his chair and looked up at them. "I was here all the time. I couldn't have killed him. This shows it."

"You have a side entrance off the garage," Jeffrey said.

"Yes, but—"

"And no camera coverage there."

He slumped and covered his mouth with his hand, shifting his head to one side and the other in frustration. "No."

Jeffrey ordered him to forward the file to an email

address he supplied, watched as he did so, and stood with phone in hand as he checked to make certain it had arrived.

"What now?" Nadine said as they battled the downpour to the patrol car.

"There's a house across the street and three more between here and the corner. You take the first two. I'll take the others."

As THE PAIR slogged through the rain, searching for evidence to place Ron Schuster at the crime scene, Barnwell plowed through interviews and emails. She had only scanned Jeffrey's questioning of Bill Parker on the afternoon of his father's murder. Now she scrutinized it, jotting notes as she did so.

She reviewed her interview with Jerry Yarborough, the agent, but found nothing new, then turned to Jeffrey's questioning of Christie Parker, the dead man's daughter. Something arrested her attention. She made another note, telling herself Jeffrey should have pursued this topic. Perhaps he hadn't grasped its significance.

She studied his interviews with Brian Ransom, the retired *Herald* editor, who'd put the lie to the story Parker had sold his family, that he'd taken a buyout from the paper in a downsizing program. That led Jeffrey to Susan Nance, the reporter with whom he'd had a long-term affair, and her ex-husband, who'd confronted Parker in the newsroom.

To avoid getting buried in details that didn't matter, she only glanced at the statements provided by the authors and attendees at the book fair. Parker dangling his secret project before the crowd that afternoon seemed to have played no role in his death.

She turned to the successive interviews with the Schusters as the detectives learned not all was as it appeared. Lydia had been the first to pick up the vibes, Joanne weeping in the kitchen while Ron dropped drunken hints that Steven Parker had been a bit too friendly. Her anger and upset when she revisited Lois Parker a few days ago. Although they'd plowed the same ground for days, Lydia read the transcript and watched the videos of every interview. She found nothing new.

She studied the interviews Jeffrey had conducted while she pursued the Bruno Vogt angle. Among them was his conversation with Jennifer Tillman, Bill Parker's student assistant. She compared her version of events with that of the theater director then read Jeffrey's account of Parker interrupting his questioning to call Jennifer, directing her to cancel the donor event. Their stories matched.

Between these bursts of activity, she took breaks to clear her head and piece the evidence into a coherent form. She drove through the rain to a deli, bought half a turkey and avocado sandwich, and returned to her desk.

To prove a case, one needed to establish a motive, a means, and an opportunity. The means were in plain sight: a round-bladed shovel leaning against the wall of the garage. Anyone entering could have used it. The killer had worn gloves. Where had they come from, and why hadn't the detectives found them? She made another note.

Opportunity was less clear. Every suspect had an alibi. Some were stronger than others, but everyone's presence seemed to be accounted for. And motive? Most murders result from lust, greed, or revenge, which often stemmed from one of the other two. But of the big three, Jeffrey had focused on what passed as love, picturing Ron Schuster as out for vengeance.

Lydia knew who had killed Steven Parker. Novak had given her the clue. She was less certain about opportunity. If everyone was telling the truth, no one had had the chance. But someone was lying. More than one, she realized.

She fired off a message to Ross Sutton, requesting that he seek a "tower dump" from a wireless service provider, then returned to the question of motive. Lust? Greed? Revenge?

She glanced through the three pages of notes she'd made. It took her a moment before she found a possible answer.

Lyle Jeffrey stepped into the small conference room, bedraggled and wearing a scowl. Whatever he was about to say stuck in his throat when she held a finger to her mouth then motioned him to sit across from her. After letting the conversation continue for a moment, Barnwell said, "I'm putting you on speakerphone. My partner has arrived, and I want him to hear this."

She pushed a button on the phone, and a hollow sound filled the room. "I'd like you to repeat what you've told me so far."

"All of it?" a woman's voice said. "I have a colloquium at six and need to grab a bite first."

"I'll summarize. A week ago, you told us your grandfather's trust fund paid for your education but that there's a residual that comes to you and your brother when you turn thirty-five. Go on from there."

"Correct," Christie Parker said. "I don't know why he set it up that way. Maybe he felt that by the time we reached that age, we would have made our own way in the world. Mother says he didn't want his wealth to spoil us."

She chuckled to herself. "That didn't stop my father from making that accusation. He thought by going for post-graduate degrees, I was avoiding responsibility. 'Will you be nothing more than a student for the rest of your life?'" she said in a deep, demanding voice.

"Were there any other provisions, apart from educational expenses?"

"If one of us had started a business, the trust would advance us $25,000. But he put a bunch of restrictions on the kinds of professions he'd fund. Insurance was a big one. That's where he'd made his money. Stuff that bored the crap out of us."

Jeffrey leaned forward as though to pose his own question, but Lydia restrained him with a hand on his arm. "Tell me about the residual," she said.

"We get what's left, no strings attached. It won't mean much to me, since our educational expenses were an advance rather than an outright gift. It's more important to Bill, but since he's younger than I, he'll have to wait longer for it."

Lydia probed her on how much she expected to receive, but she was vague. "This may sound absurd, but I haven't paid it a lot of attention. I earn a decent salary. Veronica and I own a house. Rather, our cats do." She chuckled again. "I'm thinking about donating most of it to a good cause, like the Center for Reproductive Rights. Women are under attack, as you know."

"And your brother?" Lydia asked.

"I suspect he needs it. That job of his doesn't pay much. The theater's not exactly the Schubert, and I don't think he's cut out for schmoozing wealthy people and begging them for alms."

Lydia paused for a moment, uncertain where to take the conversation.

"Is that it?" Christie asked.

Jeffrey passed her a note. "Who benefits from your father's death?"

The daughter's hesitation was even longer. "Mom, of course. She's rid of him and gets to live her own life at last. But financially, you mean? I can't think of anyone. His death doesn't affect the trust, and Mother inherits all the assets."

The two detectives made eye contact, and Lydia sat up straight in her chair. "How is their financial situation?"

Christie made a small sound, the verbal equivalent of a shrug. "Okay, I guess. I don't—didn't speak to my father, and Mother doesn't discuss that sort of thing. Why?"

"Your father had borrowed extensively over the past few years, ever since he lost his job."

"How *extensively*?" she said, drawing verbal quotes around the word.

Lydia gave her the CliffsNotes version of what they knew—cashing in CDs, taking money from his IRA, mortgaging the house.

"He mortgaged her house!" she shouted so loud the phone seemed to tremble on the desk. "That's not his to borrow on. Did Mother know this?"

Lydia avoided the question. She was here to gather information, not provide it. In the silence that followed, Christie said, "I knew he was borrowing from the trust, but that was just a loan."

Dozens of unvoiced questions passed between the two

detectives as they met eyes again. "How much did he borrow?"

"I don't know. You'll have to ask Bill."

"You weren't consulted?"

"Neither of us were. As trustee, Father could manage the fund however he chose. He invested the funds and could make loans as long as they produced income."

"Was Lois a trustee?"

"No, only my father. And before you ask, yes, Grandpa Dorsey was my maternal grandfather. Lois was his daughter, but he appointed Steven to manage the money. The patriarchy protects its interests."

She probed and prodded, but Christie seemed not to know how much her father had borrowed and what he'd used to secure the loan. They have to ask her brother for this information.

"Was Bill concerned about this arrangement?" Barnwell asked.

"Not at first, but he recently wrote something about assets being sold to fund the loans. He wanted me to fly down for a family meeting, but classes had started, and I couldn't get away. I'd promised to meet around Christmas."

Lydia continued to pursue the matter, but the daughter seemed to have told her everything she knew. "I really have to go. My students are waiting."

"One more thing, Christie. Does someone audit the trust? A bank? An accountant?"

"Yes, there's a CPA firm. I don't recall—" They heard her opening a drawer and slapping files on her desk. "Kressner and Bowie. They're on Liberty, downtown. Here's their number."

Lydia wrote it down. "I know you're busy, but you need to

do us a favor before you leave. Call him, identify yourself, and give him permission to speak to us about the trust. We can get a court order, but that takes time. Will you do that for me?"

She agreed and got off, the urgency of Barnwell's request ringing in her ears.

JEFFREY TOLD her he and Officer Foster had come up empty. "We got no answer at two homes, but the other two had Ring camera footage. We watched them both. If Ron Schuster left his home that afternoon, it was through teleportation. I'm afraid he's telling the truth. You, on the other hand ..."

He left with the sentence unfinished, made his way to the kitchenette, and brewed another pot of coffee. "How do you sleep at night?" she said.

"Clear conscience. So tell me where you are and how you got there."

"When I informed Novak the only prints found in the garage were those of the Schusters and Lois and her son, he asked if I knew what that meant. And I did."

"It means one of the four must have committed the murder. If it wasn't Ron or Joanne..."

"It has to be Bill or Lois. That made me recall something we overheard when we first arrived and were about to question her."

He filled his mug with coffee and lifted it to his lips then led her back to the bullpen. "Let me reconstruct the scene. The garage was taped off, the door half-lowered, and the crime scene van blocked any view from the street. Brandy assures me no one entered the garage but the two of us.

She referred to her notes. "When you took Bill aside, he took a moment to inform his sister. You overheard part of the conversation. What did he tell her?"

Jeffrey spread his hands, inviting her to fill in the blanks in his memory.

"That someone had entered the garage and struck Steven's head with something heavy. He speculated it was a shovel. How did he know that?"

Jeffrey didn't answer the rhetorical question; it spoke for itself.

"That put me on the track. I became convinced Bill killed his father, but I didn't have a motive. Because he was a womanizing louse who betrayed Lois? That's a possibility, but is that enough to make him murder his father? There had to be something else. When you spoke to Bill, he made it seem Steven had paid for his schooling, but Christie corrected the record, revealing the existence of a trust. Why hadn't Bill mentioned it? I called her, and you know the rest."

"The son kills the father because he gives himself a loan?" He screwed up his features as though questioning it.

"In one email, Bill asks his dad when he expects to settle up. Steven doesn't answer directly but in a subsequent message suggests his forthcoming book will be a stunning success."

"I remember," Jeffrey said. "I think Bill used the word 'trust' in that exchange. I took it to mean he trusted him. Or didn't, now that I think of it. But he meant what he said: the trust."

"As I spoke to Lois yesterday, Bill was upstairs going over the family finances. He became enraged, screamed an expletive of some sort, and bolted down the stairs, ready to explode. When he saw Nadine and me, he regained control, but I could tell he was seething. So, yes, he was concerned about how his father was spending his mother's money ... and his own."

Jeffrey nodded, acknowledging she might be on to something. "What I can't figure out though—"

Her cell phone rang. After listening, she asked the caller to hang on and ushered Jeffrey back to the conference room. Putting the call on speakerphone, she introduced both of them. "Hal Kressner is the certified public accountant who audits the Dorsey Family Trust," she explained.

She thanked him for returning the call and explained the reason for their interest. "We understand that before he was killed, Steven Parker, acting as trustee, had loaned himself some money. How much was involved?"

They waited while Kressner leafed through some paperwork and warned them the most recent audit was a year old, and that the amount might be more or less now. "At the time, it was $117,382 dollars, including accrued interest."

Jeffrey swore under his breath. "Was he making payments on it?"

"Not to that point, no."

"And since then?"

"We get paid to do the audit, you understand, not to monitor the funds on a monthly basis. But when his son asked me to look into it, I found no repayments from Mr. Parker."

"When did he make that request?"

"Two weeks ago."

"When did you report back to William?"

Kressner consulted his notes, first saying it was toward the end of the week before Parker was murdered then settling on the day before. "That Friday. I'm sure of it. I was clearing my desk for the weekend and got a call from him asking if I'd made any progress. He'd only asked a few days before. He was quite persistent."

"What was his reaction?"

"He seemed rather disturbed, particularly when I explained Steven had converted some income-producing securities to provide cash for the loans."

"What did he say when he heard that?"

"He got angry, demanding to know how I could have let such a thing happen. He didn't seem to accept I'm not the fiduciary. Our role is to make certain the annual report accurately portrays the financial position of the trust."

"And what was that position at the end of last year?"

Again, he seemed to consult his paperwork before answering. "In round numbers, it had assets of $329,000 and liabilities of $226,000, for a net of $103,000. The liabilities consist of the loan to Mr. Parker and interest-free loans to the beneficiaries for their educational expenses."

"Christie tells us she wasn't expecting much when she reaches the age of thirty-five, that most of it will go to her brother."

"Well," Kressner said in a tone suggesting she was over-simplifying, "it's true he'll receive more than his sister, but once their father's estate repays the loan, she'll get some-thing. I can prepare an estimate, but I'll need the trustee's approval."

"Is that Lois Parker?"

"Oh, no. Now that Mr. Parker is deceased, control of the trust reverts to the son."

Christie had been right. Long life the patriarchy. They thanked him and ended the call. "No wonder he exploded yesterday," she said. "He discovered how big a hole his father has dug. There's nothing left to repay the loan Steven gave himself. He stole his children's inheritance."

———

Lydia couldn't resolve how Bill Parker had driven from the theater to his parents' home then returned in time for his mother's request that he call 911. The assistant DA had blown the Schuster case out of the water for lack of physical evidence, demanding that they put the shovel in Ron's hand. She needed to do the same with the victim's son. The hour was late, and both were exhausted.

"Let's sleep on it and resume in the morning," Jeffrey said. She explained that Isabela's funeral was at ten, and she felt a duty to attend. They'd begin, he said, when she arrived.

As she puzzled over how to balance these competing priorities, Calvin texted her to meet at a local restaurant. "Tommy's joining us. Anna has to work late." Anna Molnar had been pulling double shifts for the past few weeks, not because she needed the money—though she did—but because the care facility had lost staff.

She pulled into the family restaurant on Rte. 60, which Calvin had chosen because it was Tommy's favorite. The pair were already seated, and their faces lit up when she arrived. Neither had ordered yet. Although she knew it by heart, Lydia browsed the menu while the boy chattered about a Boy Scout camping experience coming this weekend.

"Chief's taking me," he said, beaming at Calvin.

I hope people are thoughtful enough not to get shot, she told herself, not wanting to share such thoughts with Tommy.

As though reading her mind, he said, "I hope nothing happens to change that. He can't be in two places at once."

She ordered the steamed mussels, while Calvin and Tommy went for steaks. A couple near them cast curious glances. What was this boy with straight brown hair and beige skin doing with these adults, one alabaster, the other chocolate, whose only shared features were tight curls? Lydia smiled back then ignored them. She was accustomed to the looks they got whenever she and Calvin ate out. Tommy added a new wrinkle.

They quizzed him about his studies, but he was noncommittal. Everything was "okay." His favorite subject was lunch. Lydia knew from his mother that his grades were excellent. Was this the way all kids reacted to school?

"Who all is coming to your wedding?" he asked.

She named all Calvin's relatives she could recall, while he filled in the blanks, then added all her fellow cops and the few friends outside the force she had. Acquaintances, really. Would she invite them? She realized she inhabited an insular world and needed to branch out.

"Can I come?" he asked.

"Of course, Tommy. You and your mother are our guests of honor."

"Is your dad excited?"

She looked at Calvin for help, but he only returned her gaze. "I need to tell him," she said.

"Can I meet him?"

"I'm sure he'll be eager to meet you," she said, grabbing the first response she could think of.

Lydia had been putting off the day of reckoning. It was time to change that. While Calvin took the boy home, promising to hang with him until Anna returned, she entered the house, poured herself the glass of wine she'd denied herself at dinner, and called Colonel Barnwell's number. His stentorian voice, dripping with authority, barked at her over the phone.

"It's been a while since I've heard from you." The same worked the other way, she thought. "How have you been?"

"Fine," she said. "Work is going well. I'm on a new case and expect to wrap it up in a few days."

"That's good. You could have had a career in the military, but law enforcement is the next best thing."

She didn't need him to tell her what he'd wanted for her. She'd heard it many times. "I have news, Dad. I'm getting married in the spring."

He laughed, something he rarely did. "That makes two of us, kitten. I've found the most wonderful woman. Katherine is a widow too. We met at the country club. She's quite a golfer. I invited her to dinner, and we started going together. One thing led to another, and now we're tying the knot."

A parade of women had marched through his life, but he'd never spoken of marriage. He told her they both owned homes and hadn't decided how they were going to combine households. Only after he'd exhausted the topic did he say, "Tell me about your fellow."

"He's also in law enforcement. Calvin is chief of the borough force where I used to work."

"Two cops in the same family. That's quite a... No, I guess that's fairly typical, isn't it? I see lots of families in which both husband and wife are officers. It's rough on the kids when both are deployed, but usually only one goes at a time."

"We'll work it out," she said. "He's a wonderful man."

"You love him?"

"I do."

"That's all that matters. That and the fact he seems to be a responsible fellow. Kathryn's husband…"

He trailed off, telling her that his fiancé's husband had also been in the military. His soliloquy went on for several minutes, which she littered with affirming grunts. "In May?" he said, taking her by surprise. "Oh, shoot. We've booked a cruise that month. We're starting in Barcelona…"

And ending when you've finished talking, she thought. *I hope you don't bore her to death.* "But I wish you all the best. Kathryn and I both do, don't we?" Only then did she realize she had been sitting alongside him all this time, perhaps listening to their conversation.

"You too." She ended the call.

Should I cry? It seemed appropriate under the circumstances, but she couldn't waste the energy. Their relationship had been sealed the day she was attacked. They had nothing more to say to each other.

CHAPTER TWELVE

LYDIA ROLLED over and reached for her watch. 3:40 in the damn morning. She tried to fall back to sleep but gave up after twenty minutes. Tommy Molnar's voice echoed in her consciousness. "He can't be in two places at once." Sheriff Brinson had said the same about Vogt.

Trying to let sleeping hulks lie, she slipped out of bed, donned her robe and slippers, and crept downstairs. While boiling water for a cup of herbal tea, she opened her computer and logged on to the ACPD account. She wasn't certain what she was looking for but opened the reports she and Jeffrey had filed on the day of the murder and recorded their time of arrival and when they'd interviewed the two family members and the Schusters. Backing up to the original reports and the coroner's report, she drew a legal pad toward her and sketched out a timeline.

- 4:13 p.m.: Steven Parker's watch sends alarm
- 4:35 p.m.: (approx) Lois arrives home and discovers body
- 4:47 p.m.: Bill Parker calls 911 at Lois's request
- 4:51 p.m.: Scott Twp cruiser arrives

- 5:01 p.m.: CSI on scene
- 5:12 p.m.: Barnwell on scene
- 5:14 p.m.: Jeffrey on scene.
- 5:20 p.m.: Bill Parker arrives

Rachel Waldman, the acting director of the theater, said Bill had been setting up the donor reception when she left at approximately 3:45. She added this to the list. This gave him time to drive the twenty-four minutes to his parents' home and return to take the call from his mother. Had he called 911 from the theater? It provided ample time to drive home again, enter the front door, and announce his presence.

For the fourth time, she reread Jeffrey's report on his interview with the son. Bill had first called his sister. The log from his cell phone listed it at 5:26. Jeffrey had not begun to question him until after their conversation, which he'd concluded at 5:28. Shortly into the interview, he paused again, ordering Jennifer Tillman to cancel the event. This call was logged at 5:33, ending two minutes later. Jennifer had then driven from her apartment to the theater to post a cancellation notice. What time was that? She'd seen a copy somewhere. Right, Jennifer had forwarded it to Jeffrey, who'd copied it to the file. She had to hand it to the guy. He was a packrat.

She opened and read it. Direct and to the point. Sent to "unnamed recipients," which meant she'd blind-copied it to a file she kept of those either invited or attending. The message sent at...

No, that couldn't be right. She reviewed her previous entries then looked again at the heading on the email. Why hadn't they noticed this sooner?

She sat back, stroking her cheek as she wondered how to

proceed. She put the Moka pot on the smallest burner and switched from herbal tea to coffee.

Shaking her head as she realized what she must do, she fired off an email to Novak, explaining why she would skip his mother's funeral. "You've given us a break in the case. I apologize, but it's unavoidable."

JEFFREY WAS SURPRISED to find Lydia at her desk, having told him she would attend Izabela's service. Before he could ask what she was doing there, she said, "Look at this." She slid the timeline she'd developed, having typed it out, under his nose. His eyes ran down the entries until it reached the last one.

"I'm not seeing it."

She ran her fingers down the list. "Bill called Jennifer and spoke with her until 5:35. You overheard his end of the conversation. She told you she returned to the theater to do as he instructed, but it went out at 5:44. She could not have received the call at her apartment, raced to their office, composed the message, and sent it in nine minutes. It's impossible."

"Hold on a sec." He reached into his desk and thumbed through one of the many notebooks he'd filled over the past two weeks. "You're right. I didn't list the time he placed the call in my report, because it didn't seem important, but I made a note of it. 'Breaks for call at 5:33. Resume interview at 5:35.'"

"Nine minutes," she repeated. "I'm not sure that's enough to write the message and proof it, let alone drive to Oakland."

"If she has a car," he said, "which would be unusual for a student living downtown."

"She may be our key."

"Let's question her." He reached for his jacket.

"I have a better idea. Bring her here, stick her in an interview room, and leave her alone while she thinks about what story to concoct."

* * *

The woman who sat in the spartan interview room was nothing like the one he'd met in the coffee shop the week before. No more idle chitchat, charming rejoinders, or fluttering of fingers as though painting pictures in the air. Jennifer Tillman slumped in the hard chair, her long inky hair in disarray, fumbling at a medal at her neck. *St. Jude?* Lydia wondered.

It hadn't taken her a quarter hour to become undone. Ten minutes after arriving, they could hear her breathing as though she were hyperventilating. Jeffrey led the way, putting Lydia in the seat facing her and pulling his chair to the end of the table. With her back to the wall, she was surrounded, which was the point.

He started the recording, gave the date and time, introduced both of them, and asked her to state her name for the record. "What am I doing here?" she said, faking a smile.

She'd tried to grab hold of the conversation when they'd met at the university's coffee shop. He would not let her do so again. "You are at the headquarters of the Allegheny Police Department, 875 Greentree Road, in Interview Room 1. We have brought you in to answer questions relating to the death of Steven Parker. I've included my partner, who has noticed discrepancies in what you told me a week ago and what we now know. Does that answer your question?"

Based on her performance then—he now thought of it as exactly that—he expected her to respond by asking, "What discrepancies?" She did not. She stared at the surface of the table before her, which was interrupted only by the detectives' notebooks, held at angles to conceal their contents.

"At 5:33 on Saturday, October 22nd, you received a call from your supervisor, William Parker. Where were you at that time?"

"In my apartment," she said in a soft voice. "The university owns a building for upperclassmen on Boulevard of the Allies."

"And that is how far from the theater where you work?"

"About half an hour by bus. Faster if I take Uber." They asked a few more questions, establishing that Jennifer did not own a vehicle. When she went home to West Virginia, she either took a bus or rented a car. They cut her off before she could digress into the location of the rental agency or anything else to divert them from the topic.

"Going back to Mr. Parker's call, what did he say?"

"We had scheduled a donor event that night. We were premiering a new production and wanted to show our appreciation by—"

"What was the purpose of his call? Did he ask you to do something?"

"Yes, he said we needed to call it off. The reception."

"What were his words?"

"I don't recall exactly."

"To the best of your knowledge."

"I told you the first time we spoke." She waited as though that would end it. When both detectives continued to stare at her, she said. "Something to the effect that a family emergency had come up requiring us to cancel the reception, that we regretted the late notice but would reschedule in the future."

That was considerably more than Parker had said in the conversation Jeffrey overheard, but it tracked the language of the email. He said nothing but wrote himself a note. Barnwell followed his lead. Let her wonder what they'd found of interest.

"Did he describe the nature of the family emergency?" Jeffrey said.

"No."

"He didn't explain why he was in such a panic?"

"Not at that time. He asked me to send the message."

"And what did you do?"

She shrugged. "I sent it."

"From your apartment?"

"No, I don't have access to the server from there. I did it from the office."

"How did you get there?"

She opened her palm as though expecting an answer to descend from the heavens. "I took an Uber."

"The trip would be listed on the app, wouldn't it?"

She paused a beat. "I took a taxi."

"What time did you call them?"

"I got lucky. I stepped outside and flagged down a cab."

"How did you pay the driver?"

Another pause while she considered how to thread this needle. "In cash."

"Did you keep a receipt? No? Didn't you expect to be reimbursed?" Jeffrey looked toward Barnwell, who sat with her arms crossed, as though to say, "Wouldn't you?"

"So you hailed a taxi, even though Pittsburgh cabbies don't pick up fares on the street. This isn't New York. You took it to work, paid in cash, and didn't think to get a receipt." He let that sit for a moment. "How long did this take you?"

She shuffled in her chair and spread her slender fingers apart on the table. "A few minutes. I'm trying to recall."

"You weren't at your apartment when Parker called you. You sent that email nine minutes after he got off the phone."

The young woman picked at an imaginary thread on her sweater but didn't answer. Jeffrey turned to Barnwell, who'd been silent until this time.

Lydia closed the distance between them, her blue eyes boring into her. She lowered her voice, forcing Jennifer to strain to hear her. "Listen to me. Lying to us is one thing. It's a crime, but it doesn't always lead to charges. What you're doing is orders of magnitude more serious. We're conducting a murder investigation. You are impeding that effort. If you continue to do so, we'll press charges." Barnwell hesitated to make certain she had her attention. "Depending on your role, you can be charged as an accessory. That's a felony. You'll spend years in prison. Your career will be over before it begins. Your life will be ruined."

Jennifer tossed her head back and forth, as though trying to ward off an insect. "He didn't do anything. He found his dad's body lying in the garage and thought you'd say he did it. 'It's always the person who discovers the body.' That's what he told me."

Jeffrey recalled her saying the same thing when he'd first spoken with her. "You'd better tell us everything," he said.

She brightened a bit, as though it were the first day of spring after a grueling winter. She said they'd finished the physical setup at 3:30, and she was printing name tags when the acting director came into the office and told them she was leaving for a few hours. Parker decided they should do the same. "He told me to go home and freshen up. I keep my black party dress here and said I didn't need to. Bill insisted I rest, said I'd worked hard and that he wanted me looking perky. That's the word he used."

She didn't want to make the trip. At night, he always drove her back to her apartment but didn't offer to do so today. She would have to wait for the 61C bus, take the half-hour ride, then reverse course two hours later. "I told him I would, but I have a one-act coming up, so I went to the library to study my lines. It's only a six-block walk, and it was so nice that afternoon..."

"So you stayed there?" Lydia said to prevent her from veering the conversation into a side street.

"For maybe an hour, but they close at five, so I returned to the theater. I stopped and picked up a rice bowl on the way."

She finished preparations, carrying name tags, blank stickers, and pens down the flight of stairs to the room where the reception would be held. She was applying makeup when Parker called. "We're not supposed to use the backstage area, but the actors wouldn't arrive for an hour, so who was to know?"

"Tell us again. What did he say to you, and what did he want you to do?" Lydia prompted.

"He was abrupt, and I could tell he was upset. He asked me to rush to the theater and email the donors cancelling the event, citing a family emergency."

"And what else?" Jeffrey said.

"That was it. He ended the call."

"He didn't tell you his father had been found dead?"

"Not then, no. He told me to take care of it immediately. I promised I would."

"Did you reveal you hadn't returned to your flat, that you were at the theater?"

"No, I wasn't supposed to be backstage. I said I'd attend to it and hung up." Jeffrey made eye contact with Lydia, but she couldn't tell what caused his reaction.

The following day, Jennifer said, Parker told her he'd gone to his parents' home at his father's request, found him dead, and left. His reason, he said, was to avoid suspicion falling on him. If she were asked, she was to say he'd remained at the theater when she'd left.

"But he didn't," Barnwell said.

"No," she replied after giving her answer some thought. Lydia sensed she was looking for a way out but couldn't find it. "He left before I did."

THEY LET HER GO, extracting a promise not to contact Parker. The demand was superfluous, since Jeffrey had already ordered uniformed officers to bring the man in, but the warning served to underline the seriousness of her position.

The interrogation had left Barnwell with one question for her partner, but before she could pose it, Ross Sutton loomed over them, shifting his weight from one foot to the other like a little boy needing to visit the bathroom. "I got the tower dump." This was raw data from cell towers listing every phone number within range. "We triangulated two of them that place your suspect's phone within thirty yards of the theater from 11:00 in the morning until 4:50."

"He didn't leave?" Barnwell said.

A smile tugged at the edges of Sutton's mouth. Once again, he dished out information with a spoon, enjoying the drama. With his head buried in electronic gear and monitors all day long, it constituted one of his few pleasures in life.

"I didn't say that. I said his phone never left during that time."

"But..." Jeffrey said.

"You can detect slight variations in its position and signal strength through much of the afternoon. Call it a warble as the owner moves from one part of a building to another. For the hour in question, however, there's none. The phone never moved. So either he was sitting at his desk between 3:49 and 4:50, or ..."

"He left the phone," she finished for him.

"You got it," Sutton said.

"So it proves nothing."

"Not quite, although you wouldn't want to introduce this in court. If he were less intelligent, he would have turned it off. That would have been a giveaway. If he's your man, he thought this through."

Which showed premeditation, though she could picture Melissa Dawkins rejecting the information, knowing a defense lawyer would hammer home the opposite interpretation, that Bill had remained in his office, never leaving his desk.

Having delivered this disappointing news, Barnwell expected him to return to his lair, but he remained, wearing the same half-smile. Was he expecting an attaboy? Given his love of sprinkling breadcrumbs before serving the sandwich—from Primanti's, of course—she wondered what else he might have uncovered.

"You traced his car," she said.

The half-smile turned full, like the fifth phase of the lunar cycle. "We checked his registration and found he owns a 2010 Volkswagen Beetle, yellow. There aren't that many around anymore." He sniffed. "I always considered it a lady's car."

On Lydia's last case, she'd seen how, given the make and model of a vehicle, its location and time of departure from a given point, Sutton's team could track it through monitored traffic lights. They couldn't pinpoint its final destination, only the last major intersection through which it had passed. "Your man left Oakland at 3:51. We tracked it down 5th Avenue to I-379, across the Fort Pitt Bridge, and off at the Greentree exit. Its last location was at Greentree and McMonagle, six blocks from the murder scene."

Jeffrey laughed and pushed his reading glasses off of his nose. "You sure know how to lead a fellow on," he said, adding to Lydia, "Sorry."

"I'm just one of the boys," she said. "Can we get this?"

"You already have it. I sent you a map, marking each traffic light with the time he passed through. And also his return trip," he said, turning back toward his office. "He went past the theater and through a traffic light near his apartment."

Jeffrey waited until he was out of earshot and laughed. "Sutton missed his calling. He should have done stand-up. At any rate, we'll have something to confront Mr. Parker with if he ever gets here."

An officer poked his head in to announce that Bill Parker was cooling his heels—or, more accurately, his butt—in the same room Jennifer Tillman had vacated fifteen minutes before.

Parker sat with his arms folded and a scowl on his face. He looked up as they entered but broke eye contact once he recognized them. He didn't ask why they'd brought him here, waiting for them to fire the opening round.

After starting the recording and stating the preliminaries, Jeffrey said, "Where were you at the time your father was murdered?"

"At the theater. We had a reception that night, and I was making final arrangements."

"No, you left. Where did you go?"

"I was right there."

"Ms. Waldman left at a quarter to four to rest up before that night's opening performance. You told your assistant to leave then did so yourself. Where were you?"

He shifted his gaze from Jeffrey to Barnwell, seeking a refuge. She returned his stare, and he studied his hands, which stroked each other as though washing grime away. "I went to my apartment to change. It's a short walk."

"Your vehicle left the employee lot behind the theater at 3:51. You were driving. Where did you go?"

There was a moment in many interrogations when the subject realized the police knew the answers to their own questions. Parker signaled such a recognition by pulling back from the table, his eyes blinking as rapidly as an automatic weapon.

"I drove around a while. I had a lot on my mind. Big donors were attending that night. One couple in particular —they're into more traditional plays. I was rehearsing what I'd say to them if they didn't care for this production."

"And to do that, you drove where?"

"I don't recall. I wasn't paying attention."

"Northside?"

"Yeah, maybe—" A sudden twitch of his eyebrows

showed he recognized lying might not be the best course. "No, I don't remember. Just around."

Jeffrey peered at the man as though expecting him to continue. Lydia used the silence to scrawl something in her notebook. Parker cleared his throat. "Do you need water?" she asked.

"No, I'm okay." But at her suggestion, he licked his lips. She rose and left while Jeffrey let the silence hang over the room. She returned with a plastic cup and took a deep swig from her own bottle. Everything the detectives did showed they were in no hurry. They would take as much time as Parker required.

"When I spoke to you following your father's murder, you told me he had provided for your education. Do you recall saying that?"

"Not exactly. We talked about a lot. I was in shock." Pushing his half-glasses up on his nose, Jeffrey made a show of studying his notes then read Parker's words to him. "Your father paid for your college. That's what you told me. That's not true, is it?"

Parker rubbed his forehead. "It was a kind of shorthand. Dad had just died. That's what consumed me. We were talking about his personality, and I was trying to think of good things to say about him."

"You praised him for helping you. I recorded our conversation. Do you want me to play it back for you?" Parker tossed his head and waved the suggestion away. "The money came from a trust established by your grandfather. Can you describe the terms to me?"

"He set aside money for our tuition and expenses. I got my B.A. My sister decided to live off of it."

"And that's it?"

He again displayed the flash of recognition that the

detective already knew the answer. "I think we each get a settlement of some sort. When we're thirty-five, I think."

"You think?" he repeated. "But you don't know the details?" Parker didn't answer.

Jeffrey glanced at Barnwell, a silent signal for her to pick up the interrogation.

"Four years ago, your father lost his job at the *Pittsburgh Herald*. He told his family it was a buyout, but the truth is they fired him. He lived for a few months on his severance package, but it soon ran out. Neither the books he churned out nor the articles he sold brought enough to live on. He scraped together what he could by drawing on their savings and other sources. Did you and your mother know how bad things were?"

Parker crossed his arms again, his face a mask of defiance. Lois had seemed unaware the line of credit intended for home improvement had turned her father's wedding gift into her husband's ATM. If her son knew, he didn't give it away.

"A few weeks ago, you learned your father was loaning himself money from the trust. You wrote, asking him when he was going to repay it. When he gave you a vague response about the book he was writing, you called Harold Kressner, the accountant who audits your grandfather's trust. On Friday October 21st, one day before your father's murder, he provided the information you'd requested. Do you recall what he said?"

When he didn't respond, she repeated what the CPA had told them, the amount Steven Parker had borrowed over time, the fact he had repaid none of it, and the poor financial decisions he'd made as he converted income-paying securities into cash. "You were upset, blaming the accountant for the transactions when, in fact, it was your father's doing."

"If you're suggesting I had something to do with his death—"

"That's precisely what I'm saying." She thrust a copy of Sutton's map before him. "Here you are leaving the theater at 3:51, hopping on Parkway West to Greentree, and turning the corner at McMonagle toward your parents' house. You waited for his return, stepped into the garage, grabbed the shovel, and struck him over the head."

"I did not. What are you saying? That I murdered my father? What sort of son would do such a thing?"

"Eighteen minutes after arriving, you drove back the way you'd come, parking behind your apartment building. You went in long enough to change your bloody clothing then drove to the theater as though nothing had happened."

"No, you've got this wrong."

"We have you there," she said, tapping the location on the map.

He exhaled in panic, staring at the ceiling tiles.

"All right, I was there. He'd asked me to come talk to him. Said he had a plan to repay the loans. But when I arrived, he was stretched out on the floor with—" He appeared to choke back tears, but there were none in his eyes.

"You got to the house at 4:11. Your father was killed at 4:17. You left two minutes later. You were there at the time of his murder."

"No," he said.

"After you changed clothes, you returned to your office and waited for your mother to call you in a panic, having discovered the body."

He jerked as though he'd had an electrical shock. "I think I need an attorney."

"Do you need one?" Jeffrey asked. If Parker requested counsel, their questioning would have to stop. Thus, he parried the young man's question with his own.

"You called 911 and returned to the house," Lydia said. "Upon entering the front door, you called your sister and told her what had happened, specifically mentioning he had been killed with the blade of a shovel. That's what tipped us off. No one had been in the garage since your mother discovered the body. You had no way of knowing that unless you'd been there."

"I told you I'd seen the body. I didn't report it because I knew you'd suspect me."

"But you had no problem putting your mother in the same position."

"She was at a movie with a friend. There's no way you could suspect her."

"When we first talked," Jeffrey said, "you called your assistant, telling her to send out a blast email canceling the reception. After she responded, you yelled at her, or pretended to do so, because she never heard that part of the conversation. Once she agreed, you disconnected the call but put on a show for me, calling her 'a fucking student.' The woman who has spent the last several days lying for you, the one who lets you share her bed?"

This answered the question that had nagged Lydia since he'd rolled his eyes at her as they'd questioned Jennifer. Jeffrey had heard Bill Parker yell at his assistant, but she had not.

What took its place in her mind was something to which Parker had reacted. A thought formed, so sinister it was almost unbelievable. She failed to hear Parker say, "I'm not answering any more questions until I get a lawyer."

"We've heard his defense," Jeffrey said as he poured himself an afternoon coffee. The pot had grown cold, so he microwaved some in his mug, took a sip, and wrinkled his nose. Still, he returned it to his lips. "His father asked him to come to the house. When he got there and found his body, he panicked, believing we would suspect him."

"Which we do," she said, "and we have the time sequence to prove it."

"The crime scene investigators are at his apartment now, looking through his clothing for bloodstains. The search warrant also applies to his car." When she didn't comment, he said, "You're quiet."

"Rack up the interview. Let me show you something."

Jeffrey opened the file on his monitor, and she scooted her chair next to his. "Scroll forward a bit." He did so. "Here, let me do it." She leaned over him, scrubbing through the video until she reached a segment near the end. "Listen to the Q and A, but keep your eyes on him."

They heard Lydia say, "After you changed clothes, you returned to your office and waited for your mother to call you in a panic, having discovered the body."

"See it?"

"No."

"Watch him closely." She scrubbed back and reran the five-second clip.

"He didn't like that question," Jeffrey said. Lydia looked at him, watching for dawn to break. "I see. Do you think..."

"There's one way to find out."

Fifteen minutes later, a squad car pulled into the parking lot in front of the building. Lydia met the officers and the person they'd brought in. She led the group to the elevator and dismissed the uniformed pair with her thanks. Neither she nor the subject spoke to one another as they exited on the second floor.

Taking the person's arm, she walked toward the interview room where Bill Parker sat. Jeffrey had left the door open, giving him a full view of whomever passed in the hallway. As they reached it, the subject paused and looked at Parker, who returned the gaze, open-mouthed.

"Mother, what are you— Let her go!" he shouted. "She had nothing to do with this!"

"It's all right," Lois said. "They know everything."

Two days later, Barnwell and Jeffrey returned to headquarters after spending most of the day at the courthouse. They'd testified before the grand jury as it considered first the Bruno Vogt case and, after lunch, indictments of Bill Parker and his mother.

Carpenter invited them into his office, which was always more a summons than a request, and asked them how their day had gone. "Slam dunk," Jeffrey said. This was nothing more than the three of them had expected. An adage said that a decent DA could indict a ham sandwich. Much work remained before prosecutors could present their cases in court and overcome the efforts of their defense attorney to cloud the air with what Lydia, from her days in Texas, called "heifer dust."

"There's a lot we don't know yet," she told Carpenter. "Some of it we may never learn." Lois had ceased answering questions once her lawyer arrived, but their reactions when they spotted each other showed they'd planned the act together.

"Joanne Schuster says they saw Bill pulling up to the house a week before the murder. She left via the back door and didn't think he'd spotted her. We think he did. He was piecing together his father's financial shenanigans, and this evidence of his continued unfaithfulness fueled his anger. Three days later, the CPA called with the information he'd been seeking, telling him how deeply Steven had invaded the trust."

"Your theory is that Lois knew he was having an affair with her best friend?"

"At some point," Jeffrey said, "but perhaps not until that Friday. Jennifer tells us he left the office in a hurry the day before the murder. Steven was not at home that afternoon. We believe Bill told his mother everything he'd discovered, and they plotted his murder."

"Rachel Waldman followed a routine," Lydia continued. "Prior to every evening performance, she left the theater at mid-afternoon to recharge her batteries. Jennifer says it was like clockwork. Bill knew this, and his mother knew Steven would be at the book fair Saturday afternoon. She called her friend Jane Branscomb, who'd been urging her to attend a three-and-a-half-hour film. Lois had put her off, but it now provided the perfect opportunity. Bill would wait until the director left, send Jennifer home, then drive to Scott Township to intercept his father. He'd return to work while Lois came home to make the grim *discovery*." She drew air quotes around the last word.

"We have physical evidence," Jeffrey said. "The forensics team found Steven's blood in Bill's apartment and his car. He'd thrown away the clothing he wore, but he'd tried to clean his sneakers. They recovered more blood stains and matched the print to the partial alongside the body."

"Well done," Carpenter said. "You headed off in the wrong direction but eventually found your way. I've changed the color of the case on the Baltimore Board. I've also added Jeanne Holman's murder. Speaking of which…"

He picked up a sheet of paper that was on one side of his desk and handed it to Lydia. She studied it for a moment, whistled, and passed it to Jeffrey.

"Maryland State Police have reopened an investigation into the rape and murders of two other teenage girls," Carpenter said. "Both took place while Vogt was living with his sister in Cumberland. I suspect West Virginia will examine its cold cases. You may have brought justice to more than Jeanne Holman."

He did not apologize for trying to pull her back from the investigation, but his pride in the department's accomplishment was clear. "Well done," Carpenter said simply, but that spoke volumes.

WITH CALVIN OFF with Tommy Molnar for the weekend, Lydia slept late on Saturday and spent the morning cleaning house. When she attacked the upstairs bathroom, she found it pristine. Calvin had already seen to it. From the pattern the vacuum cleaner had made in the carpet, she saw he'd also done that. He had taken care of the upstairs, leaving the lower half to her.

What a guy, she thought. *I won't even have to train him.* His mother had done so. She stopped what she was doing and called Ruth Mayfield. Although the wedding was eight months off, Calvin's mother had been busy planning. "This is your wedding," she said. "Any time I overstep my bounds, tell me. I have a thick skin."

"Mom," she said, letting it slip through her teeth as casually as possible, "you are doing exactly what my mother would have done were she still here. I'm leaning on you, and I'm grateful for everything you're doing."

"Is your father excited?" Ruth had been after her to contact the retired officer. This was her way of nudging her again. How to tell her that her father had let her down at every critical juncture in her life, that this was one among many?

"I doubt he'll be here," she said. "He's planning a wedding of his own."

"Oh," she said, then after an awkward moment added, "I'm sorry."

"He goes his own way. He always has. I'm making other plans. Everything at my end will go smoothly."

Ruth seemed relieved, but Lydia joked, "And I'll be there."

She laughed aloud. "I certainly hope so." They chatted for a few more minutes, Lydia letting Calvin's mother know he was attending Scout camp with Tommy. "He loves that boy," Ruth said. "Someday, you'll have children of your own. Meanwhile, Calvin's in training."

Her father could have used a bit of that, but she didn't say so. And if she had been a boy, he might have played a greater role in the life of his child. There was nothing to be done about it, she thought as Ruth ended the conversation.

She sat at the counter for a few minutes, playing with an idea that had been rummaging through the attic of her mind for a few days. Still holding her cell phone, she went to the favorites tab and tapped a contact.

"Novak," a voice answered. "Oh, it's you. I've been

meaning to congratulate you. That is some work you've done."

"You set me on the right path," she said. "Anyway, that's not why I called. I need another favor."

"Ask away," he said.

"What are you doing in May?"

"That's a long way off. I have no plans. Why?"

"I want you to walk me down the aisle."

"Me?" he said. "Well, sure, but what about—"

"I'm asking you to do it."

"If it's what you want…"

"I do."

"I'm your man."

Yes, Chief, she thought. *You are my man. We gather around us those we can rely on.*

ACKNOWLEDGMENTS

The story is a work of fiction. Unless otherwise indicated, all the names, characters, events, and incidents in this book are the product of my imagination. While many locations referenced in this story exist, they are used in a fictitious manner, and none of the people or events depicted in these settings are real. Any resemblance to actual persons, living or dead, or actual events is purely coincidental.

The story of Pittsburgh's Mafia, retold in the first chapter, is an exception. Those interested in knowing more about the organized crime family that flourished in the post-war years should read *Steel City Mafia* by Paul N. Hodos, published by History Press.

The information on Rapid DNA analysis came from Kat Sato, a forensics scientist with over two decades of experience. Mandy Tinkey, Laboratory Director of the Allegheny County Medical Examiner, provided information and a tour of the facility. Allegheny County Police Superintendent Christopher Kearns and his deputy, Lieutenant Venerando Costa, provided a tour of ACPD headquarters and answered dozens of my questions.

Any mistakes or liberties I have taken with law enforcement or forensic practices are my own.

Jason Letts of Imbue Editing removed unneeded commas, colons, and wordiness. I thank him for his knowledge and professionalism.

ABOUT THE AUTHOR

James H Lewis is the award-winning author of ten novels. His short stories have appeared in Mystery Tribune and Yellow Mama. His short stories have appeared in *Mystery Tribune* and *Yellow Mama*.

"The Guardian," won second place in Pennwriters 2025 Short Story competition. In addition to Pennwriters, he is a member of The Author' Guild, Sisters in Crime, and Mystery Writers of America.

He is a former journalist and nonprofit executive who lives in Pittsburgh.. You can follow his writing and find links to his other novels at jameshlewis.com.

ALSO BY JAMES H LEWIS

THE LYDIA BARNWELL NOVELS

The Dead of Winter

THE CHIEF NOVAK NOVELS

Novak's Mission

Novak's Quest

Novak's Verdict

THE WORLD WAR II NOVEL

The Quadrant Conspiracy: The Plot to Kill FDR

THE ALAN RUDBERG NOVELS

Sins of Omission

Breaking News

www.ingramcontent.com/pod-product-compliance
Lightning Source LLC
Chambersburg PA
CBHW071412300726

48976CB00006B/2067